VINTAGE

INTERNATIONAL

The Beautiful
Mrs. Seidenman

The Beautiful
Mrs. Seidenman

Andrzej Szczypiorski

Translated from the Polish by Klara Glowczewska

VINTAGE INTERNATIONAL
VINTAGE BOOKS
A DIVISION OF RANDOM HOUSE, INC.
NEW YORK

FIRST VINTAGE INTERNATIONAL EDITION, JANUARY 1991

Translation copyright © 1989 by Grove Press, a division of
Wheatland Corporation

All rights reserved under International and Pan-American Copyright
Conventions. Published in the United States by Vintage Books,
a division of Random House, Inc., New York, and distributed in Canada
by Random House of Canada Limited, Toronto. Originally published in
Polish as *Pozatek* by Institut Littéraire S.A.R.L., Paris, in 1986 and in
German by Diogenes Verlag AG, Zurich in 1988. Copyright © 1988 by
Diogenes Verlag AG, Zurich.

Library of Congress Cataloging-in-Publication Data
Szczypiorski, Andrzej.
[Poczatek. English]
The beautiful Mrs. Seidenman / Andrzej Szczypiorski ; translated from the
Polish by Klara Glowczewska.—1st Vintage international ed.
p.   cm.— (Vintage international)
Translation of: Poczatek.
ISBN 0-679-73214-4 :
1. Holocaust, Jewish (1939–1945)—Poland—Warsaw—Fiction.
I. Title.
[PG7178.Z3P5913   1991]
891.8'537—dc20   90-50184
CIP

Manufactured in the United States of America
10 9 8 7 6 5 4 3 2 1

The Beautiful
Mrs. Seidenman

I

The room was in twilight because the judge was a lover of twilight. He didn't like it when his usually unfinished and hazy thoughts fell into the trap of light. Everything on earth is dark and unclear, and the judge loved to plumb the depths of the world. That was why he would often sit in a rocking chair in one corner of the immense living room, his head leaning back, so that his thoughts could sway gently to the rhythm of the chair, which he set into motion with a light touch of the foot, first the left, then the right. He wore ankle-length felt slippers with metal clasps that glistened blue against the rug when they caught the lamplight.

Kujawski the tailor watched the clasps on the judge's slippers and calculated in his head how much money he would lose buying the gold-framed painting on the wall. It showed a naked fellow with horns sitting on a cask of wine. Kujawski believed it was the devil, one of those merry devils, partial to the bottle and the ladies, that painters of old liked to depict, often against a dim and murky background. With some effort the tailor could just make out a water mill or the ruins of an old castle. They weren't very beautiful paintings to be sure, but they had their value, and the tailor was putting his money into art because he was a patriot and a man of culture.

"So you're saying, dear friend," said Judge Romnicki, "that you've had enough of this war. Yes, enough! And, besides, peace is man's natural state. We all want it, you said. . . ."

"That's what I said," the tailor nodded, looking at the devil on the cask. Suddenly he remembered that this devil was called a faun, and a sweet feeling of serenity descended upon him.

"Well, all right. Let the war end," said the judge. "At once. This very moment. . . . Would you want that, my dear friend?"

"Who wouldn't, your honor."

"Please consider carefully. I'm being absolutely serious. Peace is the most important thing, isn't it? So let us end this war. At once, without a moment's delay. Be very careful, dear Mr. Kujawski. Where are the Soviets? Let us say they're at the river Don. The British and the Americans? In North Africa. Splendid. So our dear Adolf Hitler controls Europe. And today we end the war, Mr. Kujawski. Because you were so kind as to point out that peace is the most important thing. Isn't that so?"

"But sir," Kujawski exclaimed. "How could we? With the Germans on our back like that?"

"Make up your mind, my friend. Anyway, the Germans will change. We'll have peace, we'll have peace! First the preliminaries, of course, then the peace conference, some concessions on both sides. The Soviets this, Hitler that, the British and Americans something else. But since you subscribe to the view that peace is the most important thing, then they'll have to reach some sort of agreement, that's why we have diplomats, heads of state, various government offices, overt and covert, exchanges of documents, top hats, limousines, champagne, peace to men of goodwill, Mr. Kujawski."

"Your honor . . ." the tailor muttered.

"You yourself wanted this!" the judge exclaimed. "Please, don't be shifty. There are plenty of others in the world who are. Ah, my dear friend, cheer up. . . . After all, we have peace! And because there is peace, the occupiers can't behave so abominably anymore. All right, we're not free. But we are used to that, Mr. Kujawski. After all, we were both born into slavery, and we will die in it. Oh, yes, at first they will exploit us ruthlessly. Fourteen hours of slave labor a day. A bowl of watery soup. Whippings, beatings. . . . But that will pass with time. Because there is peace, they won't have a chance to get any new slaves. They'll have to take good care of those they have already. Cheer up, dear Mr. Kujawski. A few short years, and we'll be working eight-hour days, they'll give us ration cards, there will even be coffee, tea, and why not, since there's world peace, since there has to be a common market. . . . Will the English drink all the tea of India themselves? Will the Soviets not supply crude oil, wheat, potatoes, whatever? We will live, Mr. Kujawski, under a foreign heel; it's true, no use pretending we won't, but we will live in peace. For from this evening on there will be peace in the world, and that is mankind's highest good, for which our souls long so desperately, our anguished, foolish souls, Mr. Kujawski, shamed by slavery, grown used to humiliation, abasement, servitude—not today, that much is clear, not yet, but with time. After a couple of short years, they'll give us our own schools, naturally with every single class conducted in our own language, when we'll be eating bread with bacon, and maybe even have a little bottle of French cognac now and then, maybe some herring, a Cuban cigar! Just think, my dearest friend, how many admirable qualities and noble deeds will bloom in the sunshine of this European peace. . . . How joyful will be the lives of our little slaves, our boys and girls, who will get presents of candy from their rulers, perhaps even a small painted toy. For our rulers will take good care of the children; they will introduce Ovaltine into the kindergartens, so that the children will grow healthy and strong and later make good workers, receiving a modest but honorable reward, a healthy and relaxing holiday, in accordance with the principle, *Kraft durch Freude,* meaning strength from joy, meaning that one has to rest, take care of one's health, brush one's teeth, eat sensibly, and lead a hygienic life, because that is the indispensable condition of productive and disciplined work. And as you know, dear Mr. Kujawski, *Arbeit macht frei,* work makes man free, and it makes him especially so in the sunshine of European peace. We will lack only one thing. Only one! The right of dissent. The right to say out loud that we want a free and independent Poland, that we want to brush our teeth and go on holiday in our own way, conceive children and work in our own way, think in our own way, live and die. This is the one thing we will find missing in the sunshine of European peace, which you, my friend, hold to be the highest good."

The tailor licked his lips with the tip of his tongue. The metal clasps on the judge's slippers, which only a moment ago reminded him of two tiny, twinkling stars, now seemed to him the eyes of a wild beast.

"Your honor, please. . . ." he muttered. "I want peace, of course, but under different conditions. First, Hitler must go."

"For Hitler to go, there has to be another war, Mr. Kujawski," said the judge. "So what will it be, my friend? Doesn't peace suit you anymore this evening? Are you already yearning for battle? Haven't we had enough of all this madness? Does a bloodthirsty executioner lurk inside of you—is that it? That I didn't expect, Mr. Kujawski! Haven't you had your fill of victims, of fires, of Polish and non-Polish blood being spilled in the world?"

The judge started to laugh. He stopped the rocking chair. The eyes of the wild beast went out.

"All right, my friend. We're agreed at last. Remember, Mr. Kujawski! We should always be concerned with Poland, with Polishness, with our freedom. Not with some European peace. That's bunk for fools. But Poland. Am I right?"

"Of course you're right, your honor," Kujawski answered. "I'm a dwarf not only in stature, but also in intellect."

"Never say such things out loud! The walls have ears. There might be some home-bred demiurges in there, only waiting for people to lose faith in their own reason, to begin to doubt themselves and to wonder if they don't really have, as you said, a dwarflike intellect."

"Demiurges?" the tailor repeated. "I've never heard of this. Are they like plumbers?"

6

"They're tricksters, my dear friend, who peddle mankind's salvation. Before you know it, they'll come crawling out of some hole—first one, then another. In their pockets they carry the philosopher's stone. They all have a different one, and they throw these stones at one another. Only they usually manage to hit the heads of honest people like you and me. . . . They want to arrange our future to their own liking. And they want to dress up our past to their own liking, too. You haven't come across their sort before, Mr. Kujawski?"

"Maybe I have," the tailor said in a conciliatory tone, and again greedily eyed the faun in the gilded frame.

"On the other hand," the judge continued, "your remark about the plumbers is most interesting. I hope you're not a prophet, dear Mr. Kujawski. For the day might come when they'll flush us all down the drain. Then we will truly be in a pretty pickle."

"As to the picture," the tailor resumed delicately, "I could still take this faun today. Figure the cost of the frame separately. The boy will come with a rickshaw, we'll wrap the picture up in paper, tie it with string, and it will be set to go."

"It will be set to go, Mr. Kujawski, but I'd like to hear your offer first."

"You mentioned to Pawelek that payment could be partially in provisions."

"Why, of course. That would be most welcome. I was thinking especially of meat."

Kujawski wagged his finger playfully at the judge.

"Your honor is supposed to be quite an intellectual, but you also have a good head for business."

He said this gaily, but instantly felt nervous. He wasn't certain if it was proper to speak to the judge in this way. Kujawski had more cash on him than Romnicki would see in an entire year, yet he felt awkward in the presence of this old man in the rocking chair. Not only because the judge had once been his benefactor, but for a rather banal reason: because he knew his place in the world. The time hadn't yet come when money and power decided a man's position. The tailor belonged to an era founded on a spiritual order that was as delicate as porcelain yet as durable as Roman aqueducts—a hierarchy of human souls. Everyone knew there existed an aristocracy not of birth but of the spirit. Kujawski felt uneasy and looked at the judge. But Romnicki laughed.

"I wish I did have a good head for business, dear Mr. Kujawski. I wish I did; I can't pretend otherwise," he said merrily. He was sensitive as a seismograph, with that special sensitivity poets call the intelligence of emotion, so he said also: "But fate has blessed me by bringing me together with you, and you have the head to think for both of us. I put myself in your hands entirely, whatever you propose."

And then, so as not to offend Kujawski and spoil the pleasure he took in doing business, he added firmly: "But don't think I won't bargain stubbornly, dear Mr. Kujawski."

"That's understood," the tailor answered. He thought he would overpay for the painting, just so he could sit again on the threadbare little couch in this living room, with its odor of old objects and the dust from many books.

II

Pawelek Kryński opened his eyes and looked at his hands. He always did this after awaking. Had they already turned blue, were they dead, with blackened fingernails, emitting a cadaverous stench? Or were they still his own, alive? Pawelek—that's what everyone called him from the time he was a child—was about to turn nineteen, and extraordinary things happened to a young man of that age living in those times. Already he understood well the difference between the sexes and was losing his faith in immortality. He would regain it much later, but his early manhood, like his old age, accustomed him to death. Pawelek Kryński was entering that period when love and death become a man's inseparable companions and the thought of them never leaves him.

A few years later, an eighteen-year-old displaying such fear and anguish would be merely comical. But Pawelek belonged to an era when the young wanted to be grown up. Boys of fifteen donned men's suits and demanded duties and responsibilities. They fled childhood because it lasted too long. Children had no honor, and these young men wanted honor above all else.

He opened his eyes and looked at his hands. They still belonged to him. Relieved, he collapsed again into the pillow. Henio had visited him during the night. But Henio's features were blurred, and his voice so soft that Pawelek couldn't make out the words. He only understood Henio's gesture. As always, Henio gave a signal during Pawelek's sleep. Then Pawelek would say, "Where are you, Henio?" but he'd get no answer. He didn't like this recurring dream, but if one morning he awoke with the feeling that Henio hadn't come, he was disappointed. Where did he disappear to, that monster? he would wonder.

He opened his eyes and again examined his hands. It occurred to him that he was neglecting his relationship with God. He didn't believe as strongly as he had before, or as he would again; he felt skeptical, rebellious, contemptuous, hesitant. But even as he counted on Heaven's patience, he feared its anger.

His hands were a good color, they were strong. He sighed with relief and jumped out of bed. He had many important things to accomplish today, things requiring valor and dignity. Two women appeared at his bedside. Mrs. Irma Seidenman, gold, violet, and beautiful, whom he was renouncing, and Monika, silver, dark, like a Russian icon, whom he was starting to love passionately.

Irma was Pawelek's first, boyhood love. Before the war she had lived in the apartment next door. Pawelek was thirteen when he began to love her. She was the wife of Dr. Ignacy Seidenman, a radiologist and scholar. The doctor liked Pawelek. Meeting him on the stairs, he would ask him about school, give him candy, and once he even invited the boy to his office with its X-ray machine. Irma was a golden-haired beauty with azure blue eyes and a slender figure. Even before the war Pawelek dreamed of her at night. He would awaken terrified, not recognizing his own body, which was hot, taut, aching. Irma was like an illness, she caused only torment. When she offered him candy or chocolate, he was mortified. For her he would conquer exotic lands, plunder fortresses, vanquish hostile hordes. They didn't speak the same language. He sailed toward her in a mighty ship, in a galleon with one hundred guns, in an Indian dugout; she approached him with a praline in her hand. Later, he no longer rowed a canoe wearing a feathered headdress. Irma was moving around Warsaw. A Jewish widow with a Nordic face, full of determination. It was wartime. Pawelek was finishing classes in secret underground schools and trying to earn money to help his mother. His father was in a German POW camp for officers.

Dr. Seidenman died before the war and Irma lived alone, moving from one apartment to another on the Aryan side of the city. Pawelek always had time for her. She could count on him. She was trying to save her husband's research files so that after the war radiology could develop along the lines established by the discoveries and observations of Dr. Ignacy Seidenman. Pawelek helped her in this. She was more and more beautiful. He feared for her safety and was tormented by jealousy. Irma was in her thirties, and there were many men around her.

Pawelek passed his final exams in the underground schools. He earned a little money acting as a middleman in the art trade. During the occupation, educated and formerly wealthy people with nothing to live on were selling off paintings, furniture, books. New, sometimes immense, fortunes were made, whose sources were not always clean. In part they came from the underground economy, without which the country, a mercilessly exploited hinterland of the German war machine, could not exist; and in part also from the plunder of Jewish property, for although the Germans, of course, took the greater portion of this loot, more than one valuable crumb fell into Polish hands. Pawelek moved about on that singular border between the ruined collectors of prewar days—those once well-to-do owners of engravings, canvases, and silver settings who were now forced to sell—and a small but vigilant and enterprising group of nouveaux riches, insatiable, hard, cold, boastful, among whom one could find now and then genuine connoisseurs and lovers of beauty. Perhaps they were people who were unlucky before the war—former travelers of the byroads—who now at last could step up onto the main track and retaliate against their once more fortunate competitors. In the final analysis, these were rather shady affairs, but some of the participants were people like Kujawski, the tailor, a rich man and a collector but who, to the surprise of his clients, often proved to have a good heart and a generous spirit. Pawelek stuck to him, and the tailor liked Pawelek. For a time they were inseparable. Then relations relaxed somewhat, not because of any business disagreement, but because Pawelek was kept busy with his classes at the underground university and with affairs of the heart.

He met Monika. She was eighteen, with raven hair, a silvery complexion, a cameolike profile, and the languid grace of a lazy beast of prey. In the late fall of 1942, Pawel kissed Monika. Her mouth was cold, her lips tightly pressed together, her eyes hostile.

"Never again!" she said. "Never again."

But a few days later he kissed Monika's mouth again. She returned his kiss. He nearly died. He loved her. She was beautiful, wise, good. He was nothing next to her. A pebble by the roadside. An autumn leaf. A homeless ghost. Once, in a rickshaw, he put his hand on her knee. She stiffened. He withdrew his hand. He felt the wings of death beating above him. On another day, as they were walking on Marszalkowska Street, they met Kujawski. He lifted his hat. He was a man of great delicacy and cared about good manners.

Monika said, "What a funny little man."

Pawelek acknowledged that Kujawski was a funny little man.

A week later, when they had some business together, the tailor brought up Monika.

"You're very lucky, Pawelek."

"How so, Mr. Kujawski?"

"That girl I saw you with on Marszalkowska Street. She's beautiful, definitely beautiful. . . ."

He hesitated for a moment, then shook his head and added: "Definitely? What am I saying? She is infinitely beautiful. . . ."

Pawelek acknowledged that Kujawski was a wise man, an art expert, a serious connoisseur.

He loved Monika, but he also loved Irma. They were different loves. With Monika, he wanted to spend his entire life; with Irma, a few hours. With Monika, he wanted to grow old; with Irma, to grow up. But he lived in cruel times. His dreams didn't come true. The first time he declared his love to Irma, on the terrace of a café near the Avenue Kléber in Paris, she was already an old woman. And the beautiful Monika had been dead for thirty years. Neither woman contributed significantly to Pawelek's emotional growth. The women who were to stamp and mark his life were to come later. But Irma and Monika accustomed him to death. For this he remained grateful.

But this morning, looking at his hands as he got up out of bed, gratitude was not what he felt. He was energetic and determined. Today, he resolved, he would finish once and for all with his love for Irma and would give himself wholeheartedly to Monika. He still believed that he was master of his own choices. He believed in freedom. He must be forgiven. He was not yet nineteen.

He washed himself in cold water, snorting, and was almost happy. But not quite, because he remembered again Henio Fichtelbaum. His classroom friend. The boy of the Mosaic faith. His best friend from childhood, boyhood, and early adulthood. Henio Fichtelbaum, who helped Pawelek in his math assignments. Capricious, handsome, dark, intense.

There were moments when they hated each other. Henio pouted. "I don't give a fig about you, Pawelek," he would say and storm off into the trees of the Saxon Gardens, small, loathsome, with a satchel on his back. Pawelek kicked the chestnuts in helpless rage. They detested each other. Sometimes cruel Henio would turn around and come back. Pouting, looking down at his feet, also kicking chestnuts.

"Have it your way," he would say. "We can go together to Królewska Street."

At other times, Pawelek would set off in pursuit of Henio.

"Stop! Wait! I'm coming with you. . . ."

They were Indians. They were Abyssinians. Henio would throw a plaid blanket round his shoulders and say to Pawelek, "I'm Haile Selassie! And you are the commander of my armies."

At other times Pawelek took the blanket and was emperor. They let out battle cries; the Italians fled. Henio shot from cannons, Pawelek fired pistols. They took aim with bows and arrows, threw spears.

Henio Fichtelbaum liked sweets; Pawelek liked films. They argued. Henio wanted to have some chocolate; Pawelek wanted to go to the movies. They argued because parting would have been unbearable. They were the kind of friends adults never have. They died for each other in play and were prepared to die for real because they didn't understand death yet and so weren't afraid of it. They lacked the imagination.

Later, they didn't need imagination. In 1940 Henio Fichtelbaum moved to the ghetto. Two years later, he escaped and turned up at Pawelek's, who set him up in an excellent hiding place at a watch-maker he knew. Henio Fichtelbaum moved to an attic. Pawelek kept him supplied with books and information, but Henio rebelled, whined. The ghetto experience faded in his memory and the attic drove him crazy.

"It's a prison!" Henio Fichtelbaum said.

"For God's sake, Henio, you should have your head examined. Where is it going to be any better? You've got to be patient."

"I want to go out, Pawelek."

"It's out of the question!"

"I'm going to go out!"

"You're a moron, an idiot, a fool!" Pawelek screamed.

Henio didn't go. Then, later, he couldn't stand it anymore. When he returned, Pawelek made a scene.

"But you see, everything's fine," Henio Fichtelbaum would say, cool as a cucumber. "I went out and I'm alive. Nothing happened."

"You have no conscience!" Pawelek would cry.

They were friends. Henio gave in. Not because he feared for his life, but because he loved Pawelek. But two months later he vanished without a trace. Pawelek prayed fervently. Weeks passed with no news. The whole winter passed. Henio didn't exist anymore. Only late at night, when Pawelek was falling asleep, he would appear in the darkness and give a signal. It's a sign of life, Pawelek thought, and would fall asleep. Women woke him in the morning. Irma and Monika. All three emerged from Pawelek's dreams. Only Henio Fichtelbaum was not physically present at any other time, was always horribly absent. He has died, Pawelek would think during the day. But Henio would come again at night and give the signal.

He also came later, for many years. The world in which Henio had remained behind no longer existed, but still he appeared at night and gave Pawelek the signal. But by then Pawelek thought it was the sign of death, not of life. Don't call me, he would say to Henio Fichtelbaum's shadow, you have no right. He fell asleep unafraid, for he knew that Henio Fichtelbaum wasn't God's messenger, only a good memory. Maybe they are one and the same thing, he sometimes thought.

But he firmly believed that God was also love.

For in the end it is fair to say that Pawelek was one of those favored by destiny. He survived the war and experienced love. It's an astonishing thing. He was practically a child of fortune! When he was little more than twenty, everything he had ever known went up in flames. This city had been the only world he had. Not even the whole city, just its nucleus, the several streets between the Belvedere and the Castle, between the shore of the Vistula and the Wola cemetery. The air, the sky, and the earth were different here. Buildings blocked out the horizon. As a child he had trod every square centimeter of this bit of ground. He had no other country. At its center lay the Saxon Gardens and its adjoining streets—on one side beautiful, light, and elegant; on the other noisy, ugly, and poor. No border separated these two worlds. In the shade of the chestnut trees of the Saxon Gardens, ladies in smart suits, veiled hats, and high-heeled shoes and men in trench coats, derbies, and fur collars rubbed elbows with dark-haired passersby in stained smocks and boots, shrill market women in wigs, boys with corkscrew curls and skullcaps, and weary old men with canes, in trimmed jackets, round peasants' caps, and the worn-out shoes of poor, overworked people. Sitting around the fountain could be seen the insurgents of 1914, the light cavalry soldiers of 1920, nearsighted schoolteachers who in their youth had curtsied to Orzeszkowa, various conspirators and former deportees to Siberia, prisoners of Moabit and of the fortress in Olomuniec, textile merchants from Nowolip and metal wholesalers from Gęsia, antiquarians from Świętojarska Street, young diplomats from the Brühlowski Palace, prostitutes and pious women, the unemployed and the wealthy, Jews, Germans, Ukrainians, French tutors from the former estates of the gentry, White Russian refugees, marriageable young women, students with peasant faces and empty pockets, thieves, and gossips. It was here that Pawelek argued with the cruel Henio over who had won the game of marbles. It was here that they beat up the bolsheviks, forced the Duce's crack regiments to flee, and brought down General Franco's planes, which had dared to bomb the ramparts of the Spanish Republic.

One could take a few steps and find oneself amid palaces, government buildings, limousines, the aromas of coffee and perfume. Or one could go in the opposite direction, toward Graniczna Street, Żabia, Rymarska, and arrive at the very heart of the Jewish diaspora, among small hardware shops, a noisy Hassidic throng, huge porters from the produce market in oilcloth caps and laborers' shirts, the bustle of commerce, the neighing of horses, the dusty display windows of impoverished hatters' workshops sporting the sign MODES or DERNIER CRI, fruit shops, candy shops, barber shops, shoemakers and pursemakers, street peddlers hawking jeans and bagels.

One could also walk in still another direction, toward the steeples of old churches and the musty little buildings and convents, toward the world of proletarian torment and of the rebellious dreams of the common people. It was precisely there that the Royal Castle touched the cathedral, the cathedral the Market, and the Market the Vistula and the Jordan.

This was Pawel's entire world, which in the course of a few years, as he stood helplessly by, disappeared underground before his very eyes. It literally disappeared, collapsed into ruin, burying in the rubble both people and the Polish way of life.

Pawel survived the war. Wasn't that enough? No, he still experienced love. It's astonishing. He was indeed fortune's child.

III

——————

The cell was a narrow cage. In it stood a single chair. Walls on three sides. On the fourth, facing the corridor, a door with bars from the ceiling to the stone floor. On the ceiling shone a strong, bare light bulb.

Irma Seidenman sat down on the chair, as she was ordered to do. The guard locked the door and walked away with a heavy gait.

She wasn't alone. She could hear the breathing of others, locked up in cages along the corridor. But only their breathing.

Irma Seidenman bowed her head, placed it in her hands, leaned her elbows on her knees, and, hunched over, silent and concentrated, she froze. She felt a kind of curiosity, a desire to experience every passing moment—the concentration and the silence, her own breathing, the beating of her heart.

So what Irma Seidenman had long expected had finally come to pass. Almost every day for the last two years she had been preparing herself for just such an ending. She had heard tales around town about the corridor of narrow cells. She had imagined the corridor. It turned out to be somewhat different, smaller, perhaps a little cozier, not so terrifying as in the stories she had listened to with pounding heart. Now she was in this corridor. She no longer had to fear that she would find herself here. The wall, the bars, the lightbulb, the muffled breathing nearby, and her own breathing, oddly measured and quiet. Her body rendered the corridor familiar, adapted itself to it. This was now Irma Seidenman's entire world. This is where she had to live.

All at once she thought that a life is only that which has passed. There is no life other than memory. The future does not exist, not only here, behind bars, but everywhere—in the street, in the forest, on the sea, in the arms of a beloved man. Life is that which has been realized, that which can be remembered, that which happened and passed and now remains in memory. The future cannot be my life, Irma Seidenman thought, because I am not present in the future; I feel neither hunger there nor cold nor warmth. That which will happen somewhere and sometime is still beyond me, concealed behind these walls and bars, beyond the space I occupy and beyond my understanding, somewhere in distant stars, in a cosmic predestination. My life is here, because I am here, my body and above all else my memory. Only that which has already happened is my life—and nothing more than that! Therefore, thinking about life means thinking about the remembered past: the closing of the cell door is the past, this bowing of my head, this leaning it against my arms. This I have experienced, dear God! I have experienced nothing but that which I remember. Nothing exists outside of memory.

She remembered her husband, Dr. Ignacy Seidenman, a tall, slender man whom she had loved very much, although they couldn't have children. This pained them at the beginning of their marriage, but they quickly became reconciled to it, discovering happiness together. Dr. Ignacy Seidenman died of cancer in 1938. When he died, Irma Seidenman was convinced she would not be able to live; her despair seemed beyond endurance. But after a time, putting in order her husband's scientific legacy, his work in radiology, so occupied her that the pain of her loss diminished. Later, quite suddenly and not without surprise, she noticed that she was more absorbed by radiology than by thoughts of him. At first she only felt obliged to establish order in his chaotic scholarly output; she regarded this as a moral duty, something she owed his memory. But after a time she began to notice essential gaps in his notes, photographs, descriptions of states of illness, conclusions—and she felt almost ashamed that her husband, a man so industrious and wise, had not managed to avoid a certain disorder and carelessness. She could not expose the legacy of Ignacy Seidenman to spiteful criticism. She traveled to Paris to seek the help of Professor Lebrommell. Before she had had the time to come to grips with the thousands of portfolios and envelopes, war broke out. By then Ignacy Seidenman took up less space in her life than did his archives. And it was because of these archives that she did not even think of moving to the ghetto. She was a light blonde with blue eyes, a straight, shapely nose, and a delicate, somewhat ironically contoured mouth. She was a very beautiful woman, thirty-six years old, with a sizable fortune in jewelry and gold dollar coins. She placed Dr. Seidenman's archives for safekeeping with friends, in a roomy wooden villa in Józefów, and after first changing apartments and personal documents three times to render her past untraceable, she finally settled as an officer's widow, Maria Magdalena Gostomska, in a pretty studio apartment in the Mokotów district of Warsaw. She didn't have to worry about making a living, and anyway her needs were modest; she contented herself with the life of a solitary woman who in a world gone mad nevertheless busied herself completing the work of a deceased doctor. She traveled quite regularly to Józefów, made notes in the margins of her husband's manuscripts, maintained contact with Warsaw doctors, people worthy of confidence who even in these cruel days found the time for conversation with the beautiful and intelligent woman so preoccupied with the problems of X rays and the riddles of radiology that she seemed not to notice the hell in which they all lived.

She noticed the hell. But she said that even in hell one must stay one's course as long as it is possible to do so. Now and then she reproached herself for hearing with a certain indifference the news from the other side of the wall. But she didn't have her own dead in the ghetto. She no longer had them anywhere, for the cemetery where Dr. Ignacy Seidenman lay had been leveled to the ground, the headstones stolen or used for cobbling streets. Dr. Seidenman's body did not exist, but Irma Seidenman was convinced that he himself did dwell somewhere, perhaps near God or perhaps as the spiritual energy of the cosmos or as a particle of the air she breathed or the water she drank. Moreover, he remained in her life as a memory. She saw him often, talked with him in the evenings; he came to her in her dreams. But he didn't come as a lover or a husband; she didn't feel his arms or his kisses, but only his presence, serious, silent, perhaps even a little reproachful, for Dr. Seidenman had the right to nurse a slight grievance on account of her criticisms, of those corrections she felt obliged to make in his manuscripts. Now and then she argued with him in her dreams, but she was always somehow conscious that she was arguing with herself, because he was dead, and one could not argue with the dead.

So they were together all those years, only that she lived in the very real world, with a multitude of smaller and larger cares and also with a great fear, which stemmed from her knowledge about herself, from that Jewishness, well hidden it is true thanks to her looks, her excellent documents, and the goodwill of those around her who harbored no suspicions, and even if they did, felt the pressure of two thousand years of European civilization. They were together, only that Dr. Seidenman remained somewhat on the side, luckily invisible and out of the reach of the persecutors.

Irma Seidenman told herself every day that without a doubt she would survive the war, and complete and later publish her husband's work, something she considered not only a labor of love and remembrance, but also—and this she felt not without some shame and a touch of pride—as her own accomplishment in radiology, all the greater because she had had no medical training and had achieved everything through intelligence, industriousness, and will. She felt such confidence in her ideas and observations that she intended in the future to undertake belatedly the study of medicine, perhaps even under the tutelage of Professor Lebrommell, who was also, after all, her deceased husband's mentor.

So she told herself that she would survive the war, and at the same time believed that this was an entirely absurd thought, for she would certainly be exposed and would share the fate of other Jews. She awaited that day with a kind of bitter curiosity and made a firm resolution to die peacefully, without regret, for after all she had accomplished much, and with each passing day was closer to finishing her work on her husband's papers. She very much wanted to survive for a bit longer, to still be able to complete something, to correct, to change, but she didn't succumb to a feverish anxiety for she was conscious of the fact that even if she would not be able to finish, others would. Someone certainly would finish; there were intelligent and decent people in the world who would take up her work and see it through to its conclusion. And were such people no longer to exist, then the work of Dr. Ignacy Seidenman would also lose its meaning.

So she hoped she would survive and was also convinced that she would perish, which was a most human, natural frame of mind and didn't surprise her in the least. When, coming out of the gateway on Krucza Street, she came face-to-face with Bronek Blutman, who she had heard was an informer and engaged in handing over Jews, hoping in this way to save his own skin—he had been a Jewish gigolo from the prewar dance clubs—her first thought was to settle the matter with a quick payoff.

Bronek Blutman said, "Imagine meeting in this way, dear Mrs. Seidenman. Still so elegant, well, well!"

"I won't play games with you," she answered calmly. "We can settle this."

"What is it that we can settle, my pretty one?" asked Bronek Blutman.

"How much do you want? You're a young, good-looking man, and men like you have large expenses."

"Mrs. Seidenman, my dear," Bronek Blutman answered, "neither rubles nor gold dollars can save me. I have my assigned quota."

"I don't want to get any angrier than I am already," she said. "You can fill your quota elsewhere."

"Nothing doing," said Blutman. "I'm fishing for real. Which is why we'll now go where we must. . . ."

"You're doing bad business, Mr. Blutman. I'm no Mrs. Seidenman. My name is Gostomska. My husband was an artillery officer and died in the war."

"We all died in this war," Bronek Blutman replied. "Let's go, my dear!"

"They won't be able to prove a thing."

"I'll prove it!"

Then Irma Seidenman shrugged her shoulders nonchalantly, although she felt a dreadful chill around her heart and her legs were buckling under her.

"How can they believe some little Jew, when an officer's widow will firmly deny . . ."

"Don't be funny, Mrs. Seidenman. Let's go!"

He took her by the arm. Softly and gently, for he was once a good gigolo.

"My name is Gostomska," she said loudly. A passerby looked at them and frowned.

"My name is Gostomska and I am not a Jew," she said louder still. Two men stopped.

"What do you want with this lady?" one of them asked.

"It's none of your business," Bronek Blutman replied roughly.

"You're a little Jew yourself," the man said.

"I know best who I am," Bronek exclaimed, and pulled Irma Seidenman by the arm.

An empty rickshaw was passing by. He hailed it. They got in. The two men stood on the sidewalk, expressions of fear, distaste, and derision on their faces. Bronek Blutman placed his hand on the nape of Irma's neck.

"I always had a fancy for you," he said gaily, "but it's too late now."

"Move your paw or I'll slap you!" she cried. "My name is Gostomska, Maria Magdalena Gostomska."

"Whore," Bronek muttered and laughed. But he withdrew his hand. Irma Seidenman turned to the rickshaw driver. She gave him her address. She asked that he notify Dr. Adam Korda, her neighbor, that she had been mistakenly arrested as a person of Jewish descent.

"This is a scandal!" she added with impassioned disgust. The driver replied that he would notify Dr. Korda.

Dr. Korda had no idea that Irma was Jewish. He had been her neighbor for more than a year now. As a classical philologist, he was interested in the Jewish question only insofar as it pertained to Tacitus or to the destruction of Jerusalem by Titus. From time to time he brought Irma preserves of wild roses, and they chatted a bit in the evenings about the evil, difficult times. Irma gave his name and address because he was simply a decent man, and it was important that some decent man know that shortly she would be put to death.

She didn't think any more about Dr. Korda. She also didn't think about Bronek Blutman from the moment he left Stuckler's office. Stuckler sat behind a desk, and she sat in a chair in front of it. She gazed out the wide window, which faced a blue sky.

She didn't confess. She said stubbornly, "I don't know this man. I'm not a Jew. My name is Maria Magdalena Gostomska. I'm an officer's widow. You have my documents, after all."

He had her *Kennkarte,* and he had more. He also had an old, well-worn I.D. card of the Circle of Army Families from the town of Grodno, issued in 1937. He had a photograph of a stout man in his forties in an army uniform, with a captain's insignia. The photograph was also printed in Grodno. Irma Seidenman had good documents. Stuckler was opening and closing a silver cigarette case inscribed with the gold initials *I.S.* She had received this cigarette case from her husband, Dr. Ignacy Seidenman, shortly before his death; it was her last present from him, and she had not wanted to part with it.

Bronek Blutman had shown Stuckler this cigarette case and had said with a smile, "Just take a look, Herr Sturmführer. This is probably the best proof. I S, Irma Seidenman, or, if you prefer, Ignacy Seidenman. I also knew him."

"Where is he?" Stuckler asked.

"He's dead. He died before the war," Bronek replied.

"It's not my cigarette case," she said. "I found it a few weeks ago.

You can see that it's silver. And the letters are gold. You don't just throw such things away these days."

She repeated this over and over, also when Bronek Blutman was no longer in the room. Stuckler sat lazily opening and closing the cigarette case. After three quarters of an hour he ordered Irma taken away.

She sat in the cell, and everything that had happened since morning was now her most real life.

The cigarette case, she thought. It's always some trifle that decides everything. A cigarette case, without which one can live perfectly well, which one wouldn't even notice not having. The cigarette case. Irma was certain that were it not for that damned little box she would have been let go. Although it is true that at one moment Stuckler got up and carefully examined her ears, and then quickly returned to his desk. She had heard of this nonsense about the ears of Jewish women. They had men unzip their trousers. With women, they looked for something on their earlobes. They themselves didn't know what it was they were looking for. But they were scrupulous and did not want to make mistakes. Someone in Berlin had figured out that a Jewish woman's earlobes bear mysterious markings of race. But there were no such markings. So they poked around the ears with their fingers, peered at them—and beyond that they weren't certain of anything. Stuckler returned to his desk, disappointed. But he had the cigarette case. If he did not have it, he would have let Irma Seidenman go. Of this she was almost certain.

To die because of such a trifle, she thought, is truly unjust. She did not feel in the least that she would die because she was a Jew, for she did not feel herself to be Jewish. In any case she did not consider Jewishness a defect, but she was convinced that she would die because of the cigarette case. And that idea struck her as ridiculous, stupid, vile, and odious.

IV

_____

At the end of a courtyard off
Brzeska Street stood an outhouse on which hung an enamel plate
bearing the words KEY WITH THE DOORMAN. The information was
untrue. By the end of the twenties the lock to the outhouse had rusted
and the door was shut with a hook. During the day there was a lot
of traffic here; women from the nearby marketplace used it, as did a
certain prewar masturbator sporting binoculars and a derby. But in
the evening, when the market was closed, no one came by, because
the building's tenants had two toilets on each floor, and for those who
lived in the basement the landlord, in a fit of magnanimity, had
installed before the war, right near the gate leading from the street
into the courtyard, a toilet with a porcelain bowl.

Henryczek Fichtelbaum sat in the outhouse and thought about
God. He had entered Brzeska Street at sunset, lured by the odor of
vegetables, scraps of which lay on the pavement. But he didn't have
a chance to do anything about it when he encountered the watchful

gaze of a fellow in an oilcloth cap. Frightened, he fled into the nearest entryway, looked around the courtyard paved with stones made slippery by thousands of human feet and horses' hooves, and—feverishly seeking a shelter—found himself in the outhouse. The door could be shut from the inside with a latch. It was difficult to sit in the outhouse, for it dated from the times of the Russian Empire and Czar Alexander III's policemen used to shit in it. Henryczek Fichtelbaum had heard that the czar was a man of great height and physical strength, that he Russified the Poles with exceptional zeal, and that he was highly esteemed in all of Europe. The outhouse was constructed for conducting one's business in a standing or squatting position, for in the days of empire people greatly overreacted to the latest discoveries in hygiene. But now times had changed, and Henryczek Fichtelbaum sat down on the metal step, leaned his shoulder against the wall, breathed in the aroma of excrement, and whispered:

"God, if I am to die, make it so that first I can get something to eat and get warm, because I can't stand it any longer. . . ."

He hadn't eaten in three days and felt cramps in his stomach and dizziness. He was chilled through to the bone. Mornings and evenings could be very cool still.

"God, have pity on me! Why do You keep tormenting me?"

Henryczek was very demanding in his relationship with God, as is everyone who doesn't really believe and turns to Him in special circumstances, for a last, although none too reliable, resort. Henryczek was brought up in a religiously indifferent home, on the border between two worlds, in a no man's land, because his father, the lawyer Jerzy Fichtelbaum, although he came from a family of pious Orthodox Jews, had studied law, abandoned the old milieu, and parted with the Mosaic faith. The family was Galician, poor, provincial, although Jerzy Fichtelbaum's father had belonged to people who, for that era, were educated and moved in rabbinical circles. The lawyer was a modern man, did not believe in God, and was a bit of a communist, as were many other Jewish intellectuals then who looked to communism as a remedy for all racial prejudice, forgetting quite stupidly that communism developed in Russia.

Henryczek Fichtelbaum was thus brought up in a worldly, free-thinking atmosphere, perhaps even an absurdly free-thinking one, for Jerzy Fichtelbaum wanted to be more European and libertine than the greatest European libertines in Paris, which is understandable for he came from a remote Galician backwater. Henryczek encountered religion only in school, where most of his friends were Catholics and his best friend, Pawelek Kryński, was considered to be a boy of great religious ardor—although that was an exaggeration because Pawelek also had his difficulties with God. And so it was that Henryczek Fichtelbaum grew into an impious young man whose interests ran toward the sciences, mainly mathematics, physics, and chemistry, and so toward the mysteries of the material world. Even the great shock he experienced at moving from the beautiful apartment on Królewska Street to miserable quarters in the ghetto did not incline Henryczek to deeper metaphysical contemplation.

At first, in the ghetto, he did not lack any of the necessities of life, but soon there was a shortage of everything, and after a year the lawyer's family understood that it was condemned to death. Soon thereafter, Henryczek's mother died. He was left with his father and his sister Joasia, a small tot he loved dearly. But he was young, still strong, and hadn't lost hope. He decided to go over to the Aryan side and there try to survive. He said good-bye to his father and sister and escaped from the ghetto.

That day, for the first time in his life, he thought seriously about God. He was lying in the darkness, on a damp sidewalk near the ghetto wall, and he was completely alone. A human being cannot be completely alone at a moment of trial. He needs other people, and if there aren't any, he suddenly discovers the presence of God. It is usually a fleeting presence, barely palpable, as if God had walked by in a hurry and disappeared around the corner of the nearest building. Before tackling the wall Henryczek Fichtelbaum whispered, "Help me, God!" Then he climbed over and nothing bad happened to him. So he forgot about God.

He managed well for several months, thanks to some modest financial resources and Pawelek's zealous care. But one time he made a mistake because he had become self-confident, and since he was only eighteen success had gone to his head. He went to the pastry shop on Marszalkowska Street, forgetting about his looks. Later, he justified his lack of caution by telling himself that never before had he studied his face from the perspective of racial characteristics, and what's more, no one had ever called his attention to Jewish features as something worthy of observation. If before the war he had distinguished himself in school in anything, it had been for his love of science, not the shape of his nose or lips. In the pastry shop he aroused first discreet curiosity, then alarm, and finally the violent reaction of one man, who shouted, "A Jew is eating cake!" as if a Jew eating cake in the pastry shop on Marszalkowska Street was something on the order of a dinosaur, a Russian archduchess without diamond studs in her ears, or a Jew eating cake in the pastry shop on Marszalkowska Street in the year 1942. Several people quickly left the shop. The waiter exclaimed, "Oh, Jesus! Now they will kill us all!" Only an elderly man remained calm, delivering a short, concise speech directed at the ceiling: "First of all they're going to kill the Jews anyway, and then us, so there is no reason to panic, let this young man eat his cake. I'm prepared to pay for it. Please don't get overexcited, don't prostrate yourselves, have some dignity, there's a war on, we are all doomed unless Adolf Hitler kicks the bucket in some unexpected fashion, which by the way I dearly wish upon him. So leave it be, nothing has happened, this is Poland, this is still Poland, and please don't take this hope away from me. That is all I have to say about this incident."

But another man cried out, trembling and pale, "Isn't it enough that they're murdering them, do they have to roam around town and endanger others too, complete innocents? I did not see this Jew, I did not see him. . . ."

The elderly man shrugged his shoulders and replied harshly, "But you *are* seeing him, my dear man!"

But in fact they could no longer see him, for Henryczek Fichtel-baum had jumped out of the shop and started to run, terrified as he had never been before, even more than on that evening when he had climbed over the ghetto wall, because then he had been alone and only

God was passing hurriedly nearby, whereas now he found himself in a crowd of people, felt the gazes of passersby—some sympathetic, some astonished, some fearful, some ill-disposed and maybe even downright hostile and expressing a firm resolve. And so he ran without pausing for breath, further and further away. He stopped only when he reached Pulawska Street, climbed down the escarpment toward the distant Vistula, and then quite suddenly, and without good reason, decided to escape from the city.

He spent the winter in the countryside with a kind-hearted peasant who set up a hiding place in the forest for him, fed him, gave him water, and cursed his Jewishness, which brings people so many worries, cares, and afflictions. But after a time Germans started to comb the area searching for partisans, or maybe moonshine, or maybe just Jews, and Henryczek had to flee. The peasant gave him bread, bacon, a worn navy-blue ski hat, and fifty zlotys for the road. This peasant survived the war and after death surely made it to heaven—although local people, rather small-mindedly, wished him hell, for he had joined the Party.

Henryczek Fichtelbaum returned to Warsaw toward the end of winter. He slept in attics and stairwells, in entryways and garbage dumps. He fed himself with what he managed to beg from decent people. By now he knew that he didn't stand a chance and that before too long he would have to die. This awareness again brought him closer to God, because if death was inevitable, he still had left the choice between God and nothingness.

But he loved science and searched for God only along that road. Sitting in the outhouse he made certain demands of Him, as if he considered himself to be his Creator's equal, and at the same time attempted to discover hard and fast proof of His existence.

In nature nothing perishes, he mused; in nature everything lasts eternally. But the individual elements of nature are by no means eternal, of which observation, as well as my own fate, convinces me. Here I am smelling excrement, which is the result of the transformation of matter, is part of life and is itself alive because it is composed of a countless number of cells, which die by the millions and are born by the millions so that life can go on. Nature goes on, but life has its end; individual life has its end, but the process of life, its continuation, is eternal and unending. What lies behind this? If I accept that matter is eternal and indestructible, although it admittedly transforms itself even as it endures, then I can also accept that there is inherent in it some force, some indestructible energy, and thus something that is elusive and indeterminable yet nevertheless gives it rhythm and ensures continuity. This something undoubtedly exists and certain people have named this something God! In this sense, being a material creation, I am a part of this something, and hence a part of God. Well, all right! But is a leaf a part of Him? It probably is, but it doesn't know it. I am more highly organized matter, and that is why I know that I am more perfect, but nothing more. If God were only willing also to make me less cold, then I could carry my reasoning a step further and occupy myself with the question of my consciousness as well as my moral standards.

At that moment someone walked into the courtyard and Henryczek started to panic. The man was not only drawing nearer but clearly had the intention of using the outhouse, for suddenly the footsteps stopped and a hand yanked at the door, closed from the inside with the latch.

"Damn!" said a hoarse voice. "Is someone in there?"

Henryczek Fichtelbaum didn't hesitate even for a second, because he knew that a ghost could not close the outhouse door from the inside, and answered quietly, "I'm coming out. Just one minute."

"I'll wait," the voice outside the door replied.

For a moment there was silence. But God is merciful to those who seek Him, even if they search for Him in such peculiar circumstances, amid the world's filth and indignities.

The voice outside the door spoke up again. "Well, what's it gonna be, because I've got to go!"

"Just a moment," Henryczek replied.

But the man outside couldn't wait any longer. Henryczek heard some sort of murmur, then the sounds of discharge, finally coughing, receding footsteps, and the man's words: "It's all right, do whatever you want in there!"

A door slammed in the distance, then silence.

"How could I not have believed in You, dear God!" Henryczek Fichtelbaum whispered and almost immediately fell asleep, exhausted by fear, hunger, and all the suffering of the universe, which had converged around him in the outhouse.

He was awakened by a beam of sunlight falling through a crack into the dark interior. It was cold. The sun was rising on Brzeska Street. Henryczek rose also, cautiously unlocked the door, and stepped out into the courtyard. It was empty. The pavement glistened with moisture. The pale sky was more gray than blue. A light breeze mussed Henryczek's hair, bringing with it the smell of spring. I'm still alive, Henryczek thought. He took a deep breath and the cold air stung his throat. He shivered. But the night's sleep had fortified him enough so that he didn't feel hunger as intensely as he had the previous evening. That would come later.

He looked around. The courtyard was built up on all sides, forming an irregular rectangle, wedged in between outbuildings. It was separated from the street by a run-down, damp, and dirty building. Its grimy rear windows, here and there adorned with little curtains, pots of geraniums, or sorry-looking cactuses, which in the eyes of the local residents passed for an especially beautiful, because exotic, ornament, looked directly into the windows of an equally run-down and dirty outbuilding opposite, also adorned with little curtains, geraniums, and cactuses. On the third side, the courtyard was closed off by a wall. Sheds clung to it, already half fallen into ruin, in which horses were now stabled. In future years unlicensed craftsmen's workshops would prosper there, sundry manufacturers of combs, nails, screws, or window frames—seemingly poor businesses but operated by shrewd types with a golden touch and foxlike faces who wanted to keep their heads above water in this devastated city and were successful at it for a time, until the system's iron hand, sweeping away the remains of human resourcefulness from Poland, from Warsaw, from Brzeska Street, strangled them in its awful grip. Opposite the wall and the run-down sheds rose a fence, once probably the boundary of the property, demarcated with trees, of which there now remained only some stumps and a few half-dead, dried-up acacia bushes that, in defiance of the entire world, had just put forth young shoots.

I am trapped, Henryczek thought. I am imprisoned, he thought. But deep down he knew that beyond this courtyard he would also now be forever trapped and imprisoned. This cramped, built-up space did not strike him as more dangerous than the forest in which he had hidden in the winter, and certainly not more dangerous than the streets of the ghetto, separated from the rest of the world by walls. Henryczek Fichtelbaum again breathed in deeply the cool dawn air, the smell of damp hay, garbage, and horses' urine. He did not feel uncomfortable in this courtyard, because he did not see people, their faces and looks, yet at the same time still felt their presence close to him. He was afraid of people, for every passerby endangered him, yet simultaneously their nearness represented some sort of hope.

He knew that his life would not last long, because he was a wise and intelligent young man and did not harbor illusions. He knew that he would die by a human hand, because he would be killed. And yet another man's face, voice, gaze did not fill him with horror. It is hardest to die in solitude, darkness, and silence. Death among others, in the clamor of human cries, the crush of gazes and gestures, seems less cruel. Henryczek Fichtelbaum thought that the death of a soldier during a bayonet attack is probably less terrifying than the lonely agony of a condemned man, even if he were condemned to a death in his own bed.

Why do I have to die, he suddenly thought, when I'm not even nineteen yet? Is this fair? Is it my fault that I was born a Jew, that my ancestors were Jews, that I emerged from Jewish loins? By what right was I first made a Jew so that later I would be condemned to death for my Jewishness?

Henryczek Fichtelbaum wasn't being especially original as he stood leaning against a rough wall in the shade of the outhouse from which he had just emerged. He wasn't being especially original asking himself such questions, to which he sought answers in vain. For it could well be that at that very moment, just then, in the spring of 1943, half of humanity was asking itself the same questions and also not finding answers. Later, when Henryczek's bones had been bleached white in the flames of the burning ghetto, then turned black in the rain amidst the ashes of Warsaw, and finally found themselves in the foundations of new buildings raised up over wartime ruins, various people would also ask themselves the question: How is it possible, exactly, that this chosen nation was called forth into being, that God spoke to this nation and bestowed upon it His laws, and almost simultaneously, from the very first moment of the covenant, exposed His beloved people to the harshest trials and fortune's sharpest thrusts? Could it be that they were chosen to suffer specially, so that thereby they could bear special witness?

Various people puzzled over this dilemma, in the end to no avail, for soon it became clear that God's designs were unknowable—or human interpretations of them unconvincing. At any rate, the world later started in on others and left the Jews in peace, as if their quota of suffering had become exhausted by then and the quota of suffering of others had not. It even turned out that this strange bond that linked Jews with Germans, hence Henio with Goethe, Mendelssohn with Schubert, Marx with Bismarck, Einstein with Heisenberg, was not the only one of its kind or unsurpassed in its ambiguous madness. For behold, in Vietnam people were falling like flies from gas that exceeded Zyklon B in excellence, in Indonesia the rivers quite literally ran red with human blood, in Biafra people were shriveling from hunger to such a degree that next to them the corpses on Nalewki Street in the ghetto looked like the bodies of gluttons, and in Cambodia pyramids were being constructed from human skulls whose numbers exceeded those in the crematoria and gas chambers.

People who years later came to live on top of Henryczek Fichtelbaum's bones did not often think of him, and if they did it was with a certain pride and vanity that here they were, the greatest martyrs under the sun. They were doubly mistaken. First of all because martyrdom is not like nobility that one can inherit, as one can a coat of arms or an estate. Those who lived on top of the bones of Henryczek Fichtelbaum were not martyrs in the least; at most, they were profiting from someone else's martyrdom, which is always stupid and dishonorable. Second, they did not notice that the world had gone forward, leaving far behind it the events of the war with Adolf Hitler.

Henryczek Fichtelbaum didn't know about all this, but even if God had bestowed the gift of prophecy upon him, it would have been of no consolation because at that time, in the spring of 1943, he himself, Henryczek, was about to die—and he knew that he was doomed. He was seeking an answer to the question, Why is the world so unjust and cruel?, but he came up with nothing, just like the millions of other people who later, after his death, would find themselves on the same road and headed where he was heading.

And just at that very moment he was heading toward the courtyard gate, because it was growing lighter, the sky was blue, windows were opening in the surrounding buildings, the carriage horses were neighing in the stables, and a woman ran out into the courtyard—young, pretty, dark haired, in a skirt and pink slip, with bare shoulders, threadbare slippers on her bare feet, a bucket in her hand, shivering from the morning chill. A woman ran out to the well for water, a young whore from Brzeska Street, firm, smooth skinned, nearly half naked. She came out just then into the courtyard, the heels of her slippers clicking against the cobblestones; the bucket clanged as she set it down on the boarding, the heavy arm of the well creaked as she pumped it, up and down, up and down, the water splashed into the bucket like liquid silver, the woman's large, white breasts slipped out because the strap of her slip had slid down her shoulder a bit, the water splashed again, and the woman lifted her head with a merry, roguish smile, the smile of a coquette, sure of itself, seductive, whorish, and pretty. Again the water splashed into the bucket, sprayed the stones all around, and the woman lightly lifted a shapely leg. Clearly she didn't want to get her slipper wet. And just then her eyes—large, dark, washed clean by a peaceful night's sleep on a cot in the ground-floor room, where she received her customers beneath a picture of the Virgin Mary, where during the day the breathing and groans of

34

various men who pressed down on the womb, stomach, and breasts of this girl resounded, and where at night only her calm, measured, and innocent breathing could be heard—just at this moment, when the woman raised her leg so as not to get her slipper wet, her eyes met the eyes of Henryczek Fichtelbaum.

And quite madly, without any justification, perhaps moved solely by his longing for another human being, or rather by his longing for a woman, something he had never yet had although he had desired it for a long time and dreamed of it often (even in the snow-covered forests where he hid like a wild animal, in the garbage dumps where he lived amid his brother worms, brother microbes, and brother refuse), so, moved by his longing for a woman who would distance him from death or shield him from death, Henryczek Fichtelbaum, against all reason and in the face of everything that the experience of the preceding months had taught him, stopped. Not only stopped, but turned back. Not only turned back, but approached the woman, grabbed the bucket handle, and lifted it from the boarding. The woman looked into Henryczek's eyes, then lowered her gaze to his arm, and again looked into his eyes. Slowly she nodded her head, turned around, and walked in the direction of one of the outbuildings, and he walked after her, carrying the bucketful of fresh water.

They entered a dark staircase, climbed several creaking wooden steps. She opened the door then bolted it shut as soon as they were inside. It was a small, cluttered hallway. A bare bulb hung from the ceiling. A table covered in blue oilcloth stood against the wall, and next to it a wooden chair. Further inside, a stool, and on it a washbasin.

"Over there," she said, and pointed out to Henryczek a spot near the stool. He set the bucket down. Nearby stood another bucket, full of scraps. A low door with an opening covered with a percale curtain led to a little room. It had a cot, a holy picture, a wardrobe, and a window that looked out on an old, dark wall. You couldn't see the sky. Neither could you see the well from here. Only the wall and cobblestones.

With a motion of her head the woman showed Henryczek to a

chair. He sat down. She went back into the hallway. He heard a match being struck, the hiss of a gas flame. Then the clanging of a pot, the woman's breathing, the rustle of water filling a vessel. He smelled bread. He closed his eyes. I love this world, he thought, and his eyes filled with tears.

Nothing was happening. Only a shadow was moving across the wall opposite the window, in time with the sun, which was traversing the sky. Nothing was happening, except that Henryczek Fichtelbaum was eating bread with thin slices of bacon and drinking a cup of grain coffee sweetened with saccharine. The coffee burned his lips, but he drank a lot, drank without stopping, and when the cup was empty the woman would silently refill it. And so time passed, the shadow traversed the wall opposite the window, Henryczek Fichtelbaum ate, the woman was silent, looked at him, observed silently how Henry-czek ate, watched without saying a word, as if she didn't know any words, had no language, almost motionless on the cot, still half naked, in the slip whose strap was sliding down, in the slippers she had not wanted to get wet at the well. And when he had eaten she rose from the cot and with a motion of her head ordered him to lie down. He obeyed. She covered him with a woolen plaid shawl and hung his coat up on a peg deep inside the wardrobe. Now she was the one who sat in the chair by the window, behind which the shadow wandered. Henryczek fell asleep. The woman looked at his sleeping face and thought about her village on the Liwiec River, about the sandy riverbanks where she had seen the corpses of murdered Jews, old and young, men, women, and children. She raised her eyes to the holy picture and started to pray in a whisper to the Mother of God for the safety of this young Jew, and then for her own future as a comfortable married woman, the mother of pretty children, enjoying general esteem and not afraid of the coming years.

Henryczek slept until the late afternoon, and when he opened his eyes he saw the darkening window, outside it the darkening wall, the opened wardrobe at the other end of the room, and the profile of the woman, who sat dozing in the chair. He thought that what was to happen had already happened, namely that he had died and gone to heaven. But he knew that he was alive, because he felt hunger and also desire, which probably would not be possible after death.

The woman woke up. They looked each other in the eyes. She spoke.

"So when did you get out of the ghetto?"

She had a husky voice.

"Long ago," he replied. "Back in the fall."

"Well, well," she said. "You probably want to eat again, right?"

He was silent.

She got up from the chair and went to light the stove. Again he heard the rattle of dishes.

He rose from the cot, straightened his legs, and stretched his arms, as he once used to do when he was a healthy, well-fed, happy boy, awaking in his room on Królewska Street. He felt energetic and strong. He stood in the doorway. The gas flame was roaring merrily. The woman, in skirt and slip, bare back, dark hair falling on the nape of her neck, slender strong arms, strong slender calves, stood leaning over the washbasin rinsing out the cup with water from the kettle.

Here was the center of the earth; through here passed the axis of the universe. Not only because the careening, frenzied wagon of fate on which Henryczek Fichtelbaum was heading toward extinction had paused here, not only because Henryczek was here, with his newly awakened hope. Here was the center of the earth, the axis of the universe, because here God Himself had established the core of creation, had placed His index finger centuries ago and with it had drawn the circle encompassing all the meaning of human lives. Here, where the blue flame from the gas stove roared once, flowed the stream at which a Tatar mercenary watered his horses; here ran the track along which a gangster with a tether around his neck went into Polish captivity, and on both sides of the track Jewish and German merchants set up their stalls. Here and nowhere else on the whole earth Sabbath candles were reflected with a faint yellow glow on the sheath of a Russian sword, and Polish hands broke a communion wafer in the shadow of a Prussian Christmas tree. Here and nowhere else in the universe a German poet gave beautiful names to Polish streets, a

Muscovite prince warmed up Polish soldiers for battle so that they would shoot more accurately at the emperor's guard, and Jews consumed by tuberculosis, Russian officers inspired by the spirit of freedom, and Polish deportees in chains together, conspired against tyranny. Here was the center of the earth, the axis of the universe, where stupidity was interlaced with the sublime, odious betrayal with the purest self-sacrifice. In this spot alone the wild, swarthy, and cunning snout of Asia stared from time immemorial straight into the fat, arrogant, and stupid mug of Europe; precisely here and nowhere else the pensive and sensitive eyes of Asia gazed into the rational eyes of Europe. Here was the center of the earth, the axis of the universe, where the West took the East into its arms, and the North stretched out its hand to the South. The unruly horses of the steppes here carried in their saddlebags the books of Erasmus of Rotterdam. Jewish carts, shattering their shafts in the ruts, dispersed Voltairean seeds here. Hegel passed this way in Prussian covered wagons on his way to St. Petersburg, to return later by Russian troika, with Czernyszewski, wrapped in sheepskins. Here was East and West, North and South. On this street the Tatar prostrated himself, his face turned toward Mecca, the Jew read the Torah, the German read Luther, the Pole lit consecrated candles at the foot of the altars in Częstochowa and Ostra Brama. Here was the center of the earth, the axis of the universe, the accumulation of brotherhood and hatred, closeness and strangeness, for here were fulfilled the joint destinies of peoples most distant one from the other. In these mills by the Vistula God made Polish flour for the Polish hungry, Polish flour, heavenly manna, Mosaic and Christian, of the old and the new convenant, for all the martyrs and scoundrels, the saints and the villains of this world.

Henryczek Fichtelbaum was eating bread with a slice of bacon, drinking coffee from the cup, drinking Asia and Europe—his past, fate, and destiny. The gas flame roared, the woman watched Henryczek eating, her expression serene and smiling, perhaps with just a touch of mockery in it because she feared her own goodness and honesty, knew that in the world where she lived one should not be good and honest, that in the end it usually only made one a loser, so she smiled mockingly. But Henryczek Fichtelbaum noticed only the gentleness in her face, and the slight trace of mockery he took for encouragement, temptation; so when he had finished eating and drinking he approached the woman, put his arm around her, and placed his left hand on her breast.

"What's this?" she said uncertainly. "What's this now?"

But she didn't resist, because he was young and handsome, strong and dark like herself, and also because she had never had a Jew yet, and she wanted to have everything that belonged to her world.

She turned off the gas flame, and then the light bulb in the hallway. Outside the window it was already twilight. They lay down on the cot beneath the holy picture. The woman helped Henryczek, because he had never made love before and she had many times.

Later she said, "Well, my man!"

He said in the darkness, with deep conviction, "Now I can die."

"You won't die," she said. "It will work out somehow."

"No," said Henryczek Fichtelbaum. "It can't be helped. Only I don't want to die alone. You understand?"

She nodded. She understood this very well.

"Why should I die alone and so meekly?" he asked, watching the dark window, looking out at the already invisible wall. "I would much rather cry out with hatred and contempt, so that the whole world could hear. You understand?"

She nodded again. This too she understood. But she was a woman, and so she had more common sense and acumen. She had had time to come to know people well. She did not believe that the whole world would hear Henryczek's dying cry. Those who hear the dying are only those who are dying with them. She did not believe in the strength and echo of that cry. Many years later, when she was already a widow and working as a cashier in a butcher shop—a large, fleshy, dark woman with a sour face and a loud voice—the mother of a drunken store supply man—a pale, shrewd fellow who took after his father—the mother of a petty alcoholic from the era of color television sets, furniture acquired through bribes and double dealing, dilapidated and dirty cars, rationed pork ribs, hypocrisy, political cant, police clubs, SS-20 and Pershing missiles—in other words, many years later, she would shuffle in her flat-heeled slippers and woolen coat, with a leather bag over her shoulder, weary and ill-tempered; large, heavy, but still firm enough to attract the glances of men always hungry for a woman in this world of dug-up streets, new unkempt buildings, and gawky youths in blue jeans whose eyes burned with rebellion; she shuffled through this strange, repellent world, but nevertheless how wonderful in its uniqueness, to stand near the Jewish monument in the empty square on which the winds caroused and look at the faces of those larger-than-life Jews carved in stone, nailed to the wall, with their feet as if sunk into the earth of this city. Stony and silent Jews whose voice no one heard any longer. She searched in the face of the young man represented there for Henryczek Fichtelbaum's features, but she didn't remember them. After all she had seen Henryczek in the glow of the light bulb for only a short time, and later, on the cot, darkness enveloped them both, so she was not able to commit to memory the features of the Jew whom she had loved with her whole body and soul during one wartime evening. And actually she didn't want to remember him, for he didn't play any role in her life—he had appeared at the well only shortly to disappear around the corner of Ząbkowska Street—so she couldn't and didn't want to remember him, like almost all the other people in this city, who were busy with their own affairs, with current everyday life, and unaware that they were maimed, for without the Jews they are no longer the Poles they once were and should have remained forever.

"Sleep," she said to Henryczek Fichtelbaum. "Maybe things will be different tomorrow."

But he didn't want to sleep. Suddenly he made a decision that in his mind was linked, and not without cause, to this woman's body. Suddenly he was no longer a boy, but a man, and looked differently at his destiny. He felt courageous and determined. It was this woman who was condemning him to death, a death that he would nevertheless choose consciously. Henryczek Fichtelbaum would return to the ghetto, he would not run any longer, hiding in holes, outhouses, and garbage dumps; he would return to the ghetto to embrace his fate, his head held high. I'm not a child, he thought, I'm not a boy. I'm not going to run any longer. Now I'm going to meet head on that which is written in the books. He put the palm of his hand on the woman's naked breast and felt the beating of her heart. From it he drew additional strength, became more certain of his decision.

"Your hand is cold," the woman said. "That tickles."

She started to laugh. Henryczek laughed too, and withdrew his hand. He was now strong and calm.

Behind the wall, not far away, a locomotive whistled, and then the rumbling of a train was heard. Perhaps Poles, perhaps Jews, Germans, or Russians, were riding in that train to their deaths.

V

Pawelek, sir," said Kujawski, "do you have a cash surplus?"

They were standing on the corner of Podwale and Kapitalna streets. The gas streetlight emitted a weak, violet glow. A light breeze puffed out the skirt of a prostitute crossing the street. She was very fleshy, with a wide face and pretty, light brown eyes. Pawelek remembered her from before the war. It was she who for the first time in his life had said to him one evening, years ago: "Who are you looking for, young man? A girl perhaps?"

He had become flustered, because he hadn't understood, but answered her politely. "I'm going to a friend's, Madame."

"Your friend can wait," the fat woman had said. She held a bunch of keys in her hand. When she moved it, the keys jangled loudly.

A man had started to laugh and had called out from the sidewalk opposite, "Fela, leave the boy alone. He needs a prettier girl. . . ."

Then Pawelek had understood that a prostitute had accosted him.

He had heard stories about prostitutes from his friends. He was afraid of them. Embarrassed, he ran away from the fat woman. But later, when he saw her in the streets, he politely doffed his school cap. The prostitute nodded her head with a good-humored, understanding smile. She never again solicited Pawelek. After the military disaster of September 1939, she vanished for a while, and then later appeared again, even more magnificent, enormous, in a voluminous skirt that reached down to her ankles, with a bunch of keys in her hand that jangled just as sonorously as they had in the old Poland. She usually strolled along Piekarska Street, on Podwale. This was her turf, her very own place in the world, where she alone was the goddess of love.

Pawelek, noticing the woman as she crossed the street, said courteously, "Good evening, Madame!"

"What's so good about it?" she answered, pursing her mouth. "I can't feel my legs anymore."

She turned the corner, walking heavily. She's getting old, he thought.

"You know Fela, Pawelek?" Kujawski asked. "I would never have suspected you."

"And you have no reason to," Pawelek replied. "I know everyone here. . . . I've been around here for years."

"Let's not exaggerate," said Kujawski the tailor. "You were still a pipsqueak when I was ironing your daddy's uniforms. I know these parts better than you. Fela is a good woman. So, what about the cash? Are you rich, Pawelek?"

"You have to be straight with me, Apolinary, don't pussyfoot around. What is it you're looking for now?"

"Always the same. You know that very well. But not to say a word to old Kujawski for an entire month, not even to drop by for a moment, this I don't understand. Do you really not want to earn any more money?"

"I was busy," Pawelek replied. "I've got a lot on my mind."

"You're going to have more and more."

A German soldier in an air force uniform walked by. A stout blond with a snub nose and blue eyes. His boots tapped against the sidewalk.

He walked energetically, hitting the pavement hard with his heels because he felt unsure of himself in the dark. The bayonet on his belt slapped rhythmically against his backside. Passing the two men standing under the streetlight, the soldier cleared his throat and lost the rhythm of his march. He changed feet, again cleared his throat. He stopped a bit further on, at a cigarette kiosk. An oil lamp was burning inside. The faces of the soldier and the vendor leaned toward each other. The vendor had birdlike features, with the suggestion of a hawk in the rapacious shape of his nose and the cut of his lips. Red hair above his forehead. Gnarled fingers on the cigarette box in the glow of the oil lamp. The soldier took the cigarettes, paid, and walked away. The vendor drew his head back into the booth. He probably went back again to working on his fierce, moving novel. It will come out in some twenty-odd years and Pawelek will play a part in its publication. But the wind of the uprising will by then have scattered the author's ashes.

"A certain gentleman I know might be inclined to part with two miniatures. Mid–eighteenth century. Very beautiful. But they're family heirlooms, Apolinary."

"Everyone has family heirlooms these days, even dating from the Middle Ages," the tailor sighed. "When could I see them?"

"Tomorrow, if you like," Pawelek replied. "I could telephone you."

"How much?" Kujawski said lightly, bending down to re-tie the laces on his yellow chamois boot.

"First you must see them, and then we'll talk."

"Could they be fakes?" the tailor asked. "There's a rascal in Częstochowa who makes miniatures by the dozen."

"But nobody can fool you," Pawelek replied sincerely. "You're more of an expert than the old collectors."

"Well, of course," said Kujawski. "The old collectors did business with decent people. That too was before the war. Now there's another spirit afoot in the land. All right! But I can't tomorrow. I have a meeting with an important client. Make the appointment for the day after."

"You're buying something else tomorrow, Apolinary?" Pawelek asked.

Kujawski burst out laughing.

"Nothing of the sort! I'm fitting a Kraut for riding breeches."

Fela returned. It was almost dark. She pulled on her cigarette and the red glow illuminated her face for a moment. She passed them, then remembered something.

"Mr. Kujawski," she asked, "you remember that doorman from number seven, don't you?"

"Old Kubuś?" the tailor asked.

"He wasn't so old," she replied. "Well, old or not, I'm not talking about him. The cross-eyed man who used to call me Tits! Fela Tits he called me. They killed him the day before yesterday on Zielna; there was some kind of shoot-out."

"What are you saying!" Kujawski exclaimed, although he had no idea whom she was talking about. "They killed him right there on the spot?"

"A bullet in the heart," Fela said and shook her hand. The keys jangled loudly.

"There must have been some sort of crackdown," Pawelek pronounced.

"What crackdown!" Fela snorted angrily. "He had a bit to drink and jumped a German. And another one shot him. Straight in the heart."

"A tragedy," said Kujawski. "What a pity."

"Better men than him are dying," Fela replied, turned around, and walked off heavily into the darkness. "Fela Tits," she muttered to herself, "come on now!"

"About the tits, that fellow was right. I didn't know him. But it's a shame. What are these Germans doing, what are they doing? . . ."

A moment later the men parted. The tailor went in the direction of Miodowa Street, Pawelek toward the Old Town. The tailor was thinking about the eighteenth-century miniatures, Pawelek about the man who had been killed. Did he feel pain when the bullet struck him in the heart? How does dying take place? What does a man see then?

Does he see God, does God show Himself so that the last moment may be easier, so that there is no fear? He probably reveals Himself in the final twinkle of the eye, in the last ray of light that reaches the pupil, but never earlier, because the man might survive, get well, and tell others what he has seen. So God shows Himself only at the moment when He is absolutely certain that this is death. . . .

He stopped, aghast and ashamed. You're a fool, he told himself. God doesn't have to wait for the proper moment because He knows it exactly; it is He Himself who designates it. So when is it that He shows Himself to the dying man?

He walked on. For a while longer he thought about God, about how He must now be constantly revealing Himself to various people all over the city, without a moment's rest, on a hundred streets at once, and especially in the ghetto. Then he stopped thinking about God's face. An idle quarter of an hour passed. A warm wind blew in the Market. The houses stood dark. Here and there thin, faint rays from flashlights penetrated the darkness. People were walking faster. The hour of curfew was approaching. Pawelek started to run. He thought about Henio Fichtelbaum and feared for him. Later, hot from running, looking all the time at his watch, he thought about the miniatures for Kujawski and calculated his modest percentage.

VI

_____

She was a tall woman with straight blond hair, narrow hands, and the large feet of a man. She had a prominent nose, thick eyebrows, pretty, slightly too severe eyes, and healthy teeth—although when she smiled, two gold crowns, of which she was secretly proud, were plainly visible. Perhaps that is why she smiled more frequently than her serious companions, who said of her that she had a playful nature.

When she was seven years old she had a vision. It was a winter evening. The snow crunched under the large feet of this girl, who was already tall for her age. She was returning home from school alone, for only she lived far away, on the other side of the small river. The stars were already shining against the dark sky and she couldn't see the smoke rising from the cottage chimneys, only the faint glimmer of oil lamps in the windows. She was just about to turn right onto a little wooden bridge when she had the vision. Jesus appeared before her, radiant and beautiful, holding a white lamb in His arms. She fell to her knees in the deep snow. She didn't feel the cold, only the weakness of joy and devotion enveloping her entire body. Jesus said a few words to her, softly, almost in a whisper, and she understood that she wasn't to go over the little bridge but walk further along the riverbank and then cross over the ice. Then Jesus disappeared, but before He did so He commanded her to wait in the same place the next day, and He would come again without fail. She did as she was ordered. She walked slowly, her heart overflowing with joy and reverent devotion. She safely crossed the river on hard, strong ice. That same night the bridge collapsed and two godless peasants plunged to their deaths in the river's currents.

The next evening she waited again for Jesus in the appointed place. When He appeared with the white lamb in His arms, He commanded the girl to dedicate her life to the conversion of Negroes. After that she had no more visions.

She described her experience to the local clergyman, but he was an insensitive man who kept a tight rein on his parishioners, raised pigs for a large profit, exchanged opinions with a free-thinking notary in town, and spoke with an indulgent superiority about the country people. He ordered the child to tell no one about her religious adventure.

The next day, chatting with the notary, he said, "The ignorance of my flock has reached new lows. That little one truly believes that God has nothing better to do than to look in my parish for missionaries to Africa. You would think He'd find it easier elsewhere."

But the clergyman was not a man of insight, for he didn't understand that the paths of grace are inscrutable. The little girl grew into a pious young woman, deeply impressed by her mission. At seventeen she entered a convent. At first she thought of traveling to Africa to convert Negroes, but after a time she understood that she musn't take the words spoken near the collapsed bridge too literally but rather symbolically, and she devoted herself to spreading the faith among children, teaching them the catechism. Her dedication was absolute. She was a shining example of self-sacrifice, constancy, and stubbornness. Children liked her because she was somewhat playful, or perhaps she simply understood that one didn't have to speak about God solemnly and severely like the prophet Elijah, but cheerfully, as if He were looking after the beehives, helping to thresh the barley, and driving the hay wagon hitched to two pretty roan horses. She wasn't mistaken in this, although her old clergyman, perhaps more old-fashioned than he appeared, would probably have deemed this portrayal of a God ordinary and familiar a sin.

She was called Sister Weronika, although she once dreamed of taking the name Joanna, in memory of another country girl who attained the ranks of medieval French knighthood and later died at the stake. Sister Weronika led a very industrious life. She did not spare herself. The goal she held always before her was simple. She wanted to bring to God all of earth's children—the near and the far, the white, the black, the yellow, and even those more exotic than that. If there was any coldness in her heart, then it was only toward Jewish children, for it is one thing to have never come to know God, and something altogether different to have known and to have crucified Him. The black faces of little faraway Negroes Sister Weronika deemed innocent, because they were still untouched by the hand of truth. The swarthy little faces of Jewish children bore the mark of the creed and hatred that the Saviour encountered among the people of Israel. They were the ones who had rejected God, who did not believe in the words of His Son. A high wall of distrust separated Sister Weronika from Jewish children. They emanated a foreignness. When she walked down the street, tall, large, placing her strong, masculine feet firmly on the sidewalk, Jewish children fled from her. Her white cornet, like a ship's swollen sail, glided aloofly among the black, timid Jewish dugouts. They never touched her bows, and she never sailed into their bustling harbors.

But Sister Weronika had a good measure of healthy, peasant common sense, and she realized that the world was more intricate and mysterious than she had thought when she was a girl, and that God's bewildering nature cannot be fathomed by the human mind. There were many roads given man to walk on, and many dead ends. Weronika knew that only one road led to the goal, but that the tangle of destinies, customs, doubts, dreams, and sorrows was convoluted. And this plurality was also the work of God, Creator of heaven and earth. So she prayed fervently for the souls of her erring neighbors, and she also prayed that the coldness in her own heart would melt.

When war broke out many changes took place in Sister Weronika's life. At first she felt helpless and stunned. Bombs fell on the city, buildings crumbled, fires raged. People were dying before her eyes and she could not help them. But her peasant nature, a fundamental lack of fear in the face of physical suffering—as a child, after all, she had seen bloated cows, crippled horses, slaughtered pigs and sheep, wounds from the axe and the scythe, bloody and painful illnesses, and the deaths of suffering, pious people—this countrywoman's fortitude deep inside her eventually caused her to organize the other sisters during the siege of the city. Together they learned how to dress the wounded and watch over the dying. There was more and more mercy in her heart. She thought then that giving comfort came easier to her than catechism, for those who suffer need God more.

When the German armies entered the city, she wasn't afraid of the military policemen in the streets or of the dread Gestapo. She was prepared to accept everything that God had ordained for her. Her cornet no longer looked like a sail going down the street, but like a banner of faith and hope. She took care of children who had been orphaned and lost on the roads of war. She nursed the sick and the abandoned, the helpless and the unfortunate. From early morning until late evening she ran through the streets, a hard woman with large feet, simple manners, gentle eyes. The gold crowns glittered when she smiled. The wrinkles on her still youthful face deepened. Her tongue was agile, sharp. She spoke softly and gently only to children. With adults she was often impolite, because she hadn't had a careful upbringing, had little time, a lofty purpose, and believed that God should dwell in one's heart, not in one's mouth.

She thought sometimes before falling asleep, after she had already said her prayers, that only now, after many years, was her destiny being fulfilled, and God's words, spoken by the little bridge at the river, being incarnated. True, she had never yet seen a live Negro child, but how many other people had she brought to the gates of the Church! To how many people had she brought comfort and the words of eternal love. In fact, if only there wasn't so much misery all around her, she would have felt happy. The tiny seeds of faith that she had sown with her own hands were ripening before her very eyes. What more could she have asked for?

Then Jewish children entered her life. They would arrive from the cemeteries. With a certain degree of astonishment she observed that not all the sisters were able to rid themselves of the coldness. Even under circumstances such as these a wall separated them. But she discovered new strength within herself, heard a mighty command that no one could resist. God brought it about that Jewish children came to her, lonely and weak, seeking salvation. And it was she who was to save them. From death and extinction. It was a great gift to her and to these children. She was connected to them by a sort of community of human fear and mystical longing. In the quiet refectory whose windows faced a vegetable garden, in the sunlight that lay in a wide streak on the parquet floor, or by the glow of candles smelling of wax, she taught Jewish children how to make the sign of the holy cross.

"Raise your right hand," she would say. "Yes, just like that. And touch your forehead with your hand. 'In the name of the Father . . .' and now touch your chest, and say, 'and the Son . . .' very nice, very nice. Now listen carefully. Move your hand . . ."

The children's faces were intent and sullen. They understood these signs with difficulty. Sometimes the refectory resounded with their quiet crying. Then Sister Weronika would console them.

"Joy awaits you," she would say. "Don't cry, because joy awaits you."

But not all the children understood what joy was.

It was difficult but beautiful work.

Sister Weronika also listened to the promptings of her peasant nature. She had had a vision once, but immediately afterward had found herself in her father's cottage, having to dry her older sister's shoes and stockings, peel the potatoes, look to the pigs in the pigsty. She had seen the person of Jesus as clearly as if He were alive, but her hands were busy with work until the late evening. So she realized that she lived in a world that was evil, hostile, and in revolt against God.

She taught the children the sign of the cross, but she also taught them new first and last names, and new facts about their short and complicated pasts, all of which were lies. By means of these lies the children were to arduously break through to a new truth. Below the image of the Saviour, in the presence of God, she drilled them in the great swindle, trained them in the great untruth. Three-year-olds, who knew nothing about themselves except that they suffered from hunger, shivered from the cold, and were afraid of the whip, accepted submissively their new identities. Instinct commanded them to memorize the new names, signs, addresses. They had a singular cleverness that enabled them to forget about the terror of existence.

"What is your name?" Sister Weronika asked.

"Januszek," answered a black-haired, curly-headed boy with the smile of an old dealer in cow hides.

"And your last name?"

"Wiśniewski."

"Say your prayers."

The boy said a prayer, piously clasping his hands. His eyes reflected humility, docility, and also the fear of death that lay in wait for him if he made a mistake.

But the older children carried heavier baggage. Seven-year-old Arturek, a boy of good appearance but with a bad look in his eye that betrayed the deeply embedded proclivities of his cursed race, rejected his new identity.

"What's your name?" asked Sister Weronika.

"Artur."

"Don't say that. Your name is Wladzio. Repeat it!"

"Artur!"

"Why are you so stubborn, Wladzio? Your father was a carpenter, his name was Gruszka. Don't you remember, Wladzio?"

"He was a dentist. His name was Dr. Mieczyslaw Hirschfeld. You know that very well, Sister."

"I know. I'm not denying it. But you must forget about it. Your name is Wladzio Gruszka. Your father was a carpenter."

"All right, let's say he was a carpenter. But I know what this is all about. Remember that, Sister, all right?"

"I'll remember. So what's your name?"

"Wladzio Gruszka, a carpenter's son."

He smiled, sneering. He shrugged his shoulders. He looked defiant. For a moment Sister Weronika hated Wladzio. He was slipping away from her. But this didn't last long. She thought, I won't let him go until the end of the war. If I let him go, he'll die just out of spite. . . .

In that sense he did not spite her. He survived the war. He grew into a not very tall, nearsighted man. His name was Wladyslaw Gruszecki. His biography was constructed in a refined and elegant, though not completely convincing way. He was one of those people who do not know moderation. Perhaps in his childhood he had acquired too great an ability to live several lives simultaneously and had developed a taste for it. He no longer knew how to part with the multiplicity of his beings. Wladyslaw Gruszecki's father was both a dentist and a carpenter. A stomatologist whose hobby was carpentry, as he put it in later years. Wladyslaw Gruszecki's genealogical tree showed many odd gaps near many intricate branchings. He was of noble ancestry, traceable back to pre-partition times. His forebears had held ancient Polish civil-service titles, for in his boyhood Wladyslaw Gruszecki had read Henryk Sienkiewicz's *Trilogy* many times and had taken a liking to its heroes.

He was as proper an old-time Polish nobleman as you could get. He sported a sweeping mustache. In conversation, he would interject now and then, nonchalantly, very freely, various turns of phrase dulled with the patina of age. He would say, "Dearest sir!" Or he would say, "Howbeit, now then, whither." Sometimes it was too much for even very understanding listeners.

Not only did he not spite Sister Weronika, but he developed such a taste for her teachings that he surpassed his mentor in Catholic zeal. She did not prostrate herself on church floors. He did so often. In his opinions he was peremptory, serious, and worthy of imitation. He had an anti-German and anti-Semitic complex, and opted for friendship with the Soviet Union, for he regarded friendship with the Russian nation as the foundation of a better future for his beloved country. In this he disagreed with Sister Weronika, for whom communism seemed the devil's invention, a cruel war being waged against God. Toward the Russians themselves Sister Weronika felt a moderate distaste and compassion. She remembered from childhood the Cossack patrols on the muddy roads of Eastern Poland, as well as conscription into the czarist army. She did not like Orthodox priests or the singing in Orthodox churches. The capital of her immortal soul was Rome, just as the capital of her Polishness was Warsaw. But Wladyslaw Gruszecki related to the Orthodox church with the good-natured superiority of a zealous Catholic, and to communism with the distrustful fear of a friend of old Russia. But above all he loved Polishness, its august past and its splendid future in the Slavic family. Germans he called "Krauts," Jews "kikes." He uttered some startling diagnoses, considering his origins, such as: "Kikes are ruining our country!" His attitude toward the fads of the post–Second Vatican Council Roman Church was one of reserve. It must be said that in this matter he had, for a while, an ally in Sister Weronika. She too observed with fear and doubt all the innovations that had taken root in Catholicism since the pontificate of the good Pope John. But Sister Weronika's faith was humble, so she quickly came to accept the transformations. She said that those wiser than she were deciding about the new face of the Church and she enjoined her soul to obey. After a while she discovered beauty and wisdom in the new liturgy, and also became keenly aware of God's nearness, which she had never before experienced. She was a simple country woman, and only now did she understand the significance and meaning of the Sacrifice. Before, Latin had taken her into a mysterious and hieratic world, in which she had felt frightened, a powerless plaything in the hands of God. Now she could recognize herself, her thoughts, desires, and choices. From the land of incantations she crossed into the land of prayer. The magical charm of things unknowable evaporated from her soul, and there opened before her the realm of love's great mystery. In her late years Sister Weronika drew closer and closer to Jesus, who on a certain winter evening had gone out to meet a little girl. She wasn't at all certain if she had in fact met Him then. But He no longer had to reveal Himself to her in such an extraordinary fashion. She felt His presence constantly, even though her eyes had no special power and she saw only ordinary things. She loved God and people very much in her late years.

She could not reconcile herself to Wladyslaw Gruszecki's aggressive and intolerant faith. He was a fighting Christian, and his weapon was sarcasm, of which Sister Weronika had never approved.

"A little bit more love, Wladzio," she would say in a weak old voice when he visited her, bringing cakes from the pastry shop, the smell of cologne, and a nearsighted, mocking gaze. His dark Jewish eyes lit up with a cold, unpleasant gleam whenever he spoke of Jews. He must have suffered terribly. But he was a pretender not only in his Polishness. He dressed with a studied elegance, mindful of the cut of his gold-buttoned navy blue jacket and his gray flannel trousers, which transformed him, the descendant of masters of the royal pantry and Lithuanian cupbearers, into an habitué of English yacht clubs. He smoked a pipe. Didn't drink alcohol. Didn't eat fish prepared in the Jewish manner. Never missed Sunday Mass. Collected engravings. Had his shirts custom made. Didn't marry. He was a high official in the state agricultural administration. He had finished agricultural studies. He wanted to be thought of as an intellectual. He read Proust, Hemingway, and Camus. In the original, he claimed. He also read mysteries, but this he didn't like to mention. Of Dostoyevski he would say, "Our common priest!" Of Tolstoy: "That old, wise count . . ."

"The old, wise count says that . . ."

"Our common priest wrote in his time that . . ."

He loved Sienkiewicz the most and wasn't at all embarrassed about that. But in this he was genuine.

In the summer of 1968, he expressed his joy over the fact that Poland was finally ridding itself of Jews.

"We must be a nation of a single, common, native blood!" he said.

Sister Weronika pushed away the plate with the cake she had been eating, clasped her hands to her breast, and said angrily, "Wladzio! I don't want you to visit me anymore."

"Why do you say that, Sister?"

"You're only thirty-some years old and you talk as if you were senile!"

He became flustered. In her presence he never carried off too well the role of a conservative aristocrat with deeply nationalistic convictions. Later, he would appear in a gray suit, and without the signet and pipe. He behaved with more restraint. These visits troubled him, but after all he loved Sister Weronika in his own way. She was his footbridge: Thanks to her he found his way to the old, forgotten shore. Perhaps that is why he came to see her. In the tiny parlor, where they would sit chatting about his work and her daily problems with unruly young people, he probably felt the presence of the past. In a dark corner of the room stood little Arturek Hirschfeld, a dentist's son, who did not want to be called Wladzio. Maybe he even saw the faces of his father, mother, and older brothers, whose ghosts had long ago left him, meekly yielding to the ghosts of hussars, chieftains of the steppes, and the defenders of Jasna Góra. Perhaps it was precisely at Sister Weronika's side that he rested from the pressures of old-fashioned Polishness and anti-Semitic Catholicism, which after all he did not invent himself but only imitated, full of unexpressed fears, hidden phobias, and undreamed dreams.

But sometimes in her parlor he also succumbed to the insinuations of his split personality, as if in the presence of this witness to his childhood, he was unable to free himself of the demons.

Sister Weronika was very old and sick when, for the first time, she used his own weapon of mockery. Wladyslaw Gruszecki was nearing fifty and still visited the old woman regularly, bringing cakes from the pastry shop, but he no longer knew how to talk about anything other than farming, sowing, harvests, soil renewal, nitrous fertilizers, "Bizon" combine-harvesters, sheaf binders, and the backwardness of individual peasant farms. He was a competent professional, for he had completed his agricultural studies with distinction and had occupied himself for many years with the economics of farming. But there was no question, at least for Sister Weronika, that he was the child of a Jewish dentist from the big city, had never worked the land, had no contact with the life of the countryside, did not understand the peasant way of being and style of thinking. And Sister Weronika, although she had now lived more than half a century in a nun's habit, remained a peasant woman after all and reacted to the world in peasant fashion—with that peasant realism, undaunted and stubborn, with the peasant shrewdness in arithmetic that no computers can ever get the better of. So when he complained about the shortsightedness of peasant farmers, criticized their lack of economic imagination, paraded before Weronika his program for revitalizing agriculture by a method based partly on the example of collective farms and partly on that of large private ones, as if Poland were a cross between the Ukraine and Nebraska, when he became inflamed and mocking, when he thundered and lamented, she suddenly interrupted him with a movement of a transparent, aged hand. And when he fell silent, she said, with the slightest trace of a smile: "Let me tell you something, Wladzio. Agriculture is not an occupation for Jews. . . ."

And at once she became terrified of those words, for she understood they were a blow straight to the heart. And not only to his heart. She had wounded herself with that snide sentiment, one which, as she had believed for many years, she had long outgrown. And yet there remained in her soul a thorn of peasant condescension toward these dark, ubiquitous people who trespassed uninvited upon other people's native soil.

"I'm a stupid, old peasant woman!" she cried out. "I apologize to you, Wladzio. . . ."

"What are you apologizing for, Sister?" he replied coldly and pursed his lips. "You are absolutely right!"

Once again he sat firmly in his nobleman's saddle, looking down from on high on the Jewish tenants milling around. But Sister Weronika, carried away by a storm of contradictory feelings—shame and anger, peasant stubbornness and the sweetness of contrition, love toward this aging unhappy wretch and nostalgia for the intractable boy who did not want to bend and betray himself, even in the face of certain death—cried out in a pained voice:

"Wladzio, will you finally stop provoking, will you finally stop pretending in front of me, I'm not all of Poland, I'm old Weronika, who wants to love you like when you were seven years old! Don't torture me, Wladzio. I don't have much longer to live. . . ."

Then Gruszecki started to cry. She did too. She held his wet face in her weak, transparent hands and swallowed bitter tears.

For a quarter of an hour the world allowed them to be themselves again.

But this was to happen almost forty years later, and for now Sister Weronika was busy turning Arturek Hirschfeld into somebody else. Right now they were enemies; they looked each other in the eyes defiantly. Sister Weronika was saying, her lips pressed tightly together: "Repeat it again! What's your name?"

"Wladzio Gruszka," he answered, also clenching his lips.

"Good, Wladzio," she said. She turned around and shut her eyes. God will forgive me this impudence, she thought. She was recreating human biographies, against His design. She lowered her head and prayed silently for the strength to endure, both for herself and for these children. The children watched her with curiosity.

But Wladzio Gruszka, behind Sister Weronika's back, stuck out his tongue at her. I am Arturek Hirschfeld, he thought vengefully, and I will never be some Gruszka, no-mat-ter what!

VII

The judge had difficulties falling asleep. He heard the slow chiming of the clock, which throughout the night beat out the passing of every quarter hour. Sleep would usually come at three in the morning. During the winter the judge accepted this calmly, but in the summer he felt the cruelty of insomnia. The birds were already beginning to chatter in the tree branches, the sky was growing light in the east, and he was only just then falling asleep, a sleep that would deprive him of what little of the world he was still destined to experience. He slept without dreaming, a shallow sleep, conscious that he was sleeping, listening intently to the sounds of morning, the clatter of dishes on the other side of the wall, the murmur of the awakened street, the shouts of the coachmen, the voices of children hurrying to school, the bells of trolley cars, the breathing of sleeping lovers, the barking of dogs. In the winter this was tolerable, because when he awoke a pale dawn was only beginning to tap against the window. But in the summer he opened his eyes to a flood of sunlight, to the full, ripe smell of awakened nature, so he had the feeling that he had been robbed of priceless moments of life, of which—he believed—he didn't have many left. Nevertheless he also treasured these sleepless nights, for then quiet and solitude reigned, and he could converse with himself to his heart's content, philosophize in his own fashion, and even pray in his own fashion, call upon God to judge and be judged. So he lay in a wide bed, on the left of which was a wall covered in wallpaper with a delicate, gray-blue pattern of exotic flowers and dragons, like the design on a Chinese screen from the days of his youth, and on the right a bedside table, on which stood a lamp with a shade, several books, an ashtray with a cigar stump, a plate, a knife, and an apple. His bedroom was spacious, cluttered, untidy, with the closet door always open, a settee with threadbare upholstery shiny from wear, wicker chairs, a faded rug, and a chandelier in the shape of a basket. But the judge liked this room. He felt best here, because every object bore the stamp of his solitude. When in the evening he closed the bedroom door behind him, to remain here until dawn, he rediscovered himself. Especially during the years of the occupation this room was his fortress, as if inside its threshold evil could not reach him. He undressed slowly, throwing his clothes on the chairs, as he had done his entire life, from the moment when he freed himself from the control of the rigid tutor who until the twelfth year of his life drilled him from morning to evening in neatness, precision, and exemplary manners. This was in Podole, a world now long dead, which the judge had left as a youth, from then on to confront his destiny in solitude. So he undressed slowly, finding joy in the mess. Then he put on a long nightshirt, sat down in the soft bed, and smoked half a cigar. Finally he lay down comfortably in between the sheets, clasped his hands over the quilt, gazed at the ceiling, and meditated. The clock chimed every quarter hour. Sometimes God would sit down by the judge's bed and they would converse. And sometimes the devil came. But the latter wasn't so sure of himself, so he would sit further away, on the settee, and then the judge would turn his body to face the room, lean his head on his bent arm, and, looking the devil in the eye, berate him fearlessly. The night lamp on the table remained lit. The judge hated darkness.

This evening he was completely alone. He sat in bed smelling the smoke from the cigar, which was slowly going out in the ashtray. These cigars cost a fortune during the war, but he couldn't give them up. "Cigars and dignity I will never renounce!" he would say in the company of friends. So he was sitting relishing the cigar smoke when suddenly in the other room the telephone rang. It was eleven o'clock, an evening in late spring. The window was dark, a candle burned on the bedside table because the electricity had been turned off, as happened sometimes during the occupation. The telephone resounded plaintively. The judge rose from the bed. He felt fear stealing into his heart. He walked to the door, opened it, and found himself in the dark hallway that separated the bedroom from the rest of the apartment. The phone rang again just as he was lifting the receiver from the cradle. His hand trembled slightly. The flickering glow of the candle penetrated the hallway through the open bedroom door. An enormous shadow moved on the wall.

"Hello," the judge said. "Yes ¹ . . ."

"Judge Romnicki?" answered a distant, murmuring voice, which sounded as if it were being carried by the wind. "Judge Romnicki?"

"Yes, I'm listening; who is this?" the judge called out.

"Fichtelbaum, the lawyer. Do you remember me?"

"My God!" the judge said softly. "My God!"

A quavering voice came from the other end of the line, distinct but very distant, as if it were speaking from another world. And so in fact it was. The lawyer Jerzy Fichtelbaum, an old acquaintance of the judge's, was calling. It was about his daughter, Joasia. He wanted to save his child from death.

"I'm turning to you, Judge, at the end of my life," said Fichtelbaum.

And Romnicki exclaimed, "Don't talk that way, you should never talk that way! The facts, the facts, Mr. Fichtelbaum. . . ."

They discussed the details. The judge's shadow moved across the wall, reaching up to the ceiling, flowing abruptly down toward the floor, ascending again.

"I have Volksdeutsche neighbors," the judge said softly, as if fearing he would be overheard through the wall, "but we'll find a way, Mr. Fichtelbaum. It's out of the question in my place. These Germans next door, and the building superintendent is a dishonorable man as well! But we will find a way."

Fichtelbaum insisted through the static. "I might not be able to get a connection again, Judge. I have a reliable man who will bring her across. I beg you for an address, I beg you! We will need papers. . . ."

"I understand," said the judge. "Please don't worry about that. An address, you say? Let me concentrate, I beseech you, be patient for a moment, I must concentrate. . . ."

Complete silence fell. The judge's shadow on the wall bent under the burden of the decision, for he now bore on his shoulders responsibility for a human life. Then he gave a name and an address, and Fichtelbaum cried out suddenly, "Farewell! Farewell everyone!"

The connection was cut. The judge tapped the telephone cradle once, twice. Then he replaced the receiver. He returned to the bedroom and sat down on the bed. The cigar was no longer burning.

"Here!" the judge said loudly, as if his name had just been called.

Years later, whenever he answered, "Here!" getting up from his bunk, he smiled at the memory of this evening. It was a smile at once sad and gentle, compassionate and mocking, for the judge would think then of the lawyer Jerzy Fichtelbaum, the nightshirt, the cigar, the cruelty of the world, and the candle on the bedside table. The prison guard would grumble under his nose, "What are you so cheerful about, Romnicki? Haven't they stuck it to you enough?"

Several times he reported to the warden that the accused Romnicki behaved like a half-wit during roll call.

"That's because he is a half-wit," the warden pronounced. "An old fart with mud in his head. He's not going to last long anyway."

His cellmates also asked the judge about the meaning of his strange smile. But he wouldn't answer. He had become wary with age. His former eloquence had evaporated. He trusted people less than he once had. He felt somewhat bitter, cheated by destiny. Sometimes he even thought that he had been let down, by God, by history, and also by the concept of justice that he had shaped within himself during the course of half a century, unaware that times were changing, and ideas with them. Because of this he sometimes appeared anachronistic, for whereas others accepted reality, he remained unreconciled, reproaching the world for its lack of dignity. Cigars he never mentioned. When, every morning and evening as required by prison regulations, he answered with a calm voice, "Here!" he remembered, in a still vivid, sharp, and increasingly painful manner, that although it was true that the cigars were irretrievably lost, honor remained.

Memory also remained. It was God's most beautiful gift, and he stubbornly protected it from every attempt to rob him of it. He remembered everything. Down to the minutest details. The smell of cigars and the screech of the trolley bus as it left the stop in front of the courthouse building. The color of the sky above the steeples of Warsaw churches, and against it the wings of pigeons. The rusty blotches of faded cloth on the backs of Jewish smocks. Warsaw rains. The winds, blowing over Warsaw on November evenings as the neon lights were going on. The tapping of horses' hooves on Kierbiedź Bridge, the gray ribbon of the river. Sleigh bells during snowy winters, the faces of women framed in warm fur collars. Dry summer days, when horseshoes and automobile tires left their imprints in the soft asphalt. The faces of barbers, policemen, criminals, salesmen, veterans, lawyers, carriage drivers, seamstresses, army men, artists, and children. The faces of devils and angels. He remembered everything, down to the minutest details. The fruit shop, where a soda machine hissed at the entrance and the shopkeeper emerged from behind bunches of grapes to greet the customer. The rattle of Singer sewing machines in Mitelman's tailor shop on Bielańska Street. The sentences that he handed down in the name of the People's Republic, whose mainstay was to be justice—and he treated this seriously, which is why he sparred with God, the law, and his own conscience, knowing that he held human destinies in his hands. The pattern of the wallpaper in his bedroom and the shape of fruit knives. Sleepless nights and the long nighttime conversations, when God and the devil visited him to chat about crime and punishment, the salvation and damnation of souls. He remembered truth. Every year, month, and hour. Every man with whom he had come into contact and the meaning of words spoken, action performed, thoughts thought. So he remembered truth, and that was his armor, which lies could not pierce, and through a crack, through a breach in the armor, strip him of honor. He could write all this down and publish it, to the confusion of the world that had turned against him. But he knew that one true testimony does not mean much—although it means more than a thousand false ones. That is why he remembered everything, down to the minutest details. The way the flight of birds looked then, and the shape of the clouds in the sky. The thoughts of people long dead or condemned to oblivion. Fear and valor, slanders and sacrifices, and also things falsely named and words stripped of meaning. Letters, books, speeches, sermons, cries, banners, prayers, tombstones, and wreaths. The hands of bearers of good news and the hands of informers. Heads raised up on pedestals and those in nooses beneath the gallows. He remembered the times when evil and lies showed themselves bashfully, secretively, in costume, mask, or darkness, because people wanted to pretend that they were good and devoted to truth, or perhaps they even were. All this he remembered precisely.

So he died serenely, although he knew that he was depriving the world of a trustworthy witness. But he believed that others would remain, to whom he bequeathed his memory. He died in 1956, in a small provincial town, in the house of distant relations who had taken him in when he was released from prison. In this country there are always people who will care for those who have been wronged. Ill and sapped of his strength, he would usually sit in his little room by the open window. Outside was an orchard, fragrant with the blossoms of apple and pear trees. It is precisely from there that death came to him. It emerged from among the apple trees like a gray, airy little cloud. It flowed through the open window into the room. The judge received the visitation with gratitude and relief. It happened in the early morning, in July, in lovely sunny weather. The dawn was quite cool, the trunks of the apple trees still enveloped in mist, but the sun had risen already in the east and the day promised to be hot. The first insects were buzzing, and swallows soared above the rooftops. The judge observed death calmly and with dignity, because he remembered everything. Memory, his guardian angel, was by his side. In this sense he was privileged.

But everyone can be.

Dying, he said, "Here!" and smiled gently. Then his candle went out. But the sun illuminated the judge's face during the long hours of the morning and afternoon. Only then did his relatives come into his room and see that the old man was not alive.

But that evening, when sitting on the bed in a nightshirt he had said loudly for the first time, "Here!" as if his name had just been called and he was reporting his presence to the world—he was still alive. He was more alive than he had ever been before, for he was just then exposing himself to the slings and arrows of evil, the spear of fate, and from then on he was to do battle with evil not only in his own conscience, thoughts, and good deeds, but with his whole being. He had desired this for a long time. To lay down his life for what he remembered, if need be. God did him a favor and allowed him to make the greatest sacrifice. He wasn't unique in this, it is true, but he belonged to the small minority who made such choices. It was a happy night in the judge's life.

Later there were many such nights. But starting with this one he slept well and no longer suffered from insomnia. He didn't hear through shallow sleep the voices of the world; the world existed as if he had no part in it. He slept soundly and did not care in the least about his short absence.

VIII

When Dr. Adam Korda learned of the trouble Gostomska, the captain's wife, was in, he was sitting by the veranda window reading Lucan. A young man with the look of a hoodlum appeared in the doorway and announced to the doctor that he had driven a certain Mrs. Gostomska to the Gestapo, and that she was suspected of being Jewish.

"A woman as elegant as that can't be just some Jewish girl," the rickshaw driver said, nodded his head in farewell, and left. Dr. Korda was left sitting with Lucan in his hands and outrage in his heart.

But as a classical philologist he had developed, over years of intellectual exercise, the instinct for quick, logical observation. So not even a moment had passed before he remembered that he and Gostomska had a mutual acquaintance, namely Pawelek, whom he used to encounter leaving the apartment of the artillery officer's widow. They would exchange not only greetings but also a few remarks about the day's news. It didn't surprise Dr. Korda that Pawelek, himself the son of an officer jailed in a POW camp, should visit Mrs. Gostomska, an officer's widow after all, and most probably an acquaintance of Pawelek's parents. He didn't waste any time. Abandoning Lucan on the windowsill, he went briskly into town. He informed Pawelek of the unpleasantness that had befallen the captain's wife. Pawelek took the news calmly. So calmly that the classical philologist returned to Lucan without even suspecting the torment into which he had plunged the young man.

But Pawelek had no intention of giving up. He dialed a number on the telephone and asked for Mr. Filipek. He could hear the rumbling of machinery on the other end of the line.

"This is Filipek," a man's voice answered. "What is it?"

"Mr. Filipek, this is Pawel," said Pawelek. "We must meet at once."

"Not now. After closing time. Where?"

"On Miodowa Street, in the pastry shop. All right?"

"Fine, the pastry shop. I'll be there at four."

Pawelek was waiting at the marble table right by the entrance. Filipek was punctual.

"Mr. Filipek, they've caught Mrs. Seidenman," Pawelek said.

"Don't say such things," Filipek mumbled. He wore a railwayman's uniform and held his cap on his knees.

"Mrs. Seidenman is on Szucha Avenue," Pawelek said.

"Why on Szucha right away?" the railwayman objected, not wanting to lose all his illusions. "They don't take everybody to Szucha."

"But they took her," said Pawelek.

He recounted the entire incident. The Jew on Krucza Street, the rickshaw, the Gestapo, Dr. Korda, Pawelek.

"That's all I know. . . ."

"She has blond hair," said Filipek, "and very blue eyes."

"But this was some acquaintance, probably from before the war. Some Jew from before the war . . ."

"All Jews are prewar," the railwayman replied. "We too are prewar. If he recognized her as Mrs. Seidenman, then she probably did go to Szucha."

"Please think of something, Mr. Filipek," Pawelek said vehemently.

"But I'm doing just that. Do you really think that I would leave the wife of Dr. Ignacy Seidenman to be the prey of fate? He saved my life! And now I should leave her? You don't know me very well, Pawelek."

"I do know you, that's why I called at once. I remember that you couldn't walk at all . . ."

"I walked on crutches."

"Then Dr. Seidenman cured you. I remember how I would lead you up the stairs to the second floor and how your legs would drag behind you."

"He cured me, sent me to the Truskawiec spa, lent me money. Your father also lent me some. But mostly Dr. Seidenman. And you remember his funeral, Pawelek?"

Pawelek didn't remember, because Dr. Seidenman had died in the summer, when all young people were away on holidays, but he nodded his head so as not to hurt the railwayman's feelings.

"I thought I would be the one to die first, and then he went, so unexpectedly. It was an extraordinary funeral. A rabbi walked behind the coffin, and a little further on a priest. And throngs of people. A whole crowd of Poles and Jews. He healed everybody. He was an extraordinary doctor. And the doctor's wife is an extraordinary woman."

Pawelek nodded his head. The railwayman got up.

"All right," he said. "Run along, young man. I'll think of something."

"Please do, Mr. Filipek," Pawelek said sternly, but his eyes were imploring and fearful.

"Not for you, but for her. She's worth it. And who isn't worth thinking something up for, really . . . ?"

An hour later Filipek telephoned his friend.

"Jaś," he said, "this is Kazik Filipek. I have urgent business."

"Come straight over," Jaś said cheerfully. "You know where I live."

"I do," the railwayman answered. "I'm on my way."

And he went to Maria Konopnicka Street, to a modern building where wealthy, influential Germans lived. He rang the doorbell next to a plate bearing a beautifully engraved sign: JOHANN MÜLLER, P.C. A maid answered the bell, and when he gave his name she said that director Müller was waiting for him in his study.

He was waiting. He was short, stocky, with white hair and a ruddy complexion. He was a German, from Łódź, and had been a fighter in the Polish Socialist Party, a prisoner in the Pawiak jail, and a deportee to Siberia. He once shot at the chief of military police in Radom. He missed. He was sentenced to hard labor. He returned, and again shot at the agents of the Russian secret police. Finally, with Filipek, he found his way to the Krasnojarsk Province, where together they cleared the taiga, fished in immense rivers, sang songs, and awaited the great war of nations, which was to bring Poland independence. They lived to see this war, and took part in it.

All of Johann Müller's friends and comrades called him Jaś, and mocked his German origins. "What sort of a German are you, Jaś?" they exclaimed. "I'm a German in body, a Pole in spirit," Johann Müller would answer gaily. And that's in fact how it was. Johann Müller's father, Johann Müller, Senior, was a textile worker in Łódź at a time when the city was growing and becoming an increasingly powerful commercial center. Old Müller was a German worker, and in those days German workers read Marx and belonged to the party of Ferdinand Lassalle. So the father reared the son in the spirit of socialism. What this meant in the Łódź of those years is that young Müller joined the struggle for Polish independence against the Russian empire. Everything in the nineteenth century was more or less simple. Only later did the world become complicated.

"Jaś," said Filipek, "you knew Dr. Seidenman, didn't you?"

"Yes, I knew him," replied the ruddy-faced German.

"The Gestapo have got Mrs. Seidenman," said Filipek. "And we have to get her out."

"Jesus Christ!" Müller exclaimed. "Am I the liaison office between the Gestapo and Warsaw Jews? What can I possibly do these days?"

"Jaś," said the railwayman, "you can do a lot. This is easier than getting Biernat out of the hole."

"That was ages ago!" cried Müller. "Biernat has been pushing up daisies for years."

"We must get Mrs. Seidenman out," said the railwayman.

"Her specifically, yes? And the others no? If she were some poor Rivka from Nowolip nobody would lift a finger! Look what's happening all around, Kazio. They are dying over there without any hope at all! The whole Jewish nation is dying, and here you come to me about a Mrs. Seidenman."

"We cannot save them all," Filipek said. "But we can save her. And don't shout at me. After all it's you that's killing those poor Jews. . . ."

"What do you mean, 'you'? It's the Germans!" Müller shouted. Then he added more calmly, with sadness, "Well, all right. Germans. Have a cigarette."

He held out a cigarette box.

"Why did you join them, Jaś?" said the railwayman.

"I did not join them, you know that perfectly well. I was always a German. For sixty years. And they knew it."

"So what do you need that swastika on your lapel for?"

"Precisely for that reason, you stupid man. All Germans belong to the party. I am a German, so I belong. What good would a German who didn't belong be to you?"

"Get Mrs. Seidenman out, Jaś. It's easier than the Biernat affair."

Suddenly they both felt forty years younger. In 1904 they sprang Comrade Biernat from a military-police station in Pulawy. Johann Müller arrived at the precinct in a sleigh, in a lieutenant's uniform, posing as the young Baron Ostern come to take the dangerous criminal away for interrogation. Filipek was driving. He wore an army greatcoat and propped his rifle, bayonet attached, against the coachman's seat. Young Baron Ostern ordered the precinct commander to stand at attention. He presented him with the appropriate documents.

It was bitterly cold. Baron Ostern stood by the tile stove and smoked a fat cigar. But the commander in Pulawy, an Armenian, was somewhat suspicious. A Caucasian fox. A rat from distant Asia. But the trick worked. He deliberated a long time, and in the end assigned a two-guard escort to the baron and put Biernat in chains. They had to neutralize the guards in the woods beyond Pulawy, one with a pistol, the other with a rifle butt to the head. They left them tied up on the track, in deep snow. Biernat's chains jangled all the way into Radom. Only there were they able to free him, in a blacksmith's shop near the toll gate. From there they went by train to Warsaw. Gaslight, silence, and tension, policemen on the station platform, horrible fear about whether they would succeed in getting into town, whether they wouldn't be defeated at the very last moment. But they succeeded. They reached Smolna Street, where people were waiting for them.

"It was terribly cold then, I remember," Müller said, "but I was suffocating by that stove when they were examining the papers."

"Get Mrs. Seidenman out," said Filipek.

Müller was silent for a long moment, then said, "Where exactly is she?"

"I've no idea. On Szucha Avenue. You've got to find her yourself."

"I don't know the woman!" Müller muttered. "I don't know the goddam broad!"

"Maria Magdalena Gostomska, an officer's widow."

"Details, Kazio. After all they're not complete idiots over there!"

"No, not complete," Filipek quickly agreed.

IX

At the time of which we speak Wiktor Suchowiak was thirty-three years old and slowly going to the dogs. The long life to which he was predestined would prove a failure, for as a young man Suchowiak had chosen the career of a professional bandit, which in the era of great totalitarianisms that accompanied him until his old age was bound to become a pitiful anachronism. Great totalitarianisms themselves practice banditry in the guise of law, and—to the astonishment of individual practitioners—almost always rule out the possibility of an alternative, whereas it is precisely the concept of an alternative that was once the philosophical foundation of banditry. Wiktor Suchowiak always operated according to the principle, "Your money or your life!" which gave the other party to the contract the possibility of choice. Totalitarianisms were to rob people of honor, freedom, property, and even life, all the while leaving their victims, or even bandits, without choice.

At the time of which we speak an adolescent totalitarianism raged through Europe, unusually rapacious and aggressive, murdering entire nations without pity and at the same time plundering them in an unprecedented fashion. Later the world would settle down a bit because there was no more war—at least not in Europe—and totalitarianisms practiced their trade with more discretion, rarely reaching for human life, but much more frequently for human dignity and freedom, and of course never scorning property, health, and, above all, consciousness, something that never interested professional, individual bandits because it couldn't be cashed. Wiktor Suchowiak would live to see the times when totalitarianisms at every geographical latitude and under various ideological slogans, which only served as fancy dress and decoration, practiced banditry completely out in the open, in broad daylight, to the accompaniment of brass bands and declamations sometimes not entirely devoid of lyricism.

Wiktor Suchowiak usually used a crowbar and, in the days when his lucky star was still shining, brass knuckles. He used force only in extraordinary circumstances, when resistance and refusal exceeded the bounds of his patience and threatened the success of the whole enterprise. Therefore he could not compete with the divisions of tanks and the battalions of soldiers armed with machine guns; or—in later years—with such instruments of force as electrical generators, polar winters, napalm, the blackmail of whole social groups, forced labor, apartheid, telephone-tapping, and even ordinary clubs in the hands of policemen rampaging through the streets; or mysterious kidnappings of inconvenient people, whose corpses were then thrown into clay pits or rivers; or the abductions of airline passengers who were killed one by one to extort ransom or political concessions from individuals, societies, and states.

Although it is true that the first totalitarianism with which Wiktor Suchowiak came into contact, the moment Hitler began his war, was indeed the most cruel, bloody, and rapacious, it was also the most stupid and in a sense primitive, lacking as it did the finesse of those to come. But that is how it usually goes with the works of man. We begin with coarseness, and later attain the thing of excellence, close to perfection.

But be that as it may, Wiktor Suchowiak didn't stand a chance. The choice he made at eighteen, when he robbed his first victim, was idiotic. He should have foreseen that the future of banditry belonged to legal operatives, thereby also to the police—and he should have entered their orderly ranks. But Wiktor Suchowiak never did. Not even when, already an older man and serving a prison sentence, he was encouraged to take part in building a better future on the side of law and order.

Wiktor Suchowiak was certainly not a man of honor. Isolation and individualism do not by themselves constitute human dignity. Something more is required for that. But he was without doubt a man of principles, which were the result of his profession. Politics did not interest him, and he had no intellectual aspirations. His morality was simple, as were his education, tastes, and way of life. He liked money, women, merry-go-rounds, vodka, small children, and sunsets. He did not like crowds, sweets, policemen, autumn weather, and force, if it brought him no profit. As early as the first years of the occupation he concluded that the world had gone mad. During this period he sometimes attacked his fellow countrymen, but as a rule he preferred Germans, not for any patriotic reason but out of sheer calculation. His countrymen were poor. To be sure, Wiktor Suchowiak was well aware of the risks of attacking armed Germans. But the Germans were sometimes drunk, or without all their wits about them, especially when in the company of women.

But there did come a time, however, when Wiktor Suchowiak switched careers. He saw the benefits of this move as metaphysical in nature, for Wiktor Suchowiak believed in God, and so also in Heaven, Purgatory, and Hell. For a lavish fee he smuggled people out of the ghetto to the Aryan side of town. In this way he made a good living while at the same time performing noble deeds.

As an experienced and reliable man, in whom one could place one's trust even in the most difficult situations, he boasted a large clientele. His name became well known, and he enjoyed respect even among the German guards, to whom he gave a cut of his profits. A peculiar kind of collaborative relationship developed between Wiktor Suchowiak and some of these guards, a relationship that even the most bloodthirsty of the Germans did not abuse because they knew whom they were dealing with, being well aware that any attempt to finish off Wiktor Suchowiak might cost them their lives. The bandit was a man of enormous physical strength and courage. No other smuggler of human merchandise could compare with him. The guards tried to bargain fiercely, but they always had to give in, for they lacked the strength of spirit and the determination needed to prevail. Wiktor Suchowiak never allowed bargaining. He paid what he considered proper, and cut short all their whining and threats. He was simply not afraid of them—and even if he was, they were more afraid of him.

In the early spring of 1943, smuggling people out of the ghetto stopped being a lucrative occupation, because there was no one left to smuggle. The great majority of Jews had died. Those who still remained were destitute, did not have the wherewithal to pay for the smuggling, and also stood no chance of surviving on the Aryan side on account of their looks, customs, and ignorance of the Polish language. The handful of Jews left in the ghetto was soon to die in battle, later to live on in legend.

One of Wiktor Suchowiak's last Jewish business transactions was Jerzy Fichtelbaum's daughter, Joasia. Fichtelbaum had been renowned before the war as a brilliant criminal defense lawyer. But since not all his former clients could be said to be as highly principled as Wiktor Suchowiak, Fichtelbaum could not count on surviving on the Aryan side. His appearance was disastrous. A short, black-haired man with dark, thick facial hair, an olive complexion, a classically Jewish nose, full lips, and the look of a shepherd from the land of Canaan in his eyes. Besides, Jerzy Fichtelbaum had little money left in his pockets and a lot of grief in his heart. His wife had died less than a year before from an ordinary tumor, in her own bed, which was an object of jealousy in the entire building. The lawyer was left alone with his small daughter, Joasia, an intelligent and pretty child. She had been born just before the outbreak of the war, the fruit of his later years, which only further increased his love. His son, Henryczek, was almost nineteen years old, lived his own life, and was to die his own death, unconnected with the drama of his nation and his race. He had escaped from the ghetto at the beginning of the fall of 1942 and was in hiding, without contact with his father or sister. And that is how Jerzy Fichtelbaum decided that he must save Joasia, so that he could all the more courageously and calmly prepare himself for death. It was a decision that every man of reason and understanding would have made in his place, and which many people of reason and understanding were then making.

As already mentioned, the Nazis were, to be sure, history's cruelest totalitarians, but because they had taken the lead ahead of the rest of humanity and were going for first place in the modern world, they were still inexperienced and committed oversights. For example, the telephone lines between the ghetto and the Aryan side of Warsaw operated undisturbed until the final destruction of the Jewish quarter, thanks to which Jerzy Fichtelbaum could arrange certain details of Joasia's rescue by telephone. Not only did the Nazis not interrupt the connections, but they didn't even tap the lines, which in later years Wiktor Suchowiak—and not only he—could not comprehend, given the everyday experiences of the second half of our century. But that's how it was, and thanks to that Joasia Fichtelbaum was able to survive until the present day.

One spring evening Wiktor Suchowiak took Joasia Fichtelbaum by the hand, stroked her head, and said, "Now you're coming for a little walk with your uncle."

Jerzy Fichtelbaum said very quietly, "Yes, Joasia. And you have to listen to everything your uncle tells you."

The child nodded. The lawyer added in a somewhat hoarse voice, "It's best that you go now, sir. . . ."

"Right," Wiktor Suchowiak answered. "You can rest assured, sir."

"And not a word to the child," Fichtelbaum said. "Never, not a word. . . ."

"I'll pass all that on, don't you worry about it."

"Now!" the lawyer suddenly cried and turned his face to the wall.

Wiktor Suchowiak again took Joasia's hand and they left the apartment. Jerzy Fichtelbaum, his face to the wall, moaned, but very softly, because he didn't want to cause anyone any pain, and least of all his own daughter.

"Your uncle asks you not to cry," Wiktor Suchowiak said to the little girl. "It would be best if you didn't say anything at all, just breathe slowly."

The child nodded her head again.

They went out into the empty street. Wiktor Suchowiak knew the way. The guards were paid for each shot they missed. They went through. Not even a single shot was fired. The guards were feeling lazy that evening.

But not everyone was enjoying *dolce far niente*. Not far from the wall, on the Aryan side, a certain elegant young man was circling about, known among the *szmalcowniks* as Beautiful Lolo. He was slender as a poplar, fair as a spring morning, fast as the wind, bright as the Danube. He also had a real nose for Jews, zeroing in on them unerringly in the streets, and once he caught the scent, he followed it doggedly. Sometimes the prey would attempt to dodge him, for certain little Jews knew the passageways in the city, the connecting courtyards, the stores with back exits. But Beautiful Lolo knew the city even better. Truth be told, he didn't like the little Jews from the countryside, lost in Warsaw as in a strange forest, those cowed and terrified little Jews who surrendered immediately, struck by Beautiful Lolo's first, dead-accurate glance. He took from them everything they had, and sometimes it was a downright paltry penny. But a paltry penny disappointed him, and so Beautiful Lolo would then take the little Jew by the arm, lead him to the nearest precinct, or hand him over to the next military policemen, and his last words, directed at the little Jew, sounded bitter and melancholy: "Next time, kike, you should carry more cash on you. But there won't be any next time. *Adieu!*"

Saying *"Adieu!"* he felt a kind of solidarity with greater Europe, which was his motherland.

Lolo found joy in hunting. When he came upon a Jew more worthy of attention slinking through the streets, frightened but full of determination, he would tail him, letting the Jew understand that the game was up, that he was being followed, that he wouldn't get far. Then the Jew would try to dodge about cunningly, so as to put distance between himself and the hiding place where his family was. But this maneuver would never succeed under Beautiful Lolo's watchful eye. Because at the end he would catch up with the little Jew, persuade him without any trouble at all to take a walk with him and disclose the hiding place. Then they would clinch the deal. Lolo took money, jewelry, even clothing. He knew that right after he left the Jew would switch hiding places, perhaps even squat in some basement, or try to flee the city. While he was at it Lolo would also fleece the Jew's Aryan hosts, who in their panic would give him whatever he wanted. But he didn't do this often. He was never sure of being able to strike a deal with his Aryan countrymen. This kind of Polish "Sabbath goy," who hid and fed Jews, could be doing it for profit but also for lofty and humane reasons, and that always made Beautiful Lolo anxious, for the devil alone knew if a Pole like that, molded from such noble clay, wouldn't inform the underground of Lolo's visit, if he wasn't himself up to his ears in the underground, if he wouldn't bring trouble down on Beautiful Lolo's head. After all, now and then a *szmalcownik* had been known to die in a Warsaw street from the bullets of the underground, so it wasn't a good idea to take risks. For this reason also Lolo rarely turned up near the ghetto, for not only was the competition quite stiff there, but an unwelcome eye might also come to rest on his pretty face.

That evening he was simply out for a stroll, not thinking at all about hunting. Chance brought him to Krasiński Square, and chance made him run into Wiktor Suchowiak, who was rather hastily making his way down the sidewalk of Miodowa Street leading a Jewish child by the hand. Wiktor Suchowiak was a swarthy man, dark-haired, with the good looks of a gypsy. Spotting the peculiar pair, Beautiful Lolo felt the thrill of the hunt. So he approached Wiktor Suchowiak and said, "Where are you hurrying to, Yid?"

"Dear sir, this is a mistake," said Wiktor Suchowiak.

"You're pulling this Jewish kid behind you so fast she can hardly catch her breath," Beautiful Lolo added in a jocular tone. "So stop a minute and go through that gateway. . . ."

"Sir, what exactly do you have in mind?" Wiktor Suchowiak asked and looked about fearfully. The street was empty. . . . Only from a long way down Miodowa Street could one hear the screeching of a trolley car. A barely visible, violet streak was moving in the twilight. Beautiful Lolo shoved Wiktor in the direction of the nearest courtyard gate.

"We'll talk," he said seriously.

"Sir, I am not a Jew," Wiktor Suchowiak protested.

"That remains to be seen," replied Lolo. "Show me your dick."

"But the child," Wiktor Suchowiak mumbled.

"Don't you bother me about the kid!" Lolo shouted. "Show me your dick!"

"Joasia," Wiktor Suchowiak said calmly to the little girl, "turn your face to the wall and stay still!"

Silently, Joasia obeyed her uncle. Wiktor Suchowiak unbuttoned his coat, leaned his head down slightly, and then abruptly hit Lolo in the jaw with his bent elbow. Lolo staggered, cried out, and leaned against the wall. Wiktor Suchowiak gave him a quick jab in the stomach, and when Lolo bent over, drove his knee into his groin. Lolo moaned, took another punch to his jaw, then another to his nose. Blood spouted. Beautiful Lolo slid to the ground. Wiktor Suchowiak leaned over him, but just then caught Joasia looking, and called out, "Turn around! Do as your uncle says!"

The child turned around. Wiktor Suchowiak said quietly to Lolo, "You piece of shit, next time I'll skin you alive! Now hand over your measly pennies."

Beautiful Lolo was bleeding profusely, was in terrible pain, his thoughts were muddled, in his heart he felt bitterness and terror.

"I don't have anything, sir," he mumbled. A powerful kick rolled him over face down to the ground. He felt the chill of cement beneath his cheek, and his tormentor's agile hands going over his entire body. Wiktor Suchowiak found the wallet and change purse. His gestures were calm. He carefully counted the bills.

"Whom did you work up today?" he asked. "I pull in this much dough in a month."

He was lying, because he made more, but he saw no reason to let the bleeding assailant in on his business. He threw the change purse down near Lolo's head.

"Here, for the trolley," he said. "And steer clear of me!" He took Joasia by the hand, saying, "That gentleman got sick. His head got all mixed up."

They walked out of the gateway. With difficulty Beautiful Lolo pulled himself to his feet. But he couldn't walk yet. He leaned against the wall and just stood there, breathing heavily. Blood was still flowing from his nose. He was sore, humiliated, and full of hatred.

These two men were to meet again in twenty years. Wiktor Suchowiak had just been released from prison, prematurely aged, an outcast and a reactionary. Yet the state authorities, fired by the mission of improving human nature, did not just cross off this unfortunate product of capitalism. Wiktor Suchowiak was referred to a factory producing building materials, where he was to take a job operating a concrete mixer. Never in his life had he had anything to do with concrete, with the exception of the floor in his prison cell, but he had a quick mind and a strong character, and so he hoped that somehow he would manage. And after all, he didn't expect much from life anymore. With his letter of recommendation in hand, he went to see the personnel director. The director received him curtly, as was his custom with new workers who had a shady, criminal past. He read the letter, scowled, and put the piece of paper down on the glass desktop. The desk was wide, a bit worn. The director too was a worn-looking man. He had a swollen face, and his soft, fair hair was balding slightly. The room was sunny—a summer day, a cloudless sky. Wiktor Suchowiak watched the director in silence.

The director said, "Have you ever worked with concrete?"

"No, sir," Wiktor Suchowiak replied. "But a man can learn everything."

The director nodded. Rather skeptically.

"What did you do time for?" he asked.

"It says right there," Suchowiak replied. "Assault and battery."

"And what did you do that for, Suchowiak? Isn't it better to work honestly for your country, for society? I think, Suchowiak, that I won't be disappointed in you. They send me the likes of you, and then all I have is trouble—but I like the way you look, so we'll take you. For a trial period, of course. That assault was probably the first one, right?"

Wiktor Suchowiak smiled, and replied, "No, sir. The second. The first time I worked over a *szmalcownik* during the war, on Miodowa Street in Warsaw."

The director suddenly turned pale, bit his lip, and looked attentively into Wiktor's eyes.

"What are you talking about?" he said softly.

"About us," replied Wiktor Suchowiak. "I gave you a proper thrashing then!"

"What are you talking about!" the director shouted. His hands were shaking. "What do you think, Suchowiak? That a criminal's word means something around here? That your slander will change anything around here?"

"I don't think anything, but I know life," Wiktor Suchowiak replied. "Once they start digging into your past, you piece of shit, you won't get away. Will they believe me? Sure, they'll believe me. They have a hell of a powerful yearning to mete out justice. No damn Party is going to help you then, no rank."

"Not so loud," the director growled. "What are you doing this for, man? What are you doing this for? I've given you work, you can live here snug as a bug in a rug. And if worst comes to worst, I'll be able to defend myself. . . . I'll deny it! Sure as there's a God, I'll deny it!"

"Don't talk so much, you piece of shit," Suchowiak interrupted, "because you don't know what you're talking about. To whom will you deny it? To those Russian thugs from the security police? Better men than you break down there. But who says I'm going to run straight to them? Did I say that?"

"Sit down," said Beautiful Lolo. "Sit down, you lousy whore. . . ."

"If the director asks me to, then I don't see why not," replied Wiktor Suchowiak, and sat down in the chair in front of the desk.

They talked a long time. Even the secretary became worried.

Twice she was putting through a call to the director and twice he called out sharply, "Don't put them through! . . . I'm busy."

Finally they parted. It cost Beautiful Lolo a pretty penny. And as a farewell, Wiktor Suchowiak patted him on the cheek. In a caressing way, but manfully, because it hurt. It hurt Lolo in his heart. He was left behind in his office, as he had been twenty years before in the gateway on Miodowa Street, with a feeling of impotence, humiliation, and a terrible hatred.

Wiktor Suchowiak took a better-paying job in another establishment on Beautiful Lolo's recommendation. They never saw each other again.

After several years Wiktor Suchowiak became disabled and collected a modest pension. He suffered from bone marrow disease and moved about with difficulty. He lived in a large room on the outskirts of town, in an old and damp building. His only pastime was looking out his window onto the street. But it wasn't a busy street. He watched young women with children; men hurrying to work or to the pub; quarrelsome, snooping old women who gossiped in the little square. At first he too would sometimes go down there, sit on a bench, and chew the fat with the old folks. But he felt worse and worse, and in time rarely left the house.

In the evenings, when he couldn't fall asleep for hours, he would cry softly. He didn't know why. But the tears brought him relief. And when late at night he would finally drift off, he dreamed of the war and the occupation. People often dream about the best moments of their lives, and so he was not an exception, although a Freudian analyst would have had little use for him. Because when Wiktor Suchowiak dreamed of a wardrobe, it didn't mean in the slightest that he wanted a woman. A Jew was sitting inside that wardrobe, and was saying to Wiktor Suchowiak, "I thank you enormously for what you have done for me!" And Wiktor Suchowiak would reply with dignity, "I didn't do this for love of you, Mr. Pinkus, but because I was well paid! Now sit still, sir, because the lady who lives here is about as frightened as Hitler's ass!"

Is there anyone in this country who after all those years wouldn't want to have such sweet dreams? But only Wiktor Suchowiak and perhaps several dozen other people had them. Dreams such as these usually bypass the well-fed combatants. The wise and all-knowing Morpheus distributes them among impoverished teachers in small towns, old retired judges, engineers, railwaymen, or gardeners, and sometimes also among salesladies and prewar pickpockets. But you can only learn about what these people once did by listening carefully to the words they speak occasionally in their sleep.

X

———————

The tailor Apolinary Kujawski oc-
cupied a five-room apartment with a balcony near Marszalkowska
Street, on the third floor facing the street. Tall, tile-covered stoves
stood in the rooms, with the one in the living room being of particular beauty, decorated with rosettes and a little iron door in the shape
of a palace gate. On the ground floor of the same building Kujawski
had his atelier, somewhat dark but spacious, with three separate
rooms. In the front room he received his customers, took their mea-
surements while they inspected themselves in the mirror. In two rear
rooms worked the journeymen, and three Singer machines rattled
from morning till evening. Steam rose in thick clouds as heavy, hot
irons pressed moist linen to the garments.

Kujawski was an honest man, of short stature, balding, nearsighted,
with a soul not devoid of romantic raptures, a simple intellect, a small
and shapely foot. He had a tendency toward a certain studied elegance,
elegance as understood by a man brought up before the Great War

in a small town in the former province of Plock, where the majority of the population was Jewish. Accordingly, he wore dark suits and stiff collars, patterned ties, chamois boots in a shade of yellow, and brightly colored vests, either in green or deep red, depending on his mood. On the third finger of his right hand he sported a signet ring with a stone, and on the little finger of his left hand a ruby.

For Kujawski was a very wealthy man, and enjoyed among the officers of the German Wehrmacht, and in part also among the German police forces, the reputation of being the best trouser maker in Warsaw. They came to him from as far away as Lwów to order their riding breeches and dress trousers.

Kujawski wasn't a man of great personal courage, so he didn't try to turn his acquaintance with so influential a clientele to the advantage of Polish national interests. But because he was nevertheless a patriot, he spent generously in discreet support of the opposition movement. He also supported artists. He paid large sums for literary manuscripts, which were to be published after the war. He bought canvases from masters of the brush, storing them in his apartment with the profound resolve that in a free Poland he would turn the collection over to a museum, where of course they would hang with the donor's name engraved on the appropriate plate, or even right on the front of the building.

Kujawski made his fortune thanks to extraordinary circumstances and his reputation for being a reliable man. Years before, right after the Great War, when he arrived in Warsaw in search of work, he moved around from one tailor's shop to another, never staying in one place for long because he was a man of radically Christian views and didn't want to work for Jews, while in his profession the Christian establishments had more than enough available hands. He lived during that time in a basement near Miodowa Street, lonely, short, and angrily proud because of his poverty. He eked out a meager living ironing suits for the men who lived in the same building, as well as mending the clothes of the neighborhood poor. One of his most influential customers in those years was Judge Romnicki, an original and a sage, who grew to like the little tailor.

One day, when Kujawski was delivering the judge's corduroy trousers to his apartment on the second floor, the judge said to him, "Mr. Kujawski, I've found full-time work for you."

"You're making fun of me, Judge," the tailor replied.

"I'm not in a joking mood. You've heard of Mitelman?"

"Mitelman? The one from Bielańska Street?"

"That's the one. I've been ordering clothes from him for thirty years. A great artist with the shears and a man of irreproachable character. He is ready, on my recommendation, to employ you, dear Mr. Kujawski."

"But sir, I am a Christian tailor."

"Don't talk nonsense, Mr. Kujawski. Does one baste differently in the Christian way than in the Jewish?"

"That I cannot say, but they have different customs, which—"

"Mr. Kujawski," the judge interrupted, "I took you for a reasonable man. Mitleman is prepared to take you on. For full-time employment. He's got several cutters working for him, a dozen or so helpers. A large establishment. The best clientele in Warsaw. What more do you want? In several years' time, if you apply yourself, save, you'll be able to open up your own shop. And you'll finally be able to get married, Mr. Kujawski, because it is high time you did. . . ."

"I'll never get married, Judge."

"That's your affair. Well then, what will it be?"

Kujawski asked for some time to think it over, assuring the judge that by evening he would bring him his answer. He didn't harbor a distaste for Jews, but they were alien to him. He grew up among them, but at a certain distance. They aroused in him curiosity and fear because of the dissimilarity of their language, customs, appearance. In his native town Jews comprised the overwhelming majority, but the Christians considered themselves superior, perhaps precisely because, although being in the minority, they nevertheless felt themselves to be favored by the world. It was a hierarchically constructed world, and everyone knew his place in it. Jews were below Christians on the ladder because of the very fact of their Jewishness—and Kujawski did not inquire into why this was so. It was that way from the most distant times, probably from the day when the Jews crucified Jesus. God Himself established such customs on earth, maybe to punish Jews for their nonbelief, their stubbornness, and their betrayal of Him.

Kujawski was a deeply pious man, and he believed in the same way as others around him. He prayed, attended church services, received the Holy Sacrament, gave himself into the care of the Virgin Mary, loved Poland (which was truly Catholic and suffered on the cross of slavery just like Jesus Himself and hence had the right to the name "Christ of Nations"), did not respect the Orthodox and sinister Muscovites, the Lutheran and brutal Germans, and also the un-Christian and noisy Jews, but naturally he disrespected them all in different ways—the Muscovites because they were his persecutors, because that was Siberia, the whip, paddy wagons; the Germans because they were his enemies from time immemorial, perhaps they did know more, perhaps they did work better, but they scorned Kujawski for being a Slav, and for this he paid them back with hostility and derision; and he disrespected the Jews because they in turn were below him, always wanted to outsmart him and dupe him, whereas he felt himself to be more native to this soil than they, more in his own roost than they. They were strays, whereas he grew out of these ancient Polish roots, these were his rivers, his fields, forests, and landscapes, in the midst of which they appeared only as wanderers. So Kujawski was irritated by shady Jewish dealings, by Jewish buildings and shops, because they took up space that belonged to him, and into which he himself had difficulty fitting. He felt sometimes that he had to elbow his way into his own house just to find a corner in which to lay his weary head.

Kujawski agonized terribly for several hours, but in the evening he returned to the second floor and announced to the judge that he would accept the job at Mitelman's on Bielańska Street.

"I'm tired of being poor, Judge," he said, as if wanting to justify that here he was, laying down his arms, putting the Polish scythe into a corner, and taking up the Jewish needle.

Judge Romnicki said, "Well, thank God you have some sense in your head, Mr. Kujawski."

Kujawski was a talented tailor, and Mitelman the master of masters.

The owner of the popular firm on Bielańska Street found the small and enterprising Christian worker much to his liking, all the more so as it was also in Mitelman's interest to employ at least one goy, for this gave him access to even the most squeamish clientele. He sent Kujawski to the best houses, because in the best houses, even in the most liberal, progressive, and refined ones, a Christian artisan did not disturb a certain immemorial moral order, even if at the same time he might not fit fully into the European concept of how the world works. So Kujawski earned a decent living, but he did not make his fortune. He remained in the basement.

But in 1940, Mitelman was getting ready to move to the ghetto. One rainy and windy day in the fall, toward evening, he appeared in Kujawski's basement and said, "Apolinary, I'm going into the ghetto. I have a warehouse full of the best cheviot in all of Warsaw, you know that. I have one hundred and twenty-five bales of Rapaport woolens from Bielsk, and I also have bales of cloth from the Jankowski firm, those that we chose together right before the war. I have the kind of shop . . . I don't need to say any more. I'm going into the ghetto. You're the only Christian in my firm, and you will keep all this for me until better times."

"But Mr. Mitelman," Kujawski exclaimed, "where will I keep all of this? In this basement?"

"Did I say anything about keeping it in the basement? It's a fortune, after all. Take a bit from it, buy a shop, earn money, guard the stores, bring some of the profits to the ghetto, because I trust you like my own father. And when the war ends we'll go into business together, Mitelman and Kujawski, it can even be Kujawski and Mitelman, or Kujawski and Company, I don't care anymore, but it will be better for you, however, if it's Kujawski and Mitelman, because the name carries some weight, they know me a little around town."

And that is what happened. Tailor Kujawski became the keeper of tailor Mitelman's fortune. They met in the courthouse building on Leszna Street for as long as it was possible, and Kujawski brought Mitelman money, and he also brought food; he brought a good word; he brought his sympathy, friendship, advice. Mitelman grew weaker and weaker, and Kujawski stronger and stronger, but he didn't rejoice in this in the slightest because he knew that a terrible injustice was being done, that Jews were suffering, dying, perishing, and that this punishment for their sins was beyond human imagining, even if they had sinned grievously, not having faith in the word of the Saviour. Furthermore, even if Jews had sinned, then certainly Mitelman himself had not sinned much, for he was a righteous man, good, generous, fair, and devout, although in a Jewish way, which wasn't to be recommended.

Kujawski was not a man of inordinate intellectual ambitions, and now and again he even felt a certain distaste for his own intellect, reproached it for its narrowness, and said, "I am actually an idiot, but is it my own fault that I'm an idiot? And if I myself know that I'm an idiot, then I'm probably not such a complete idiot!" Thus, in short, he did not possess philosophical aspirations, did not plumb the mysteries of human existence, and did not judge the world, but he nevertheless realized that hell had broken out around him, that evil had triumphed, and that one had to oppose it in the most effective way possible. He made trousers for German officers because whether in his trousers or without them they would still be doing what they were doing—after all no one shoots from his breeches. They can have bare asses and they'll still be killing those poor Jews; they can have bare asses and they'll still be shooting Poles; and as far as the Russian frosts are concerned, somewhere near Moscow—well he, Kujawski, doesn't make sheepskins for the German army; in his breeches they'll freeze their asses off not only near Moscow, but even near the Warsaw suburb of Rembertów; and so he had no pangs of conscience about earning his living from the Germans, especially as he was at the same time inspired by the romantic and patriotic ambition of bringing aid to those in need, to the wronged and the persecuted.

Suddenly, in the spring of 1942, he became the proprietor of an immense fortune, because Mitleman the tailor simply died in the ghetto, and his only son, Mieczyslaw Mitelman, was shot down a few days later on Rymarska Street. And that is how the tailor Kujawski came to possess the fortune amassed over the years through the industry and labor of a Jewish cutter and the toil of his journeymen. There was no doubt in Kujawski's mind that this fortune was his in part only, but he was not at all certain to whom the rest belonged. Certainly not to the Germans! To the Jews? But where were the Jews? And which Jews would have the right to tailor Mitelman's fortune? So maybe it belonged to the Polish nation? Kujawski was confronted with a dilemma. But for now there was a war on, both Jews and Poles were perishing, and the fortune in his keeping was growing, thanks to the demand for breeches and dress trousers for the officers of the Wehrmacht.

The tailor decided that the collection that he would donate to the future museum should bear the names of two donors, namely those of Apolinary Kujawski and Benjamin Mitelman, and resolved also to fund a poetry publishing house called Kujawski and Mitelman. He consulted on this matter with Judge Romnicki. The judge was from time to time his client, but not in the old sense. He no longer ordered suits, but sold off works of art, mainly paintings, which he had acquired over the preceding decades.

Now and then Kujawski also let Pawelek earn some money by being the middleman in certain transactions, although the tailor was fully aware that Pawelek was less knowledgeable in matters of art than he was himself. For Kujawski had an inborn artistic sensitivity, and a multitude of beautiful and valuable objects had passed through his hands. He even did business with dim-witted German officers, buying from them fragile porcelain, candlesticks, miniatures. He liked to swindle them and did this whenever he could, for he knew that the objects they offered him for sale were almost always stolen.

In the end Kujawski found a certain kind of harmony in his wartime existence. Living surrounded by works of art brought him pleasure. Money gave him self-confidence. He now frequented the most cultured homes as a welcome guest. Elegant ladies offered him their hands to kiss and treated him with sympathetic understanding. But he knew that he mustn't take too many liberties because in spite of everything he remained a tailor, and all these people were the nation's elite. They were educated, well-read, at ease with themselves, proud, courteous, and above all very refined, wise, and beautiful, even in their disagreeable impoverished circumstances, even as they were selling off their last bibelot, silver épergne, or old book. That is why he was unable to bargain with them. And they, despite appearances and everything that was said of them before and after, had a peculiar sense, not in the least a business sense, not a commercial one, but simply an ethical one, thanks to which they knew that Kujawski would never cheat them and would never mock their poverty. Because a mysterious thread of dependence bound them to him, paradoxical and yet of great consequence, springing from an ancient core of Polishness, of Polish history and culture, from that unique skein of Polish yarn, a thread of dependence and community that enjoined the tailor to respect them and be grateful for being able to help them survive. Because if they didn't survive, then he too wouldn't survive, for there was in them something which neither they nor he could define, that permitted him to be a Pole as long as they existed in Poland—and not a moment longer!

And this is how Kujawski found blessed harmony in his life. Only one thing made him anxious. Namely that it seemed as if the Lord had turned away from Poland, exposed it to too harsh a trial. For what could Poland be so terribly guilty of, when, after a century of slavery and suffering, she was reborn after the Great War and survived barely twenty years? There is no doubt that not everything in Poland was as it should be, but then where was it as it should be? Were things as they should be when powerful France defended itself for barely one month and capitulated so ignominiously, practically falling on its knees before Hitler? Were things as they should be when the Soviet empire, stretching clear to the ends of the earth, collapsed with a bang under German pressure in the space of two months? And, after all, it had been the Soviets who together with Hitler had carried out the partitioning of this ill-fated Poland. For that sin God had rightly punished them; they had to flee from the Germans all the way to Moscow, and it was only there that they somehow managed to come to their senses and put up more effective resistance. So what is it about Poland and the Poles that they must suffer again, as never before? Why does God try Poland and the Poles so cruelly?

These questions gave Kujawski no peace, for it appeared to him, as it did to many others on this earth, that God governs human history. He was not to live to see the day when they explained all events without exception with the help of the scientific method of dialectical materialism, and even if he had lived to see it, he wouldn't have believed in that method, for according to it he was a petit bourgeois, a dim-sighted piece of work from the periphery of the classes, whose character, intellect, and habits were shaped by the tailor's shears, the Singer machine, and spools of thread, and thus an unconscious, unfinished product of the sociological version of human fate, bungled by the course of history; whereas he himself, Kujawski the tailor, knew perfectly well that he had received a soul from God, that he should listen to his conscience, which was just as unique and uncommon as the conscience of Benjamin Mitelman, Judge Rom-nicki, Pawelek, or even the German Geissler, for whom he was making a pair of breeches with a leather patch on the ass. He knew that he should listen to his conscience, which was his only weapon against all the wrong being done in the world, and if dialectical materialism knows nothing of this word, but only of social condition-ing, then it itself must contribute—whether intentionally or not—to that wrong, to the world's corruption, even if in theory it wishes to save the world, in spite of the conscience of the tailor Kujawski and the designs of God.

But he didn't live to see those days, which were to come only when his remains had already lain for years in a mass grave, among those of the many others shot down in a street execution in the fall of 1943, when his collections had been consumed in the fire of the Uprising and dispersed by the wind sweeping over the city's smoldering ruins, and his soul was tasting the joys of communing with God, and also with the soul of Benjamin Mitelman and the souls of those pleasant, worthy persons whom he had assisted by buying their works of art to the very end, or almost to the very end of his life, convinced that he would one day be able to make a splendid donation to a museum in independent Poland.

His last day was like a mirror image and abridged version of his entire life, beginning with the moment of childhood. As a boy he had been lively and restive, stealing pears in the evenings from the local rectory, never sitting still in one place for long. And that's how it was that morning when he awoke, restless and anxious. He paced aimlessly about his rooms, went out onto the balcony despite the rain, returned again to the living room, only to appear a moment later on the ground floor, in the atelier where normal, everyday work was going on, again climbed the stairs to the third floor, paced around the rooms, distracted somehow, swollen with something and yet empty, oddly thirsty for the world and its mysteries, which were still concealed from him.

Around noon he entered his youth. He marched to the Saxon Gardens with a springy, brisk gait, which looked comical to some passersby, for what they saw was a little man in a dark overcoat, little yellow boots, with a little cane, who looked like a comical dandy from a small town in the former province of Plock, with overly long sideburns cut at an angle, cheeks a little too powdered after shaving, rings on his fingers, and an amusingly dancelike step that was a bit too long for such short little legs, which nevertheless wanted to move in a very masculine fashion, with a glide, with a certain grace, with the kind of self-assurance that a tall and slender build gives a man. So the tailor Kujawski was walking along, already somewhat calmer, on his way to see the judge, to exchange views about the current situation, and perhaps also to persuade him to sell a most beautiful miniature on wood, representing sixty-eight figures of people and animals gathered at a Flemish country fair in the middle of the seventeenth century.

But he never got there, because on Niecala Street policemen grabbed him and threw him into the hole, and when he tried to explain that he sews trousers for the German high command they dealt him a blow on the back with a rifle butt so painful that he lost his breath, became dizzy, and immediately fell silent. That is how he entered his middle age. In the cell he maintained his silence, and when he did speak on several occasions, it was only in the hope of consoling and calming his companions in adversity. He knew already that it would be his fate to die against the wall of a Warsaw building. He was familiar with this business of public executions which had been raging all over town for some time now. He was afraid of death, that is certain, but his personal dignity did not allow him to show his fear.

He passed the night in prayer and meditation about the world. That is how his old age began, something he hadn't yet experienced when he was still a tailor on Marszalkowska Street, because he was only forty years old and had big hopes for the future. But on that last night he bid all his hopes farewell. He greeted the dawn cheerfully and calmly. This ordinary tailor, the most banal man under the sun, in point of fact rather absurd in his cheap vanity, maybe even downright stupid, who still secretly believed that the best thing for rheumatism was to sleep in bed with a cat because with time the rheumatism would enter the cat and completely abandon the afflicted limbs. This ordinary and simple man from the former province of Plock—who in his childhood sang patriotic ditties, didn't like Jews too much, detested Muscovites, was fearfully contemptuous of Germans, and of other people knew little or even nothing—this little Christian tailor, who made his fortune from bales of Jewish cheviot and then dreamed naïvely of his lofty role of patron of the arts, was granted a few hours before his death the miracle of true enlightenment. Things hitherto hidden he saw quite clearly, in their full essence, significance, and transience. And even this miracle was somewhat banal, as was everything that pertained to the tailor Kujawski. Because it is commonly known that at the end great wisdom is given to decent people and taken away from villains. For what is man's greatest and least easily attainable wisdom if not the ability to call good that which is good and evil that which is evil? And it is in this that the ordinary tailor, who had an excellent hand with the scissors, surpassed later philosophers and prophets. And even had he not been so skilled he would have surpassed them anyway, because he carried in his heart a good measure of justice, goodness, and love of his fellow man. So as he died against the wall of a Warsaw building, he was dying in a very dignified and beautiful way, having beforehand forgiven his murderers because he knew that they too would die and that death would not absolve them of infamy. He forgave all people and he forgave the entire world, which he recognized as being badly organized and in revolt against God's designs, for he surely wanted a world in which every man would be free irrespective of his race, nationality, world view, shape of nose, way of life, and shoe size. Kujawski actually thought then about this question of shoe size, because he didn't operate in philosophical categories but resorted to the wealth of his own banal and maybe even downright foolish observations, made from the perspective of a tailor who spends his time fitting people for a pair of trousers. And what of it, since after all he proved to be more insightful than those prophesying saviours and improvers of the world who were to come after him and once again count people's bones, track down their origins, if not racial then certainly those of their class, putting collars on them the way one does on performing bears, so that they would always dance to the victory tune played by the accordion in the Gogolian troika running wild across Europe, powerful and unbridled.

He died against the wall of an apartment building, and when the executioners threw his body onto the lorry and drove away, a woman dipped her handkerchief in the tailor's blood, which was congealing on the sidewalk, and bore it away with her as a symbol of human martyrdom.

That is how he entered into the pantheon of national heroes, although he didn't desire it in the least and even in the final moment it didn't so much as cross his mind that he was a hero. He knew, in that final moment, that he was a good man, and he wished the world well, his fellow men, and also Poland, which in his own provincial way he had loved dearly all his life. But he didn't know that he would be a hero, and had he known he would have expressed the firm wish to be crossed off the list. Later it was already too late! Contradicting his ideals of freedom and mocking his simple tailor's life, they placed his death upon a pedestal, as a model and example. But it was never fully explained what this was to be an example of. Whatever the case may be, he had gone out with the purpose of taking a walk in the Saxon Gardens. Were these walks of his supposed to be exemplary? Or perhaps instead the way in which he handled the scissors? Or his fondness for fake signet rings with coats of arms? It was never made clear. Only his death was to count, as if a death meant anything at all separate from the life that had preceded it.

XI

_____

Dear party comrade Stuckler, I wouldn't come to you to argue about some Jewish woman."

"He's a reliable informer," Stuckler replied. "He moved around among Warsaw Jews for several years. He knew them all well. . . ."

"Maybe he did, comrade Stuckler, but this person is an old acquaintance of mine."

Stuckler smoothed down the hair on his temples. He looked up at Müller with calm, slightly sleepy eyes.

"And even if she is an officer's widow?" he said softly. "What's the harm in detaining her?"

"I'm not here about a Polish officer's widow, but about a friend of mine," Müller said emphatically. "You've got nothing on this woman. She's ended up here by mistake."

"I'm not excluding that possibility," said Stuckler and picked up the telephone receiver.

In a quiet voice he gave the order to bring Maria Magdalena Gostomska. He replaced the receiver and turned to Müller.

"Party comrade Müller," he said, "I admire you. I've been in this town for barely a few months and already I feel tired. One must have extraordinary strength of character to get accustomed to the Polish environment."

"It's been so many years," Müller replied. "I've spent almost my whole life here. They are really not so bad. Just between you and me, some of them are a little disappointed now."

"Disappointed?" Stuckler echoed slowly.

Müller nodded his head thoughtfully.

"There were many here who for decades counted on us. They felt closer to us than to the Muscovites. They often call Russians Muscovites here, you know. I'm not a political man, party comrade Stuckler, but too great a harshness towards them doesn't seem right. Especially now, in the face of wartime events."

"They are Slavs," said Stuckler.

Müller cleared his throat. How will she act? he thought. Is she sufficiently quick to understand our mutual game? He felt moisture on the nape of his neck. I'm playing for high stakes, he thought. But she's playing for still higher stakes. If only she can play it right.

Stuckler smiled faintly.

"A horrible city," he said. "A savage city. I'm going on vacation in a week."

"Where to?" asked Müller. His tongue was stiff.

"Home," Stuckler replied. "I come from Saalfeld, in Thuringia."

"A very beautiful area," said Müller.

Stuckler nodded his head and closed his eyes.

I must jump up violently from the chair. Talk a lot, loudly. I'll walk up to her with a cry of surprise and joy. I can't speak in Polish in this situation. . . .

"I like to ride," said Stuckler. "I go on long excursions in the saddle. It's very relaxing."

"Here also?"

"Very seldom, unfortunately. I can't allow myself too many free moments, too much recreation."

"The service," Müller said with a sigh. "When you come down to it, this is still the front."

"Yes. This is the front," said Stuckler.

Will they bring her with a translator? I've made a mistake. I didn't find out from him whether she speaks German. If I speak Polish I'll arouse suspicion. I know too little about this woman.

"But now I'll be able to rest," said Stuckler. "Maybe I'll even take some therapeutic baths. Did you know, party comrade Müller, that we have many mineral springs in Saalfeld?"

"I hadn't heard of that," Müller replied. "Do they work for stomach ailments?"

I'll jump up from the chair and I'll cry out that my feelings are hurt. Why didn't you use my name, my dear Mrs. Gostomska?

"That too," Stuckler replied, "but mainly they just strengthen the entire organism. I've been feeling exhausted lately. Maybe it's nerves?"

"It's no wonder, party comrade Stuckler."

The door opened and Müller felt faint. A handsome blonde in a gray walking suit entered the office, elegant, slender, with a pale complexion and huge blue eyes. A burly SS man appeared behind her. Müller rose from his chair.

"Not to use old Johann Müller's name, my dear madame, how could you possibly!"

Jesus Christ, he prayed, *Jesus Christ!*

"I knew this was all a mistake, Mr. Müller," she replied calmly and in fluent German. "I didn't want to worry you."

"My dear Mrs. Gostomska!" he cried.

He didn't see her eyes, he was looking somewhat higher, above her head, still in fear that something terrifying would happen.

Stuckler sat motionless behind his desk. Suddenly he said, "Your name is Gostomska? A Polish officer's widow?"

"Of course," she replied.

"Mistakes happen," said Stuckler. "But we correct our mistakes."

On the street he took her arm. They walked quickly, in step. A gray-haired, ruddy-complexioned short man and a slender, pretty woman taller than he.

"I don't understand any of this," she said. "And I feel a little weak."

"We can speak Polish," he replied. "There's a pastry shop on Koszykowa. We can go in there."

They looked like an odd couple on a strange, slightly too hurried walk. He told her how he came to find himself in Stuckler's office.

"My God," sighed Irma Seidenman. "I barely remember Mr. Filipek."

It seemed to her that she was walking arm in arm with her husband, Dr. Ignacy Seidenman, because it was he after all who had gotten her out of the cell in the Gestapo. Müller felt the touch of her hand on his arm.

"Thank you," she said very softly, and he felt a sweet sensation. "I will always remember this day. And never, never in my life will I walk on Szucha Avenue."

Maybe she hadn't been mistaken when, sitting in the cell, she contemplated her existence as remembrance of the world, and only as remembrance of the world. If her life was no more than that which had passed, she had the right to presume that she would never again walk on Szucha Avenue, and that this day in April would remain forever deep in her consciousness. But life is also that which hasn't yet happened. It is a laborious movement forward, until the end of the road. In the course of the next twenty-five years she walked every day on Szucha Avenue, and even inside the building where the cells were. And she almost never thought about this day in April, about the night spent behind bars when she waited for death because of an idiotic cigarette case bearing the initials *I.S.* Every day she entered the ministry building, where she occupied an important post, and didn't even remember that the museum of martyrs was housed there. When circumstances reminded her of this, she felt a certain discomfort. Her life was that which had happened, but not only what had happened in all finality, but also that which had not quite happened yet, which was still in the process of happening. That is what she thought about. Only that is what held her attention. She often had tormenting dreams, but not about the war and the occupation, not even about Dr. Ignacy Seidenman, who still existed somewhere in her memory, in its farthest recesses, although no longer as a husband but rather as a sign and symbol of a past long buried beneath ashes, a sign of something good and valuable that once filled her life, later to disappear into the shadows under the pressure of everything that was slowly coming into being, in suffering, anticipation, and bitterness. But in that very suffering and anticipation lay the meaning of everything. It occupied Irma Seidenman's entire mind, because she was an active, ambitious, and wise woman and wanted to shape reality with her own hands, to feel the roughness of it with her fingertips and also its smoothness, of which there was no lack, particularly in moments when something was finally happening to make room for things still to come.

It seemed to her sometimes, to her own surprise, that she had within herself a strange instrument that somehow resonated improperly, like a cracked fiddle. Perhaps, she was wont to think many years later when she was already a very old woman, perhaps that fiddle of hers had cracked precisely during the war, on the night she spent in the cell on Szucha Avenue, or even earlier, in the summer of 1938, when she had learned at dawn over the telephone that her husband, Dr. Ignacy Seidenman, had just died. Something in that instrument sounded false, and Irma knew it, because she had a very musical existential sense. When she brushed her gray, slightly dirty-looking hair (it often happens to light blond hair with age) and looked at her wrinkled face in the mirror, sitting in a pretty, sunny room near the Avenue de la Motte-Picquet or when she looked through the newspapers on the terrace of a café near Avenue Bosquet, where nearly every day she drank a *citron pressé,* a lonely old Jewish woman on the streets of Paris. When this happened, thirty years from the day when Stuckler allowed her to leave the Gestapo building accompanied by old Müller, it was not Stuckler that she remembered, or the cell with bars, but only a small office with a desk the color of dark honey, two telephones, a palm in the flowerpot by the window, a rug, chairs upholstered in blue fabric—this small room she remembered perfectly, and the face of her secretary, Mrs. Stefa, and above all the faces of those three men who behaved so coarsely and were so derisive when they appeared in her office in April of 1968 to remove her from it.

And as an old woman on the streets of Paris she didn't remember at all, or maybe she didn't want to remember, that during the war, in that very same building, she had repeated stubbornly, "My name is Maria Magdalena Gostomska, not some Mrs. Seidenman! I am an officer's widow, I am not a Jew!" She didn't remember that incident at all, but a completely different one, which took place in the same building, perhaps even on the same floor—she couldn't even be sure about that—a completely different incident, in other words, when she said harshly to those three mocking and unyielding men that she would not waste her breath talking to them, that she would speak only with their superiors, people responsible for the country, and that they would surely understand her situation, her position, irrespective of the idiotic fact that her name happened to be Gostomska-Seidenman, Irma Gostomska-Seidenman.

The three were nodding their heads, and one said, "All right, all right! Let's not waste any more time. . . ." She took her purse, but when she was reaching to pick up the briefcase that contained still unread documents, something she usually did as she left her office so that she could work a little more at home, one of the men said emphatically that she should leave the papers, that there was no need to take them. "You won't be coming back here, love," he said. And he had been right. She didn't come back. But later, after many years, she was aware that that internal instrument was broken—she heard the false note in herself—because Stuckler would appear to her as a barely visible shadow. Stuckler was a phantom, a symbol, an inconsequential phenomenon, whereas those three who came to her office and didn't let her take her briefcase, and also Mrs. Stefa, who turned her face to the window when Irma crossed the outer office accompanied by the men, were reality, were life that happened in all finality,

1947.

Returned to
you from —

Mr. + Mrs. ·
Caplin· (They
loved it...)

David

although interrupted violently in one quick moment, brutally and vilely.

And that is all she remembered. She didn't remember Stuckler, Müller, Mr. Filipek, Pawelek. She didn't remember Dr. Adam Korda, but only those men in her office; Mrs. Stefa's silhouette against the window, and also the bloated, swollen, ill-disposed faces of those she spoke with later; the hands of customs officials on her baggage, papers, books, and notebooks. She remembered only this as she looked into the mirror in the room near the Avenue de la Motte-Picquet, as an old woman, a lonely Jewish woman on the streets of Paris, for whom the thought of Poland was like a wad in her throat, like a gag. She told herself sometimes: I am unfair! That was my native country, so I am being unfair! But a moment later, swallowing with difficulty the *citron pressé*, she would add, with relief: But why should I be fair, since I am an old, wronged woman, from whom they took everything only because she was called Irma Seidenman? And she no longer wanted to be fair. People have a right to be unfair when God afflicts them with misfortune.

But when she walked in the direction of Koszykowa Street supported by the arm of Johann Müller, she did not yet know that in the course of the twenty-five years that were still to come she would cross the threshold of the building on Szucha Avenue every day, or that she would leave that building in a paradoxically comical and pitiful manner, because there where her Jewishness had now nearly detained her forever, it would later become the cause of her being let go. And just as now her Polishness had been the cause of her being let go, later it would certainly have been the cause of her being retained. As she walked supported by Johann Müller's arm, she did not yet know that in thirty years' time, brushing her dirty gray hair in the room on the Avenue de la Motte-Picquet, she would be a tragic figure, but tragic in a completely different way than she was now, on the corner of Koszykowa Street, miraculously escaping death in the Gestapo building on Szucha Avenue. She didn't know about all of this, and she didn't yet know the thoughts, feelings, and dreams that would come later—in an entirely different world—devoid of all connections with the reality surrounding them—Irma and Müller—as they entered the small pastry shop, took their places at a small table, and ordered a pastry each from a tall, dark-complexioned waitress whom Müller addressed as "Dear madame!" because until recently she had been the wife of an illustrious writer and herself a pianist well known all over Europe, and before long was to become the corpse of a nameless woman buried beneath rubble.

"I won't be able to swallow a thing," said Irma Seidenman and pushed away the little plate with the pastry. "I'm only now starting to feel faint."

"I'm a stupid man," Müller said. "Here I am feeding you cake, and you haven't had anything to eat in two days. . . ."

"I'm not hungry," she replied. "I'm somehow . . . bursting. I can't explain it."

"Nerves," said Müller. "It will be all right by tomorrow. You must go to bed. Sleep this off. . . ."

"That's out of the question, I won't be able to fall asleep. I don't want to be alone now. . . ."

"Perhaps you'd like to visit some friends?"

"No, no. . . . Actually I don't know. I feel completely rattled."

"I will let Filipek know that everything is in order."

"I know him so little, sir. But of course, I want to thank him with all my heart."

Suddenly she started to cry. She bent her head and tears ran down her cheeks.

Müller said softly, "Go right ahead and cry. Go right ahead and cry."

The dark-haired pianist approached them and stroked Irma's hair with sympathy, as she would a little girl's.

"Tears are good for you," she said, "but I'll bring you something that's really foolproof."

Irma Seidenman raised her wet blue eyes.

"Foolproof?" she said. "My God!"

She took out a handkerchief and wiped her face. Then she blew her nose loudly, as if she wasn't at all the elegant and cultured widow of a doctor, or even of an artillery officer.

The waitress placed a glass of brown liquid in front of her and said, "Drink this, Madame."

Irma Seidenman drank it.

"It's terribly strong!" she exclaimed and smiled. The waitress nodded.

"You see, I told you. That's my 'Gestapo potion.'"

"I'd very much like a taste myself," said Müller. "I hope you'll allow me."

"But of course," the waitress said.

Time was passing. Müller telephoned Filipek, the railwayman. He informed him that Mrs. Gostomska was feeling well, and that the whole affair had been a success. He returned to the table. He drank one more glass of the Gestapo potion. He listened to Irma Seidenman, who was talking about her stay in the cell on Szucha Avenue. Time passed. They were no longer strangers. If I were twenty years younger and the times were different I would fall in love with this woman, Müller thought. But now it's enough that she is saved. Suddenly he burst into loud laughter. Irma Seidenman looked at him with surprise.

"It just occurred to me," he said, "that all of this is very extraordinary. My life is extraordinary. Doesn't the party badge on my lapel bother you?"

"But I know who you are," she replied.

"But this isn't a masquerade, my dear lady. It's the truth. I am a German, a real Johann Müller. Do you understand that?"

"I understand," she replied calmly. "There are all kinds of Germans. Everyone knows that, sir. . . ."

"Today everyone knows it, but if this war continues, if this whole mess continues, Poles will forget that there are all kinds of Germans. And who will I be then? What will happen to me then?"

"You're not speaking seriously," Irma Seidenman replied. "Hundreds of people know you here. Please, you shouldn't be afraid. . . ."

Müller frowned lightly.

"I'm not afraid of anyone, my dear lady. Fear? No, it's not about fear! I'm thinking of my, let us say, affiliation. Where do I belong? Here or there? It's not about me, because I know that I belong here. But after the war, in independent Poland, will other people recognize as self-evident that I belong here? After everything that is now happening between Germans and Poles, will Poles see that?"

"But of course," said Irma Seidenman, although she suddenly felt uncertain, or rather fearful because of the harm that might come to this man.

"My dear lady," said Müller, "Marshal Pilsudski referred to me as 'my fat little Hans,' he called me 'little Hans.' Do you know that I met the marshal more than forty years ago, and that I used to transport his underground papers from Lódź to Warsaw? He would say, 'Little Hans should go. He can lead every Muscovite around by the nose. . . .' My God, how long ago that was!"

"And did you lead the Muscovites around by their noses?" she asked. "Like today you did Stuckler?"

He passed his hand over his red face. He became a bit pensive.

"I thought of only one thing all night," he said. "What approach to take with Stuckler. . . . This may seem strange to you, but it was actually very simple with him! It wasn't that way with the Muscovites. . . . Stuckler is a German. And I know more about Germans than anyone else in Warsaw. A certain party comrade Müller comes to see him, he's the director of a large parts-and-repairs business, a functionary of the Rüstungskommando. He comes and says that some dirty little Jew nabbed a lady friend of his on the street, suspected of being Jewish. Stuckler is a German, and Germans are straight and narrow. If you allow me I'll go even further. Germans are flat as a board! Without imagination, without hypocrisy, without duplicity. They ordered Stuckler to exterminate Jews, and so he exterminates them. If they order him to respect them, in no time at all he'll be kissing your hand and treating you to the best French cognac. Discipline, accuracy, dependability in every job they do. In crime as well, unfortunately! So what do you think went through his head when I showed up and said that an acquaintance of mine, Mrs. Gostomska, and so forth and so on? He thought that there had been a mistake, that you must be sent home, and that that informer must get a proper going-over. . . ."

Irma Seidenman listened with her head slightly inclined, by now quite calm, preoccupied with Müller's words, as if he were speaking about someone else, about an interesting but quite alien affair that didn't pertain to her in the least.

"Yes," Müller continued. "I thought all night about how best to play the game with him. I was sure of one thing only, that one had to play it with a lot of noise, without any hesitation, without a moment's reflection. I was afraid whether or not you would understand this and behave in the right way. But he's a German. With a German it would have worked out somehow in the end anyway, even if there had been complications. He's not a Muscovite, my dear lady, he's not a Muscovite.

"And if I had had to pull it off with one of them? That would have been a completely different matter. Elegant, narrow at the waist, like a marriageable young woman, sleek, polite. Supple. Quick. Gentle. 'How happy I am, my dear Ivan Ivanovich, that you were so kind as to pay me a visit!' That would be the beginning. And cognac, of course. I tell him this, that, and the other. He listens politely. He smiles. He has delicate hands, feminine. He moves them about on the desktop, and there isn't one little piece of paper on the desk, not a single document, nothing at all. I speak, he listens. I finish, he is silent. He smiles and remains silent.

"What is a German thinking at such a moment? He hesitates, because after all they've already written up a report about your case—there's a folder, some documents are now lying on a shelf—but on the other hand director Müller says that there's been a mistake, the mistake must be repaired, and Germans don't make mistakes because it's not in the German style. What the German is thinking I know well.

"But what the other one is thinking—I don't know. Nobody knows, even another Muscovite doesn't know. Silence. I start again from the beginning. He listens courteously. He looks at his fingernails.

'Dear Ivan Ivanovich, it's so pleasant chatting with you.' Finally he says to me, 'One little moment, Ivan Ivanovich, we'll show you this Zajdenmanka!' And he treats me to some more cognac. And then a woman appears, maybe a blonde even, maybe even blue-eyed, but not you at all, a completely different person. And he watches. I play out my little scene, he smiles. Then he says to this woman, 'Thank you, Niura. You can go now.' And he turns to me with a doleful expression, deep concern in his eyes; he is practically weeping. 'What do we need this mutual unpleasantness for, dear Ivan Ivanovich? All for the sake of one little Jew girl? Think it over, Ivan Ivanovich, because otherwise we'll get very angry. . . .' And when I start to mutter something or other, he is suddenly no longer elegant, feminine, soft, but all at once a beast, a tiger has crawled out of him; he's already pulled a whip out of some drawer, he's already cracking it over my head, he'll hit me or he won't hit me, but in any case he's screaming atrociously the whole time, repeating the most vulgar expressions with gusto. He has splashed the glass of cognac into my face, his eyes are dark, narrow little slits, again and again he whirls the whip about, threatens me with paddy wagons and Siberia. 'I'll put you in chains, you son of a bitch! You'll die like a dog in exile, you son of a bitch,' and after a while he's sitting again behind his desk, his smile gentle, warm; he has poured more cognac, he pats my hand. 'Ivan Ivanovich, let's let bygones be bygones, I only implore you—never again, never again. . . .' And in the end, when he has walked me to the door, he adds with a melancholy expression on his face, 'I love people, Ivan Ivanovich, and my heart bleeds when they are harmed, believe me, sir. But this is a higher injunction, a higher injunction. I'm searching for philosophical justifications, as it were, and often I really do not find them. If you visit me sometime we can chat about these subjects; I'm in need of a sympathetic soul, of the companionship of a wise man who has given thought to a thing or two. . . .' And that's how our affair with the Muscovite would have ended, dear lady, if not worse. . . ."

Irma Seidenman listened to this story as if from a distance. Now, with the passing of time, she felt closer again to the cell on Szucha

Avenue, to that night of great reckoning and anticipation. That is probably why she answered, when Müller had finished, "And yet those Muscovites are different; there's just no comparison. I'm most afraid of the Gestapo."

"It stands to reason, my dear lady," Müller replied. He wanted to add something, but fell silent. A stream of unpleasant thoughts carried him away. They were painful thoughts, for he felt the bond with Germans, his Germanness, as he had never felt it before. The weight of it crushed him. We lack that pinch of folly, we are so very sober. Maybe that is why I went off to live here among the Poles, because I always had that bit of folly, that impulsiveness of the imagination, which a real German doesn't feel. Touched by the hand of folly, he ceases to be a German. He renounces his blood and his native soil. To be the best in every field, to be peerless—that is the German ambition. To compose most beautifully, to work most productively, to philosophize most wisely, to possess the most, to kill most efficiently! Well, yes, he thought with bitterness and pain, but after all that is the truest folly. Uninhibited thoughts and actions, seeing life as a dance, or as a song, is not folly. German insanity lies precisely in the dead-sober ambition, in the unrelenting effort to be first in everything. This woman is right. There is nothing more cruel. No Muscovite hypocrisy can compare with this straight and narrow, unwavering passion for leadership that has branded the German mind. She is right. The Muscovite's hypocrisy is terrible and destructive, but after all it is never perfect, one can always find some flaw in it, some crack, through which a bit of ordinary, human soul trickles through. If history ever imposes on Germans the duty of hypocrisy, they will become the most excellent hypocrites under the sun. Dear God, how much must a German such as I suffer, an unfinished German, formed not at all in the German manner but with some kind of a defect in the heart, who sees all this through the Slavic experience, a German infected with the blessed disease of Polishness, which is beautiful precisely in that it is imperfect, unfinished, unrealized, uncertain, searching, flighty, capricious, unbridled, quite like a madman being led by the hand by an angel?

"You are probably right," he said to Irma Seidenman, although she was lost in her thoughts and wasn't listening to his voice. "You are probably right. Because a Muscovite lacks perfection, he is always short of something, he will always neglect to do something, so all this effort of his for absolute dominion over man will in the end prove fruitless. But what is worst is that all of you will always be here between the hammer and the anvil."

Leaning over the table, suddenly strangely old and sad, he realized that he had sacrificed a great portion of his life to a lost cause. He didn't worry about his own future, but about the future of this country, to which he had tied all the hopes of his youth and of his mature years. His personal fate appeared to him all at once as unworthy of attention. And he wasn't mistaken. Providence proved quite kind to him. In the fall of 1944 he found himself in the ruins of the city. He heard the increasingly loud rumble of Russian guns from the other side of the Vistula and was indescribably afraid of meeting those who would say to him, again with a hypocritical smile like they had thirty years before, "Well, well, Ivan Ivanovich, here we are, back on our old dungheap. . . ." Not for a moment did he believe in the transformation of the Russian soul, in Russian communism, in Russia's revolutionary reincarnation. Communism was alien to him, repugnant even, because first of all, to his socialist mind, it was lacking in all rational ties with the workers' movement as he knew, loved, and respected it from the days of his youth, and, second, this communism was tainted by the Russian soul. It was above all else Russia—tyrannical, dark, and unbridled—with her Asiatic attitude toward the world, her mysterious melancholy and cruelty.

So Müller fled from Warsaw and from Poland, not because he felt himself a German, connected with the German republic of Adolf Hitler, but governed by a blind fear of the Muscovites, Siberia, the whip, and captivity. He still experienced a lot and suffered a lot, an old man stripped of all illusions, a castaway without a country thrown into alien landscapes. He left behind him in Łódź the graves of his German parents and of his Polish and Jewish comrades. He was all the more lonely because he didn't find fellowship with the other

Germans who settled, as he did, in Bavaria, fleeing in the migration of peoples that ensued from the new division of Europe that moved the borders of states the way one moves furniture in an apartment. All those who considered themselves to have been driven from their homes still felt themselves to be Germans, and, most importantly, wronged Germans, something that Müller did not accept to the end of his days because he felt himself to be only a little bit German, and a little bit still a Pole.

He sympathized now and then with his German countrymen, but he didn't absolve them from sin and didn't consider them history's victims but rather people co-responsible for Hitler and for all the misfortune that befell Europe as a consequence of the war. So he lived alone, without financial worries after several years of poverty, but silent and not understood, always facing toward Poland, whose new sufferings filled him with sadness. He felt helpless and mocked by the course of world events, a shipwreck run aground in the shallows, far from home port. The Poles with whom he had contact after the war didn't know him, so they weren't especially communicative, let alone friendly. There were nights when Müller ardently desired to return to his Germanness, in it to find solace and relief. He would then sedulously go over in his head all the Polish shortcomings and vices, Polish sins and stupidities. He could draw up quite a long list, as could every man who has come to love Poland deeply. And precisely for this reason he felt all the more strongly—against his own will almost—a Polish patriot, because he knew Polish weaknesses, all those Polish shortcomings, rascalities, idiocies; the flightiness, the snobisms and confusions; the xenophobias, delusions, myths. He saw them even more clearly than the most authentic Poles, because the thinnest of partitions always separated his mind from Poland, the spider's web woven from the genes of his father's and grandfather's German traditions. So he enumerated Polish sins in order—so he believed—to distance himself from Polishness, to make it repugnant to him, to dig between himself and Poland an impassable chasm, and all the easier rediscover himself again on the ground of genetic Germanness.

But he quickly abandoned this activity because he realized it was fruitless. The more critical Müller became toward Poland, the more deeply he yearned for it, the more strongly he loved it. His love was made more ardent by the thought that he could not—as before—take part in Polish events, and while Poland suffered he took carefree walks amid magnificent Alpine landscapes, lacked for nothing, quenched his thirst with choice beer, satisfied his hunger with choice dishes, lived in a pleasant, comfortable house, and above all was free, was master of his actions and thoughts, did exactly what he wished. No one looked into his pots, and even less into his heart and head, for the period of democracy had come to Germany, a democracy so decent, universal, and dependable as was possible only in Germany. And so German democracy did not bring Müller peace either, for he found in it again that tyrannical perfection without which Germans cannot live. Just as years ago in the pastry shop on Koszykowa Street, he was again visited by the thought that Germanness consists precisely in this drive to bring everything to perfection, in demonstrating if not excellence in everything, then at the very least the desire for excellence. So again he felt unwell. He missed that incompleteness, ambiguity, uncertainty of things and thoughts through which the weakness of human nature shines in its eternal searching for something that is unnamed and inexpressible.

When he was very old and sickly, and had taken to sitting on the terrace of his Alpine home, he thought—not without a certain mean-spirited satisfaction—that the Germans were now once again Germans to the full, that in the West they had perfected their Americanism, and in the East their Sovietism. And old Müller shook his head over his own sorry fate. When the time came for him to die, he saw the city of Lódź, Piotrkowska Street, on it a socialist parade, and in the parade young Johann Müller, surrounded by Polish, Jewish, and German comrades, all of them marching bravely with cries of "Long live Poland!" straight toward the mounted Cossacks assembled at the end of the street, ready to charge, swords and whips raised high above their horses' necks.

XII

The front doorbell rang. Pawelek looked at the clock. It was almost nine. Pawelek's mother cast a frightened look at her son, who was sitting at the table, his hand on a book, listening to the silence that fell after the ringing ceased, the silence of an evening in an empty apartment, separated from the rest of the world by blinds of black cardboard and heavy poppy red curtains. Now only the grandfather clock, made by the firm of Gustav Becker, was ticking quietly in the corner of the room, its golden weights and chains glittering behind the glass. A gaslight framed in a metal crown glowed pale blue above the table. Pawelek's fingers moved on the book, and his eyes ran again in the direction of the clock, which trembled somewhere deep inside its mechanism and began to strike nine measured beats.

"But it's past curfew," his mother said in a whisper.

They both stood up and looked at each other.

"I'll open it," she said. She was a pretty woman, with delicate, expressive features like those on an old cameo. A wave of fear welled up within her, a feeling she'd grown familiar with over the last few years and which paralyzed her each time she heard the doorbell ring, steps on the stairs, words spoken in German. Her husband, an officer in the September 1939 campaign, was in a German prisoner-of-war camp. Each day she watched her son, and the sight of his ever more masculine, slender silhouette terrified her. She wanted him to remain a child, and as that was impossible she wished upon him some gentle but visible deformity, perhaps one short leg or crooked shoulders, and would have been happiest if for a time he could have become a dwarf. But he was not a dwarf, but a strong and well-built young man. He was about to turn nineteen. He didn't speak much to his mother and was rarely at home. His companions were other tall and well-built young men—and she was certain that this Pawelek of hers was plotting something, scheming against her in some way, risking his life, so she trembled with fear, love, and hatred. She reproached herself for her former thoughtlessness and her big mouth, for all those fairy tales and Polish legends that years ago she put into her child's head. She reproached herself for those little poems and prayers, songs and reminiscences, by Mickiewicz and Grottger, Pilsudski and Father Skorupka. She cursed all those battles of Grunwald, Byczyna, Psków, the Praga massacre and Napoleon, Olszynka Grochowska and Malogoszcz, the ramparts of the Citadel, *The Pawiak Ten,* the Magdeburg fortress, the miracle on the Vistula, and above all else she thought ill of her husband, who, although he sat behind the barbed wires of an *Offizierslager,* nevertheless still roamed around the house, working Pawelek's hands when the latter wound the grandfather clock by pulling the weights and the chains; when he took books down from the library shelves to read them; and doubtless came to Pawelek at night while he slept to talk to him all the time about Polish responsibilities. This absent husband also came to her at night, but in a different way—without his uniform, sword, and four-cornered cap—and most often actually completely naked, a bit violent, smelling of tobacco and cologne as he had twenty years ago, when for the first time she felt his cavalryman's weight upon her, immediately after a victorious battle—the youthful weight of a soldier who had won a war and captured his woman. She received this husband shamelessly and greedily during the nighttime, wished to prolong his presence in her dreams, but in the daytime she didn't like him one bit, was afraid of this unruly ghost who tempted Pawelek and drew him over to his side, to that other dangerous shore where men similar to him were assembling, while meantime she trembled on her shore in loneliness and fear.

Pawelek walked out of the room and disappeared from her view. She heard his steps in the dark corridor, and then the rattle of the bolt, the clink of the chain, and finally the bang of the door being opened. This is the end, she thought, it's the Gestapo come for him. She stood motionless, a pretty, middle-aged woman with light hair above her forehead, large blue eyes, slender fingers that she clasped together in a gesture of fear. She heard the blood throbbing in her temples and said to herself that she would not survive this trial. God should not punish people so severely and demand that they still continue living.

She heard an unfamiliar masculine voice in the corridor, speaking Polish, cheerfully and freely. Pawelek appeared in the doorway, and behind him a little girl, whom a tall, dark-skinned man with the face of a criminal was holding by the hand. You're an idiot, Elżbieta—she told herself—you're a stupid woman, Elżbieta! Only now did she remember that it was probably today, or perhaps tomorrow or the day after, that Joasia Fichtelbaum was to arrive in her house, the little sister of Henio Fichtelbaum, Pawelek's best friend from school, the capricious Henio, a boy just a bit too sure of himself, arrogant because of his excellent grades, whom her husband had never liked. For her husband in general was somewhat reserved toward Jews, far though he was from advocating any violent methods, of course, for after all he was a product of the struggle for independence and a European education, he was a true gentleman, with that light, nineteenth-century veneer of progressivism and liberalism whose ambition it had been to transform the world into a planet of universal brotherhood. So her husband was far from advocating violent methods, but he spoke of Jews with a certain reluctance, a lordly forbearance, perhaps, but without warmth, rather caustically.

So this was Henio's little sister, the daughter of Jerzy Fichtelbaum, a well-known lawyer, a man of great charm and culture. She had enjoyed talking to him whenever they met at various school functions. Once she had had coffee with him on the terrace in Lazienki Gardens, having run into him by chance during a Sunday walk. The boys were riding ponies while she spoke with the lawyer and his wife—whose face she could no longer remember for she was too worldly a woman to remember a Jewish lawyer's wife she had met once during a Sunday walk in Lazienki Gardens—she was drinking coffee and talking of Pawelek's friendship with Henio, which in her eyes somewhat ennobled Henio, made him more worthy. And what joy she had felt, what warmth in her heart, when Judge Romnicki—whom she called "our Marcus Aurelius from Miodowa Street," because knowing Latin from her youth as well as ancient history she considered the judge a philosopher and a citizen of genuinely Roman virtues—how glad she had been when the judge turned to her, of all people, in this delicate and beautiful matter, at once ancient and modern, beseeching her to take in for a day or two a Jewish child, the daughter of the lawyer Jerzy Fichtelbaum, whom after all she knew.

She agreed at once, for this was a Christian act, Polish and humane, magnificent from any perspective, and as it entailed risk, also conferring upon one's life a kind of hallowed glow. She didn't do it out of vanity, for no one ever lays his head on the block out of vanity but out of a need in her own heart, which was good, tender, and sensitive to wrong. At night she asked her absent husband if she had done the right thing and he answered yes, adding that it would not behoove the wife of a Polish officer in German captivity to act any other way. And so this child now appeared on her doorstep, pulled up onto dry land from the depths of the cruel sea of violence and crime. She was a pretty four-year-old girl with curly hair and large, dark eyes. She stood in the light of the gas lamp, listening intently to the last strokes of the clock, which was beating out nine o'clock. All the gates in the city were just now being locked, and the woman, something having just occurred to her, looked anxiously at the tall newcomer.

He nodded his head lightly and said, "Well, my dear lady, the goods have been delivered."

"Please, come in," Pawelek exclaimed. "You seem to have blood on your coat!"

"It's oilcloth," the man replied. "It won't leave a stain."

Pawelek's mother took Joasia by the hand.

"How tiny she is," she said. "She's probably very hungry."

"I don't know about that," the man replied. "But I'll have a cigarette, if you don't mind."

He pulled out a heavy metal cigarette case, took out a cigarette, slid the filter between his lips, and lit up.

"My God," she said, "but it's past curfew. . . ."

"The curfew doesn't bother me," he said, "but I'll leave in a minute."

"Oh, no!" she exclaimed. "Please, sit down."

He sat down in his coat, holding his cap on his knees.

"You can rest assured about Joasia," she said. "I'll see to everything."

"That's not my affair anymore," the man said. "What's to happen next with this little one, I don't know. I've done my bit. . . ."

"But of course," she replied, with an excessive eagerness that at once struck her as inappropriate. She looked into this man's face and wanted to commit it to memory, yet this desire was accompanied by a kind of distaste, fear, and embarrassment. She said to herself that she must remember this face because it belongs to a brave man who risks a lot bringing help to the persecuted, but at the same time she felt the need to memorize the features of the man who appeared in this empty house where loneliness and longing were the air she breathed. After all, Pawelek was not a man, he would never be one, would remain a child forever, a big child who would one day have children of his own, but would nevertheless still remain a child.

The man's face appeared rather blue to her, perhaps because of the dark stubble on his cheeks and the light from the gas lamp. He lifted his head, they looked into each other's eyes.

I shouldn't look at him, she thought, flustered, and turned to the child.

"Joasia, I'll make something to eat in a minute."

Joasia nodded her head.

Pawelek said, "She looks a little like Henio, doesn't she?"

"Only Henio wasn't so pretty," she replied.

"Mother, don't use the past tense!" he cried.

She sighed sadly. "But it's been so many months since he's given any sign of life. . . ."

"If you're talking about the brother of this little one," the man said, "he's not on the other side of the wall."

"He's hiding somewhere in the countryside," Pawelek exclaimed. "He's strong, intelligent. And anyway . . ."

He stopped because he was worried. He had not thought of Henio for a long time now. Henio had vanished suddenly, in the late fall. They had parted one day on Koszykowa Street, in front of the public library. Pawelek had brought Henio some money.

Henio had been in good spirits, and had said, "I've decided to have some fun today!"

"Don't behave stupidly," Pawelek had replied. "Go back to Flisowski's place. There's nothing worse than hanging aimlessly around town."

"Why aimlessly?" Henio Fichtelbaum had cried. "I'll go to the pastry shop, maybe I'll meet a beautiful girl who will take me home, and after the war I'll marry her and we'll go to Venezuela. . . ."

"Please, Henio," Pawelek had said with a touch of anger. "You're a grown man after all. Things are not too bad for you at Flisowski's. . . ."

"Leave me alone!" Henio had yelled. "It's easy for you to talk. What things, damn it! I sit up in the attic like a bat, the old man comes twice a day and leaves the food. He's deaf as a post, I can't exchange a single word with him. Can you even begin to imagine what it's like being shut up like that, with only a tiny window, all you can see is a patch of sky, always the same patch? Not a single little branch, not a single face. . . . At night I can hear the mice scratching up there, Pawelek. Only mice. And I cannot walk at all. Three steps to the left, about face, three steps to the right, about face! And quietly, on tiptoes, so no one will hear. . . ."

"Henio!" Pawelek had said emphatically, as if he were speaking to a small child, "you are safe there. Do you know how hard it was to find such an excellent hiding place? I had to really twist Flisowski's arm to get him to take you in for a while. . . . And besides, I'm now looking for—"

"Oh, stop talking so much!" Henio had interrupted angrily, and his capricious lips had curled in an expression of distaste and disdain. "I know that you're doing what you can. But after all you can walk around town, meet people, ride in a trolley car or a rickshaw, alone or with a girl, with your hand on her knee. I've had enough of this, damn it!"

"I don't have my hand on her knee!" Pawelek had shouted, because Henio had touched a wound festering in his heart. "And it's not my fault that you're sitting at Flisowski's. A week ago you went to the barber's. What are you going off to the barber's for? It's—"

"What am I, a gorilla?" said Henio, full of anger and resentment. "Am I supposed to go around looking like a hairy ape just because you locked me up in that attic?"

"I locked you up? Me?"

Henio Fichtelbaum had waved his hand.

"All right, not you! But from time to time I have to move a bit, breathe, look at people! You don't understand this, Pawelek, but this is ecstasy, I tell you, sheer ecstasy, just to be able to walk around on Koszykowa Street, without any special purpose, just to walk around."

"You're not allowed to do that," Pawelek had said firmly.

"I know! I'm meek as a lamb, after all. You would never have been able to order me around like this before, chief! I'll be obedient. But now and then, let's say two, three times a month, I have to come down from that damned attic."

"Only on condition that I go with you."

"Have you lost your mind?! I'm not going to endanger you!"

"Of course," Pawelek replied. "But let's say that when you go out I'll walk a few paces behind you, I'll be on the lookout. . . ."

"Don't go around playing detective, Pawelek! You want to follow me? What for? If something happens, you won't be able to help me anyway."

"But I'll know what's happened to you, where you are. . . . Maybe then something can be arranged."

"There's no more money left for ransom, Pawelek."

"One can always get money somehow. And remember, no more barbers! All kinds of people go there, you're in an enclosed area, immobilized, with that damned sheet under your chin. . . ."

"That barber was telling Jewish jokes, you know. I was roaring with laughter."

"You know what, you sound as if you had absolutely no idea of the seriousness of the situation!"

"Probably," Henio had replied. "But be so kind as to keep in mind that it is after all *my* situation."

Pawelek hadn't wanted the tension to escalate again so he had given him a forced smile.

"All right, Henio. Please, go back to Flisowski's now. I'll drop by the day after tomorrow and we can discuss the details of your outings."

They had shaken hands. Pawelek had gone into the library, and Henio had turned around in the direction of Marszalkowska Street. That was the last time Pawelek saw him. Because when he showed up at Flisowski's at the appointed time, it turned out that Henio Fichtelbaum hadn't come back to the attic. The old clockmaker Flisowski was quite pleased with this turn of events.

"Mr. Kryński," he said to Pawelek, "you can tell your friend not to show up here anymore. I have enough troubles of my own and I want to live to see the end of the war, whatever that end will be."

"But Mr. Flisowski," Pawelek exclaimed, "this is impossible! We had an agreement!"

"You can argue with me all you want!" the clockmaker snapped.

"I've had my say and that's that! If you ever have an older man, a calm older man who sits quietly, doesn't whistle the 'Tango Milongo,' doesn't knock on my ceiling to be let out to use the toilet ten times a day, doesn't yell in my ear that he has an ugly view from the window, when you have such a sedate, older gentleman, then I may even take him in for a while. But that pal of yours, never again, as sure as there's a God in Heaven!"

From that late fall day Henio Fichtelbaum disappeared, and Pawelek consorted only with the memory of him, with the ghost of his friend, who he assumed had been killed, although in the corner of his heart he nursed the hope that Henio was safely in hiding somewhere and thinking about his friend Pawelek. But in the course of the long winter that hope had grown weaker and weaker, and by the spring had completely melted away. Yet now, when his mother declared that Henio had not been as pretty as his little sister, Pawelek protested. Henio *is,* he thought, Henio is alive. In this way he chased away the demons.

In a few days' time the telephone will ring in this room. Pawelek will pick up the receiver, gazing at the golden face of the clock, and will say to himself that it's seven o'clock, a pretty April day is beginning.

"Hello!" he will say, looking at the clock's dark hands.

"It's me," he will hear a soft, distant voice.

"Henio! My God! What are you up to?"

Tears will run down Pawelek's face, as if he was not a young man of nineteen but a small boy in a little velvet suit with a lace collar.

"I'd like to see you," he'll hear the distant voice say.

"Of course, Henio! Listen, this is very important. Joasia is well, everything is all right with her, she sends you her greetings."

For a long while all he'll hear will be a monotonous hum. He'll call out anxiously, "Henio! Can you hear me?"

"Yes, I hear you. I too send her my greetings. I want to see you."

"Where are you?"

"In town."

There will be another long silence, and then Henio will say, "I'm going back there!"

"Where are you now? We have to see each other."

"Yes. At nine o'clock on the corner of Książęca Street and Three Crosses Square, all right?"

Just then Pawelek will hear a crackling noise and the connection will be cut. He'll keep calling out, "Henio, do you hear me? Henio!" But there will be no answer.

And this will happen in a few days. The telephone will ring, the clock will say seven, a bright morning outside. It is written in the stars. Just as it was written in the stars that Pawelek would say to the man in the oilcloth coat, "Please rest a while, and we'll fix something to eat."

"There's no need," he replied. "Give some to the kid, but I'm not hungry. I'll be going soon."

"That's dangerous," the mother said. "They shoot without warning."

"Don't you believe that, ma'am. They could shoot their own people that way. They always check your papers."

"And you have a pass?" she asked.

"I have everything I need," he replied, and started to laugh. She had never heard such a laugh. There was cruelty and danger in it. She looked again into the man's eyes. And she thought that he could read her thoughts. She felt her cheeks burning, and now was afraid of both of them, of the man and of Pawelek. She was afraid that Pawelek would notice the strange state she was in, that peculiar excitement and fear.

But Pawelek took the child by the hand and said, "Joasia and I are going into the kitchen and we'll make delicious things to eat there. . . ."

"Oh, why," the woman said meaninglessly, then sat down abruptly at the table, across from the tall stranger. She didn't have the strength to escape his gaze. He stretched out his hand with the cigarette case.

"Will you have one?"

She shook her head. Only now did he look around the room. He examined the cupboard, the console table, the porcelain behind glass, the framed photographs, then the heavy poppy red curtains in the windows, the slipcovers on the chairs, the damask tablecloth. His eyes were blank and without curiosity, but to her it seemed that when he was looking at the decorative tiles on the stove and at the stucco on the ceiling, he was doing this as if he were undressing her, as if he were looking at her breasts, her belly, her naked shoulders. What is happening to you, Elżbieta? she thought. He's a monster after all, a brute, a man of violence! She wasn't mistaken. He was brutal and violent, and there were those who thought of him as a monster. But that is precisely the kind of man she wanted, the kind she was waiting for, shocked at herself and terrified. They were silent. Even if he were to stay by her side for many years, they would still have nothing to say to each other. They would be man and woman, man and woman at every moment—and nothing more! But he didn't stay. He had his shady affairs to conduct at the very edge of the world, where there were no more human beings left but only beasts and ghosts. He put out his cigarette, rose from the chair, tall, powerful, with a bloodstain on his oilcloth coat.

"I'm off," he said and twisted his lips into a smile. "Please say good-bye to the kid for me. And my best to your son."

"But perhaps after all . . ." she said.

He shook his head.

"There's too little time, lady. Always too little time!"

He put the cap on his head, pulled the peak down low. His face was transformed, he looked more gentle now, as if the cap's shadow hid his crimes.

She walked him to the door. On the threshold she said, "There's no light on the stairs, sir."

"I'll manage," he replied.

She gave him her hand. He lifted it to his lips and kissed it. She slammed the door shut behind him and leaned against the frame, breathing heavily and rapidly. She felt the moisture of his lips on her hand, and it made her tremble. She heard his footsteps receding down the stairs. I hate him, she thought. Monster! I've been humiliated. . . .

Thirty years later, when she was an old woman, she still hadn't put aside this hatred. She no longer remembered his face, but she remembered herself. And thirty years later she still felt the humiliation. Whenever she later encountered such strong-bodied men of simple bearing, who behaved with a self-confidence stemming from physical strength, a sense of authority, cleverness, or even the most ordinary stupidity; whenever she later encountered such plebeians, who were casually superior toward her, or with whom she felt herself insecure because of her fragility, femininity, weakness, because of history—which pushed her to the side, into the ditch, off the embankment, while they walked straight down the middle in those coats of theirs, made out of oilcloth, leather, or nylon, in peaked caps, hats, or bareheaded; when she saw their faces, craggy somehow, roughly hewn; when she watched as they smoked cigarettes, holding them between their thumb and index finger with the lit end turned toward the inside of the palm; whenever she heard their steps, set into motion by the weight of large bodies, or smelled the odor of their skin, penetrating and sharp, that smell of sweat, tobacco, and things illicit, she always remembered that evening when she had taken in under her roof Jerzy Fichtelbaum's daughter. And she felt the humiliation. But taking a Jewish child under one's roof then, in the spring of 1943, was a beautiful and praiseworthy act. Why did she feel so humiliated? What had happened that evening that after so many years it should return to haunt her with such bitterness and revulsion?

She sat at the table, looking at the hands of the clock, listening to Pawelek saying something to the child in the kitchen, and tried to think about her absent husband, in German captivity for more than three years now, among hundreds of other officers like him, who had abandoned their wives to defend their country, a country that could not be defended, a country destined to be abased, wronged, and destroyed. Why, she thought, for what sins?

She placed her hand on her breast. She felt the well-known shape beneath her dress, which nevertheless always seemed alien and unpleasant, since it didn't really belong to her, but to a man. She was orphaned. She was in part dead. Why am I dead, she thought, when, after all, I've committed no crime?

That thought somewhat sobered her religious soul. Don't be ridiculous, Elżbieta, she said to herself, death is not punishment for sins but a reward, the passage to eternal life. Don't be ridiculous!

This brought her relief. She didn't want to see herself as ridiculous. Rather, she was sad and disappointed. She sat awhile longer, gazing at the clock. The thought flashed through her head that that man might go out on the street, fall into German clutches, and spill the beans about where he had taken the Jewish child. Fear seized her again, but it lasted only a moment, because she knew that that man would not fall into German clutches, that the likes of him simply don't, and even if he were to, he would never say a word. She trusted him, hated him, and felt humiliated.

And then she got up from the table, went into the kitchen, and to her own surprise found joy and peace of mind again. With tenderness she undressed the small Jewish child and bathed her, cheerfully humming melodies from her youth.

XIII

At five o'clock in the morning, at daybreak in the fog and springtime chill, he was riding in a streetcar over the Kierbiedź Bridge. The car rumbled. People stood crammed together, sleepy, numbed. A sharp, penetrating odor of fear and hopelessness rose above their heads. Only that odor has remained, in trolley buses, streetcars, and coaches manufactured by Chausson, Berliet, Ikarus, and San, and in the train compartments as well. Human fear is different now, as are human hopelessness, exhaustion, dreams, and longings, but the smell has remained the same.

The streetcar rumbled over the bridge. Below flowed the river. On the sandy right bank a solitary man with a fishing rod in his hand walked toward the stone dike. The last man who had not given up hope.

Filipek, the railwayman, had a long way to work. He lived in the Wola district, and commuted to the engine house in Praga. Twice daily he crossed the city. In the morning and the afternoon, or in the afternoon and the late evening. He didn't like to work the second shift. The return trips always made him nervous. He had a pass, of course, but his faith in it was limited. He knew the worth of documents. As a young man, in 1905, he had worked in the technical department of the Revolutionary Faction. He knew how to forge even the most sophisticated documents, the kind that opened up the gates of the Citadel and Pawiak prison. Yet those were still idyllic times, the twentieth century was only just beginning, and people hadn't yet felt its rhythm. Much water would flow down the world's rivers before the eyes would comprehend, the ears would hear the truth, the lips would speak it. In 1943 the railwayman Filipek put no faith in documents, even if they were stamped with the word *Ostbahn*. A policeman would turn the pass around in his hand with an expression of distrust. But he was a German policeman. The sight of the swastika aroused within him feelings of respect and a certain moderate measure of magnanimity. But with one careless gesture one could destroy the equilibrium of his soul, stir up violent passions. One could say just one word, a quite innocent one even, but one which to his ears would sound like a challenge. The pass would then cease to exist, and a moment later so would the man who carried it.

Water continued to flow down the rivers, and a new breed of policemen appeared. They didn't want to see any documents. They would hold them up between their thumb and index finger, reluctantly, mockingly, now and then with disgust, and they didn't need to read them. They knew everything in advance, without any documents. You can't go through here, please move on; you cannot go out, sir; you cannot go in, ma'am; what's written is written, and what's said is said! Policemen of this type didn't have to read documents. They only read instructions, carefully, with immense concentration. It was uphill work, laborious, painful; sweat poured down their faces. Even the most unfeeling man couldn't help but be moved at the sight of this discipline, the goodwill evinced by this new breed of policemen, who were overcoming the great obstacle of the written word, running their fingers along the lines of type, helping themselves with their lips, even with the tips of their tongues, conquering with indescribable hardship the intellectual Himalayas of instructions in order to absorb their profound political, social, and cultural content; to absorb it forever and ever, or until the next day when a new set of instructions would appear—that new Mount Everest of bureaucratic eagerness and resolve to transform the world—and again they would undertake their labor, hammer into their heads a knowledge that was mysterious and inaccessible to laymen, pounding themselves on the forehead with their fists so that later they could pound their neighbors with clubs—although within reason and methodically, without evil intent, without a thirst for blood, in a manner that was, so to speak, administrative and educational—with the goal not of depriving a man life but of awakening reason, in the most broadly understood interest of the state, in accordance with the content of the instructions memorized the other day, memorized in between the plastic riot shield and the color television set, in the glow of a lighter, in the greenish glow emanating from an electronic watch, similar to the glow that in the nineteenth century emanated from fresh tombs.

Consequently, having no confidence in the most dependable passes, something that put him ahead of his times, railwayman Filipek tried to work the first shift. There was yet another reason why he did—a hidden and lofty reason attesting to his courage. Filipek was up to his ears in the underground, and in the evenings he worked in a clandestine printing press because he was an expert on various types of printing machines and devices and knew how to make from an ordinary household wringer astonishing contraptions that were useful to the resistance organizations.

Many years later various people tried to imitate the skills of railwayman Filipek. Thirty-year-old girls, who walked the streets of Warsaw dressed in the costumes of Peruvian peasants, and thirty-year-old boys in jeans, with the beards of old men and the imaginations of small children. They imitated him earnestly but incompetently, and sometimes downright comically, because to make a printing machine out of a wringer one must not only screw the screws in correctly, one must also understand what true, cruel bondage is, one must have experienced the Muscovite whip and the dungeons of Szlisselburg, the German cells on Szucha Avenue and detention camp barracks, Siberia, deportations, forced marches east, Pawiak, Auschwitz, street executions, Katyń, the snows of Workuta and the steppes of Kazakhstan, Moabit and the forts in Poznań, Montelupich, Dachau, Sachsenhausen, the shores of the Jenisej and the Irtysh rivers, the wall of the Warsaw ghetto, of Palmira, Treblinka; one must have experienced all this with body and soul, have it engraved on one's skin, carry it around in one's bones, in one's heart; one must taste, like railwayman Filipek had tasted, the years of watchful, sleepless nights, when every murmur seemed to be the steps of death, every rustle the wind outside the prison cell window, and every whisper a deportee's prayer or the farewell on the threshold of the gas chamber. To turn a wringer into a printing machine it's not enough to suffer from humiliation, hypocrisy, lies, truncheons, arrests, accusations, threats of banishment, the lawlessness of the powerful and the defenselessness of the weak, the pride of the state and the abasement of the citizen. That does not suffice to turn a wringer into the printing machine of a truly free man. On such a wringer one can yell, curse, demand, threaten, weep, and mock, but one cannot speak calmly about the world and about human dignity. If one's cup of suffering hasn't run over, one's dreams will remain unfulfilled.

So railwayman Filipek was riding to work, as he did every day for many years, only this morning he was in an especially good mood. During the night he had successfully transformed one more wringer, and the previous afternoon he had received news from Jaś Müller that Mrs. Seidenman had been saved. Jaś Müller, as always, had proved infallible. Filipek looked out the streetcar window, saw the dome of the Orthodox church on Zygmuntowska Street, and felt moved, for memories from the days when he was fighting against the yoke of the Czar washed over him. But on the sidewalk in front of the church stood military policemen in oilcloth overcoats, helmets with swastikas, and leather belts around their stomachs with silver buckles adorned with the inscription *Gott mit uns!*

Is God really with them? Filipek asked himself. His good mood vanished. Where is the Virgin Mary of Jasna Góra, Ostra Brama,

Piekary, Kobryń—from cities near and far—if in the course of one man's life, on the corner of Zygmuntowska and Targowa streets, in the capital of the nation that at one time stretched from sea to sea, ruled over Gdańsk and Kudak, Glogow and Smolensk; if before the eyes of one man, a mustached, skinny railwayman with overworked hands and a bare head; if in the life of this one man, within his living memory—in his powerless presence, full of a desperate humiliation, on the corner of those two streets—there have stood a mounted Cossack from the steppes, a Prussian officer with a monocle in his eye and the Iron Cross on his breast, a beefy military policeman with a swastika, a vigilant Red Army man in a loose blouse with a tommy gun over his shoulder; if in this ordinary place but a holy one after all because absolutely unique; before the eyes of only one man, during his lifetime, in the course of thirty years, a Cossack and a Prussian, a Nazi and a Red Army man, were changing the guard here, then where was the Virgin Mary from those cities near and far, the queen of this nation? But maybe it is the nation's fault? Perhaps it hasn't yet matured to the level of Europe, of Asia, perhaps it hasn't reached its own potential?

Was this country merely the territory for foreign armies to march across, the land behind the front lines, the strip of ground between them? The last trench of Latin Europe, facing the eastern steppes but at the same time a defensive rampart in the face of the Teutonic deluge. The outpost of the free world, squeezed in between tyrannies. A narrow band of hope, separating Prussian pride from Russian ignorance. A little river between cruelty and hypocrisy, bestiality and deceit, contempt and jealousy, arrogance and flattery, screams and murmurs. The borderland separating the shamelessness of undisguised crime from the cynicism of concealed crime. Only a strip of land, a piece of ground, an outpost? And nothing more?

Pawelek, the railwayman thought, I envy you. You will live to see other times. Poland will no longer be like a nail in a pair of pliers. It will be independent again, and yet better than during that other, recent period of independence, because it will be without the blue police, the *sanacja* movement, the hurrahs of the jingoists, without the pettiness, conceit, peasant poverty, labor revolts, superpower ambitions, ghetto benches, Rzeszów strikes, those murdered at the Semperit factory, those destitutes digging in the coal pits; without hungry intellectuals and unrestrained colonels; without provincial clergy, the prison in Brześć and the camp in Bereza, anti-Semitism, Ukrainian riots, the smell of pickled cabbage, the ubiquitous herring of the poor, homeless vagrants, boastful bourgeoisie; without chimneyless cottages and boarded-up villages; without bankrupt theaters, expensive books, cheap prostitutes, dignitaries' limousines, and the Front of National Unity. I envy you, Pawelek! You'll have a Poland of glass houses, our Poland of the Polish Socialist Party, a workers' and peasants' Poland, without dictatorships of any kind because dictatorship is bolshevism, cruelty, atheism, and the end of democracy; you will have at last, my dear Pawelek, an independent, just, and democratic Poland, a Poland for all Poles, Jews, Ukrainians—even for Germans, damn them, even for them too. I won't live to see this, Pawelek, because they're going to catch me in the end! How long can one dodge, conspire, play tricks on those scoundrels who have trampled Polish soil? I've told you more than once, Pawelek, that I've played tricks all my life. I played them during Nikolai's days, during Stolypin's, then during Beseler's too, and how! Can you guess, Pawelek, when it was that I wasn't doing time? I did time in Pawiak even before the revolution of 1905. I cleared the taiga in the Krasno Province. And whyever not! During the days of Emperor Wilhelm I ended up in the same police station where I had done time under the Muscovites. That's just the kind of weird Polish, and Polish socialist, monster I am. So, it goes without saying, I also did time in independent Poland. And why on earth not? I did time on Danilowiczowska Street, detained for interrogation, because during the May 1 demonstrations I defended the communists. One should fight communists, Pawelek— they are a dangerous, deceitful mob—but never with a club, never with a club! So when the police started instructing them with clubs to love their country, I put up a good fight. They shut me up, naturally, for a certain length of time. I also did time in '38. And why on earth not? On account of the Socialist Party's agitation against the elections, which the colonels wanted to stage for themselves at the workers' expense. So I did time, what else? . . . You yourself have to admit, Pawelek, that one doesn't end such a life in bed. It won't be long before the Krauts have me by the collar. And they don't play around. It's up against the wall or off to camp, to certain death. . . . So I won't live to see an independent, just Poland, Pawelek. But you will for certain, because . . .

Filipek interrupted his internal monologue because he had arrived in front of the engine house, and being a man of a peculiar mold, an old-fashioned social democrat, he separated politics and the struggle for the interests of the workers from professional work. Near engines he thought only of engines, near boilers only of boilers, and it would never have occurred to him that one could throw down the welding torch in any old place and declaim in favor of planting corn or in honor of some girl who had laid herself across the railroad tracks in order to demonstrate her pacifist inclinations. For Filipek, a party agitator who didn't know how to adjust a monkey wrench was above all else a bungler, and he did not listen to bunglers and had only scorn for them because they offended the dignity of the working man. If Filipek hated anything in the world with his whole soul, then it was probably the bungled, the tawdry, the cheap, and so also those little loudmouths and demagogues who had only contempt for the worker, held his work cheap, slighted his toil, all the while dolling themselves up in the feathers of the working man's advocates. It is that which most indisposed Filipek toward the communists. He was horrified by the fate of some of them, revolted by the ideological quarrels that ended in death sentences, because he had grown accustomed to other ways and measures. His comrades respected one another, were united not only by the struggle but also by personal friendships. When they quarreled, they didn't spare sharp words and reproaches, but it would never have occurred to any of them to set thugs upon their political opponents. But it is not these matters that played the largest part in railwayman Filipek's opinions. Like every worker who feels his class deeply and is proud of the dignity of labor, Filipek reasoned practically. First and foremost he was an honest working man. Only work determined the respect he had for others. The professionalism, accuracy, decency of work. The wise, honest spirit that guided the worker's hand, his fingers, the strength of his muscles. The honor of the hand, the ethics of the hand. It is that which ruled Filipek's judgments. And the communists before the war were not workers but traveling salesmen of the socialist revolution. They were not workers by profession, because their profession was communism, factionalism, agitation, and igniting the fuse of revolt. Filipek never saw a communist at a machine, busy working, his hands soiled by grease or oil. They were not workers, because their only field of interest was human consciousness, human angers, illusions, and fears. They were not workers but exorcists, utterly enthralled by the magic of words, gestures, shouts. For this he did not like them, did not respect them, although he admitted that this one or that one was brave, prepared to make great sacrifices for his idea.

When Filipek found himself in the engine house, he thought only of work. He worked as best he could for all the hours he was there, until dinnertime. He knew that the locomotive he was repairing might very well carry German arms and ammunition to the front, and in that case it would be beautiful if the boiler exploded, or the pumps went berserk, but it might equally well happen that the locomotive will be pulling cars filled with thousands of innocent people, dear to railwayman Filipek's heart, and so every detail had to be soundly executed, every screw screwed in just right.

Several years later, with a crowbar and a pickaxe, drenched in sweat like a caveman, subsisting on a bowl of soup and a piece of bread, with fever in his eyes and hope in his heart, Filipek was digging his way through the rubble of Warsaw. The Germans didn't put him to death, although they did get to him just before the Uprising and he went through the hell of the camps. In May of 1945 he was back in his native city. An emaciated old man in concentration camp stripes. He didn't sleep nights. He was tormented by coughing. He suffered from dizziness. His hearing was failing. But already by fall he found a shovel, then a pickaxe. Never before in his life had he worked so hard and with such self-sacrifice. Communists or no communists, Stalin or no Stalin, what's important is that we have Poland back. That's how he talked. In 1946 he took part in the May 1 parade and cried, seeing the red and the red-and-white banners. A happy heart was beating then inside his weak body. Next day he met Pawelek in the ravine of ruins on Krucza Street, and they fell into each other's arms.

"We have Poland, Pawelek!" railwayman Filipek called.

"We have Poland," Pawelek replied.

Then they reminisced about their dead. There were more of them than the living.

"So little Monika died in the Uprising," Filipek muttered. "Such a pretty little thing she was. . . . But you're young, Pawelek, some time will pass and you'll start to love another young lady. Don't be angry with the old man for saying such things, it's just that I've come to know life, I've seen a lot, it will be like I say. . . ."

He fell into a prophetic mood and prognosticated about glass houses. Pawelek listened respectfully, for he had great esteem for Filipek, but without special enthusiasm because the spirit of the Polish Socialist Party was not his spirit; he shunned politics—they filled him with a kind of disgust—and he saw peculiar things in Warsaw and in Poland, which augured neither glass houses nor socialist happiness. But he kept silent. For what did this poor worn-out laborer have left besides his illusions?

He had his common sense left. His hearing was weak, but his eyesight was devilishly sharp. His enthusiasm was crumbling. They were agitating again. Nothing but agitating. Agitating everywhere. They tried to persuade Filipek that he had climbed down from the trees only yesterday, that the world was emerging from nothingness, and history counted only from today. History is older than you, he replied, and I too was here before you. . . .

When three years later, in the winter of 1948, Pawelek visited Filipek, who was by then an invalid, the railwayman no longer mentioned the glass houses. He lay pale and emaciated on the sheets, smoked cheap cigarettes from a wooden holder, sipped a prune compote from a jar, and said:

"Filth, Pawelek. I have never said about Polish affairs that they were smeared in filth, and now I'm saying it. Everything's filthy, Pawelek. They've even spat on their own Gomulka. What kind of people are these, what kind of people? The minute the commune touches anything it immediately fouls it up. I never thought that before. They were never as they ought to be, that I always knew, but to do such things, such things . . ."

Pawelek remained silent. He gazed at old Filipek's emaciated face and again bid farewell to the departing world, which was never to return. This was probably the last man from that world, a survivor of several wars and revolutions, a prisoner of emperors and despots, a victim of history's horrible tricks or perhaps of a farcical anecdote told to the world by God, whose title is Poland.

Few people walked behind railwayman Filipek's coffin. Those still left alive from his distant family, Pawelek and his mother, the beautiful Mrs. Gostomska, and three aged common workers. Perhaps they were the only ones left in this new workers' Poland? Filipek lay in his coffin and knew nothing. Or maybe only then did he know everything, but it had seemed to him all his life that after death he wouldn't know anything because he didn't believe in God but in socialism and ardently to the end.

But on that April day, when he was returning home by streetcar over the Kierbedź Bridge, death was still far away. Still before him were a handful of suffering and a pinch of illusions.

XIV

The lawyer Jerzy Fichtelbaum
heard the noise in the courtyard and understood that the moment he
had been waiting for had arrived. He was surprised that he felt neither
fear nor despair. The state of his soul was quite different from what
he had imagined it would be during the past months. Then, whenever
he had closed his eyes and listened intently for this moment, which
was sure to arrive, he had experienced a very unpleasant sensation of
falling into an abyss, into darkness, into an indescribable coldness. As
if he were sinking into the infinite universe, which he knew, being
an educated and well-read man, to be devoid of light and warmth.
An ice-cold shaft without end, and in it, falling faster and faster
toward infinity, the lawyer Jerzy Fichtelbaum, spinning all alone, like
a bird without wings, or an insect, through the pull of gravity, farther
and farther and faster and faster, until he was completely out of
breath, in an ever-thickening darkness, coldness, and emptiness. It was
a very unpleasant sensation, and he wished that it wouldn't last long,

but with each day it lasted longer, finally becoming a horrible torment that haunted him even in his sleep.

But now it suddenly turned out that when the noises, which were without a doubt the harbingers of the coming of that dark universe to the third floor of the building, resounded downstairs, as Fichtelbaum waited in the empty room, he accepted everything very naturally and calmly. He didn't feel any anguish, and something so odd happened to him that it must have come from the outside; it didn't originate from within him, but came precisely from that noise, which was slowly moving up the stairs; it didn't originate from within him, but from that universe slowly clumping upward, which opened and shut the doors of the deserted apartments, turned over chairs, ransacked the closets, shoved the stools about. The lawyer listened intently and discovered a certain rhythm in this, the ticking of an enormous clock, which was measuring his own time as no other clock had until now.

I should close the door, Fichtelbaum thought, but then he immediately remembered that the lock had been broken for a long time, the key was lost, and the bolt had fallen off. The door onto the staircase was therefore ajar, and the lawyer, standing in the middle of the room, saw a ray of light falling through the crack onto the floor, and it was through that crack that the sounds of the heavy-footed universe approached.

Well, all right then, the lawyer thought. So I'll see the boots first.

He decided to sit down. He picked up a wooden chair standing against a wall, moved it near to the slightly open door, and sat down. The chair creaked and the lawyer became terrified. But he quickly grew calm again. I don't have to be afraid any longer, he thought. This is all behind me already.

Still, he sat motionless, because he didn't want the chair to creak. He heard the noise one floor below. He knew that this wouldn't last much longer now, because the apartment below had been vacant for several days.

He sat motionless.

"Put on a hat," a voice said.

Fichtelbaum flinched.

"Put on a hat. A pious Jew wears a hat," the voice said.

I must be going mad, the lawyer thought. What voice is this? Am I hearing the voice of God?

But it wasn't God yet, just the lawyer Fichtelbaum's father, Maurice Fichtelbaum, who had died at the beginning of the twentieth century. He was speaking now from the nineteenth century, from the time when he was still alive. Fichtelbaum saw his father in a pretty, spacious room whose windows gave out on a garden. Beyond the garden stretched fields of barley, and on the horizon the dark line of the forest was visible. Maurice Fichtelbaum stood near the window, with a beautiful black beard flowing down to his chest and a gray hat on his head. He was a very good-looking man; he wore a coat made from a dark fabric and dark trousers. A heavy silver watch-chain glittered at his waist, and a pair of glasses dangled on another chain just below his beard.

"Put on a hat," Maurice Fichtelbaum said to his son. "You can do at least that much for me before you die."

And he took off his own hat and handed it to his son.

"And you, Father?" the lawyer Fichtelbaum asked very softly. "Now you don't have a hat."

"I have no need for one anymore," the father replied.

The lawyer remembered that his father had bought this hat in the nineteenth century, in Vienna, when he had gone there with Rabbi Majzels for a conference of Jewish charitable organizations. After returning home Maurice Fichtelbaum showed the hat to his little son and the lawyer remembered perfectly that the inside leather band was stamped with the seal of a certain well-known hatmakers firm near Kärtnerstrasse. He couldn't remember its name, but he saw across the great distance that separated him from the nineteenth century the oval sign on the band, which proclaimed, K. UND K. HOFLIEFERANTEN.

Jerzy Fichtelbaum shrugged his shoulders.

What sort of hats did they furnish the emperor with, he thought skeptically, when the emperor always wore an army uniform? He probably even went to sleep in a uniform.

Just at that moment the crack in the door widened and a boot appeared on the threshold. And at that moment too a small but useful miracle occurred. Jerzy Fichtelbaum raised his eyes and saw on the barrel of the gun pleasant, cheerful sunshine falling into the large room through the window looking out onto the garden, the barley fields, and the distant forest. The lawyer's father stood by the window, with his beard, in the hat made by the emperor's outfitters, with a watch-chain at his waist, and glasses dangling beneath his spreading, dark beard. He held the lawyer by his hand, and the lawyer was also wearing a hat and also had a black, beautiful beard flowing down to his chest, although he was still a little boy.

XV

He stood by the veranda window and carefully observed the street. He was short, balding, slight. His figure contrasted with his features, which were sculpted with powerful strokes of the chisel, as if God had been working angrily and impatiently. It was a peasant's face from the old canvases of Kotsis or Chełmoński, where strength is interlaced with oafishness. So he stood by the veranda window, observed carefully the street in front of the house, and felt pain in his heart. For so long, so incredibly long, he had been able to exist at a distance from the current of events, on the dry shore. He wasn't cowardly, he was simply not that interested. Only years later would it turn out that everyone without exception had been interested. He belonged in reality to that group of people who accepted the loss of independence with sorrow, looked upon the occupiers with revulsion, were filled with terror at the world's raging cruelty but positioned their own existence on the sidelines, occupied with the cares of everyday life or—like himself—with the inner life, with their spirituality, at a remove from ordinary things, all the more removed the more the ordinary things became evil and inhuman. Throughout the preceding years he had lived among ghosts, in friendship and harmony. He was a classical philologist not only by training and taste. Latin and Greek rendered him a man absent from the world. In those days this was still possible. He lived alone, in the pleasant, cultured company of the classics. He took walks, holding Thucydides, Tacitus, or Zeno by the arm. He ate with Sophocles and Seneca. Living people he barely recognized and he was perfunctory in his contacts with them, for although they were in fact necessary for living, they were also uninteresting and loud. He was thought to be absentminded. Stories were told about him of which he knew nothing, because those around him considered him not a partner but an object of conversations.

He came from a village near Kielce, where his parents and grandparents farmed the land of others in return for a roof over their heads and a piece of bread. He didn't remember his mother at all and recalled his father, a man of a fearful temper whose anger stemmed from misfortune, without love. He abandoned his father and siblings at the age of ten and went off to live the life of solitary poverty. But he had in his soul a hatred of destitution and humiliation, of the country village, the weeping willow and the hazel grove, the furrow of arable soil, smoky fireplaces, peasantry, vilification, mutual lamentation. The likes of him grew into rebels or into loners, focused on themselves. He had a choice between social revolution and flight from a poorly arranged world. Positivist poets wrote poems about people like him. And Zeromski did too. He worked on construction sites, near wells, with horses. He went hungry. He suffered. And he studied with a peasant doggedness. He got lodgings in tiny shacks in return for chopping wood, carrying water. He got food in eating houses in return for washing the dishes and the floors. He completed the classical high school with honors, and was accepted to university free of charge. His Golgotha lasted twenty years, because on top of everything else he had to live through the Great War and the year 1920. Only after that did he stand on his own two feet, but he always lived in poverty, proud and solitary, a doctor of philosophy, a classical philologist, the son of landless farm hands, who through his own work, determination, and strength of character had lifted himself up not only above his own station, but above millions of other people who, unlike him, were born under a lucky star. He had only himself to thank for everything and he needed nothing from the world. He was content with a modest existence, derived an income from occasional Latin and Greek instruction, and also did any other work that came his way because he wasn't afraid of any job, having already come to know them all in his youth. He didn't like the world that had been given to him. Therefore he abandoned the world of people and visible things, and moved to the warm, sunny climes of antiquity.

When the war broke out he did not fear for the future. Solitary people who live in the world of the imagination do not experience the everyday worries of their neighbors. The war and the occupation did not reduce Dr. Adam Korda's circumstances, nor did they deprive him of the privilege of his walks with Cicero. He wasn't in the least a cold and pitiless visionary. The sufferings of others filled him with sympathy. But everything that was happening around was after all not his affair. He did not study, like many did, the direction of Hitler's armored incursions, because he was more occupied with the question of Anabazis and the Gallic Wars. Perhaps during the times of the occupation he felt even more confident than before in the world of delusion and unreality because everything around him was after all unreal, far from the accepted norm.

People talked of his terrifying and at the same time comical adventures. He found himself in a police roundup and didn't notice it. Asked by the military policeman for his identity papers, he couldn't grasp what it was that the man really wanted, until finally the policeman, who was probably bored or else had a soft heart, waved his hand and ordered him away.

"How did you manage to get out of that roundup?" asked an acquaintance, who had witnessed the incident.

"What roundup? Ah, yes, indeed. I don't know, really. I was deep in thought."

He avoided people, and so perforce also the war which they had unleashed. He was interested in ancient wars, hieratic, proud, and without bloodstains, sculpted in white marble. He found in them a kind of moral order that didn't exist in real life. And so he didn't care about real life.

He grew to like his neighbor in the apartment next door. A very beautiful, calm lady, an officer's widow. He had distant relatives outside Lublin, visited them sometimes and brought back jars of preserves and bottles of fruit juices. Now and then he permitted himself to offer a jar of preserves to Mrs. Gostomska. She would thank him with a captivating smile and reciprocate with a packet of tea, which was no small gesture. Sometimes he would pay her a visit. She had great feminine charm and was interested in antiquity. He had never before met such a quiet, reticent, concentrated person. He was grateful to fate for having brought him into contact with her. Suddenly, she fell into bad straits. Suspected of Jewish descent, she was arrested by the Gestapo. She was in danger of death.

It was the first time Dr. Korda had come into such close proximity with the threat of death. Only yesterday Mrs. Gostomska had answered his greeting with a smile, and tomorrow she would no longer be alive, having been tortured by the Gestapo. It wasn't death itself that seemed terrifying, but the waiting for it, the hours of helpless waiting. Mrs. Gostomska was counting on Dr. Korda's help. She had sent word to him. He didn't remain idle. Immediately he undertook a course of action. But he didn't have high hopes. What could a young man, Pawelek Kryński, their only mutual acquaintance, do? What could he do if everything people said about the Gestapo and about Szucha Avenue was true? And they didn't go around spreading lies, for there was a cruel war underway; Dr. Korda had heard about the tortures, the executions, the concentration camps. Wasn't his acquaintance, the classical philologist Dr. Antoni Kamiński, in Auschwitz? Dr. Korda regularly sent food parcels to the camp. He denied himself many things so that he could send Kamiński the packages. What could a young man do to save Mrs. Gostomska? Dr. Korda feverishly searched his memory for people who might prove helpful.

But he had few acquaintances and no friends. For the first time in his life his solitude, the loner's way of life, weighed heavily upon him. So much, after all, depended on other people, without whose helpfulness and efforts Mrs. Gostomska will without fail soon die. There is no doubt that she is not a Jew. An utterly ridiculous suspicion. If not for her very light hair, Mrs. Gostomska would look like Diana. But does this mean anything to the people on Szucha Avenue? Whether she's a Jew or not? After all it's not only about Jews!

He stood in the veranda window and carefully surveyed the street. It was a good observation post. If Mrs. Gostomska returned he would be bound to see her. He stood there in his knickerbockers and lace-up boots, small, balding, motionless, with a painful anxiety in his heart. He felt impotent and weak. He didn't think of the Gallic Wars but about the one outside the window. When evening fell he didn't turn on the light. He moved the chair close to the window, sat down, and continued gazing out into the darkness. Only at midnight did he realize that it would be impossible for Mrs. Gostomska to return at that hour. He covered the window with a blackout shade and curtains and went to bed. He fell asleep near morning, but awoke almost immediately and again took up his position by the window. He had a whole day of waiting ahead of him. And a terrible loneliness because the ghosts of antiquity had left him. Every now and then he napped briefly, his forehead leaning against the windowsill. He would wake up stiff. Perhaps he had missed Mrs. Gostomska's return? He listened carefully for sounds from the apartment next door. There was silence.

The hours crept by on tiptoes behind his back. It was a spring day, full of sunlight and birdsong. In the early afternoon Dr. Korda felt that he must do something, that he could not remain motionless any longer. He hadn't eaten for hours, but he always ate little, attached no importance to meals, and so he didn't feel hunger. "Eating is a barbarous thing!" he said often. In this he wasn't being in the least antique but simply the descendant of landless peasants of the Holy Cross Mountains, who contented themselves with very little—a potato, a bowl of thin soup.

He left his observation post and went out into the street. He paced about on the sidewalk in front of the building, for what else could he do? Inside of him he felt an unfamiliar barrenness, a swollen emptiness. Suddenly he decided to have a cigarette. Incredible, he thought feverishly, incredible. But he was already heading in the direction of the kiosk, which huddled on the corner against the wall of a building.

"A packet of cigarettes, please," he said.

"What kind?" the vendor asked.

"I don't know. Inexpensive ones, please."

They were cigarettes of the Haudegen brand. He opened the box, smelled it, slipped one between his lips. Then he remembered that he didn't have any matches. He went back to the vendor. Finally he lit the cigarette. He inhaled. He started to cough. Incredible, he thought, incredible. But he continued to smoke. He strolled along the sidewalk, a small man in knickerbockers, a jacket with the shirt collar out, lace-up ankle boots, and smoking like a steamship on the Vistula. He no longer felt the burden of emptiness in his chest, but a sharp, stabbing pain. A cough tormented him now. He returned to the apartment. He threw the cigarette stub into the toilet and flushed. Again he stood by the window. The day was waning. She's no longer alive, Korda thought. It was a terrible thought. But with every passing moment he grew more and more certain that Mrs. Gostomska was dead. Finally, he gave up. He left the window and sat down at the table. What is happening to me, he thought; it's just one human being. Just one human being. After many years in a completely different world, a metamorphic, immature, and moderately cruel one, here he was, still struggling in this thicket. Of antiquity only rubble remained, only then was antiquity finally demolished. Just one human being, he thought, just one. He was terrified by the world, which had appeared so suddenly, had burst out like Minerva from the the head of Jove, enormous and omnipresent, upon a desert of destruction and smoldering ruins. He suddenly saw himself robbed and duped. This world offered an ease that had never been offered to Dr. Korda. Everything that he had attained through indescribable hardship, through renunciations extolled by the poets, all at once was within the reach of every hand. Shepherd and barbarian were storming the acropolises that Dr. Korda had been scaling alone, with the sweat of his brow, in humiliation, through an enormous effort of will. He didn't feel envy, but disillusionment and fear. He was afraid of plurality. What was the value of a world that was not redeemed through the sacrifice of a solitary man, in which everyone had something or nothing, equally and identically, without distinction. . . . Just one human being, just one human being, he repeated, just one. Where do the stars shine, that shine the same for everyone? he asked himself. Where do my winds blow without me? Who besides me will look into the eyes of my death? Who has seen my gods, lived through my fears, dreamed my dreams, experienced my hunger, laughed with my laugh, and cried with my tears?

Only then did antiquity collapse into rubble. One human being. Just one human being.

So the first load of dynamite was set off under the Doric column at the moment when Dr. Korda sat down at the table and thought that Mrs. Gostomska was certainly no longer alive. A human being had been killed. Only humanity remained. Is that possible? he asked himself. He didn't want to reconcile himself to the death of an individual. He got up and again went to the window. The gods hadn't deserted him, because just then, in the falling twilight, in the final glimmers of the sun sinking behind the rooftops, he spotted a familiar silhouette. Mrs. Gostomska was walking down the sidewalk. She appeared somewhat tired, but as always elegant and beautiful. He wanted to run out to meet her immediately, but then thought better of it. It wouldn't be polite, he said to himself, she needs solitude, time to concentrate. I will keep watch here, on the other side of the wall. He was seized by gaiety. He sang quietly to himself. Suddenly he felt hungry. He went to the kitchen and ate bread, drank milk. Then he discovered the packet of cigarettes in his pocket and threw them into the garbage.

XVI

"I'm going back, Pawel," Henio said.

For the first time he didn't say "Pawelek," but "Pawel."

And Pawel answered with a certain coolness, "Where are you going back to, Henryk?"

"There."

Henryk pointed to the dark cloud rising above the ruins of the ghetto. It was reflected in his eyes.

They were standing by the wall of a building on Książęca Street, and they could see before them a square surrounded by low houses, a round church, and the long perspective of the Ujazdow Avenue. Trees on the avenue were turning green. It smelled of spring and of the ruins after a fire.

They both understood that suddenly they had become adults. They were no longer boys. And they weren't surprised. One of them, at any rate, was to die soon. In the proximity of death even children age quickly.

"There's no sense in your going back there," Pawelek said. "It's certain death."

"Probably," Henryk replied. He was never certain of anything. He was too good a student, first in mathematics and science. "Probably," he repeated, and shrugged his shoulders lightly.

Pawel came to the conclusion that there was no longer any point in wasting words. Henryk will go back there. His resolve was unshakable. Would I go back if I were in his place? Pawel thought. Probably yes, he answered himself. But they could no longer compare their conditions. They had reached a crossroads. They were standing close to each other, they were best friends, they had lived together through more than ten rich years of childhood and youth, and yet at this moment they both understood that something was separating them. They were on opposite sides now, a high wall was rising up between them. Such walls fall only at the sound of the trumpets of Jericho, but the trumpets of Jericho were silent.

"We are probably seeing each other for the last time," said Henryk, and again lightly shrugged his shoulders.

Pawel was silent.

I cannot stop him, he thought. So he'll go. We are no longer as close as before. Henryk is taking something from me. I cannot hold on to that which he will take with him when he goes. And that which is mine in him will die on the other side of the wall. Now there will be less of Pawelek. Perhaps there will be none of that old Pawelek whom I liked so much because he was an amusing, headstrong boy and I was never bored when I was with him. Henryk is taking Pawelek from me and they'll both go to hell. It would be good to keep Henio for myself. That Henio who just now took off somewhere and is hiding in the entryway to a building on Książęca Street, waiting for Henryk to leave. Keeping Henio is the only thing that I can do.

He looked at Henryk's face. It still bore traces of Henio's features. Increasingly weak, pale traces. Already they had vanished from Henryk's eyes, but they still remained in the rosy cheeks, in the capricious, lightly curled lips, in the dark, thick hair above his brow. One must retain this.

Commit to memory every detail, even the slightest. This double-breasted coat, in herringbone, long, with wide, padded shoulders, with the middle button on the right side coming off, hanging by a thread. That button will fall off before Henryk reaches the ghetto, but for Pawel the thread will never break, even fifty years from now. Henio's shoes. Black boots, carefully laced, slightly worn. A navy blue ski cap with a shiny visor. A black woolen scarf, tied with a knot at the throat. Henio's hands. Small, girlish, with pale, slim fingers. Henio's ears. His nose, eyebrows, forehead. Rosy, slightly puffy cheeks. The lips a little too voluptuous, which would have been Henio's undoing, one way or another.

To remember Henio. And also his shadow, barely visible against the white wall of the building. And the pigeon on the windowsill above Henio's head. I will take him, thought Pawel, I will save him.

That is what he thought, with triumph and bitterness.

But what was he memorizing Henio for? So that he would carry that boy around with him through the long, dark tunnel of the coming years? Why was he memorizing him, since they were never again to speak in the same language? Of what use is a silent man, who doesn't know words, who is unable to name things or mete out justice?

Pawel was memorizing this Henio with his double-breasted overcoat and slightly worn shoes so as to argue with him constantly later, inundate him with questions to which Henio, always silent, never answered, a capricious Jewish teenager with red, voluptuous lips with whom Pawel walked shoulder to shoulder forty years later to Stawki Street, flowers in his hand, the blood throbbing vengefully in his temples, military policemen in blue uniforms at the end of the street—a completely alien world, with no connection to Henio, a world that no longer had a single stone, a single particle of air, a single drop of moisture from the world of that Książęca Street on which Pawel is saying good-bye to Henryk, on which Pawel is memorizing Henio, so that just as Saint Christopher carried the mysterious infant he can carry him on his back across the roaring, dangerous stream. But Saint Christopher had only to take a few steps and he was already on the other, safer shore, whereas Pawel will be bearing that burden of his, this silent Jewish youth, for entire decades, through all the days of savagery, cant, stupidity, and hypocritical high-mindedness that still await him.

And what will remain of this adventure at the end of the journey? An old man will walk up to the building on Książęca Street, stop beneath the white wall, nod his head. He will look at Henio. Henio will be a rosy-cheeked boy in a double-breasted overcoat with a ski cap on his head. Not a single wrinkle, not a single gray hair. The dead do not age. "And what was the use of taking you through all this misery, Henryczek?" the old Pawel will say. Henio will shrug his shoulders. Perhaps he will also just say that one familiar word. He will say, "Probably . . ."

"Good-bye, Pawel," said Henryk and stretched out his hand.

"Good-bye, Henryk," said Pawel.

I'm not going to like this scene, Pawel thought with a sudden rage. If we both survive, it's going to seem ridiculous.

But whatever the danger they were facing, it was not the danger of being thought ridiculous. Later various people tried hard to make that scene look slightly ridiculous, in films and on the television screen, and in fact now and then it did look ridiculous because of the artistic shorthand—a heroism not of this world—in which it had to be portrayed. In a tainted world of hackneyed slogans, hypocrisy, petty trading with the dead, and endless gabbing about the future, such a scene was truly an anachronism, and thus ridiculous, like Julius Caesar on a bicycle.

But of course they couldn't foresee this, standing against a building on Książęca Street, two young men who loved Marshal Pilsudski, spoke often of Romuald Traugutt, dreamed about the cavalry charge at Rokitna. They were only taking the first uncertain steps on the marshy ground of totalitarianisms and both were ready to die rather than be mired in it up to their necks.

"I'll go now," said Henryk.

Pawel was silent. The pigeon flew off. The figure of a woman with a green scarf around her shoulders loomed deep in the entryway. The bell of a streetcar on Nowy Świat Street, its red shape emerging from around the corner like a tin dragon, a toy for little boys, for Henry-czek and Pawelek.

He walked away. And disappeared at once. Pawel looked at the sky. It was very blue—an April sky. Only somewhere on its periphery, above the rooftops, a dirty trail of destruction drifted slowly by.

Is it possible that even then he had the impression of a beginning, not of an end? Is it possible that at the very moment when Henryk's silhouette vanished from his eyes he understood that a new chapter was beginning, one without end, which would last for the rest of his life? Later he would be convinced of this. On that very day, he often thought later, I understood that the time of partings, good-byes, and eternal fears was beginning. But it wasn't just partings. It is true that Henryk's walking away was Pawel's first good-bye. There would be many more. Perhaps they were even more wrenching then, but not felt so intensely because later he was never again nineteen, an age when every departing person takes with him nearly one's entire world, leaving behind only worthless crumbs. Later he even learned to glue his life together from shards, for which no reasonable person would give a tinker's damn. He wasn't the only one to learn how to do this. And yet it wasn't just a matter of parting. Yes, Henryk was indeed his first friend, and when he walked away he took with him Pawel's childhood and the best moments of his youth. But why was it that later, after many years, Pawel remembered not only the figure of the boy in a double-breasted overcoat vanishing around the street corner, never again to appear in the world of the living, but also that dirty trail of smoke in the sky, like a rusty rag suspended above the rooftops of Warsaw? Why was the sky to seem to him from that moment on dirty, faded, even if now and then it was lit up by some heroic conflagration?

A dozen or so months later, when Henryk was long dead, the entire sky above the city, from one end to the other, was streaked with trails of smoke and the glare of fires. Pawel did not then remember his parting with Henryk, he didn't even remember yesterday, or the last hour. He lived in the midst of combat, on a barricade in the Uprising. He thought about his machine gun, which was part of his existence. The most important part, on which everything else depended. And yet then too he was accompanied by a feeling of hopelessness, again he was parting and saying his good-byes. Houses and streets, parks and squares, monuments and people were leaving him. With each hour of the Uprising there was less of him; he was shrinking and growing smaller, sinking into the depths and disappearing, like this city. Later they were to call this treason, later still a beautiful madness, in the end a tragedy, in which Pawel became entangled innocently and without the right to choose. He, however, never felt himself to be a traitor, a madman, and even less an extra in a drama that was not his own. He didn't have much to reproach himself for, since after all he had been trying to do his duty. As far as others were concerned, he was never certain whether they did theirs, and whether they really wanted to. But he had no desire to sit in judgment on his neighbors, even if they sometimes judged him.

The sky always seemed to him dirty and devoid of forbearance. Perhaps it was because for a certain time he doubted God. But later too, after he had already regained his faith, he did not regain hope. He was always haunted by the feeling that he had lost something of great importance during the war. He would dream of Europe's cities, which he didn't know and had never seen. He dreamed of cathedrals, castles, bridges, and streets. He felt good during these dreams, only to experience a kind of loss upon awakening. Later he traveled to Europe. A foreign visitor from distant lands. And he lost his dreams. Those cathedrals, castles, and bridges existed, to be sure, but they did not belong to him, he did not find himself there. My European consciousness no longer exists, he told himself with sorrow; perhaps even it never existed, perhaps it was merely a delusion, a desire for an identity that had never been given us? He found within himself a kind of a barbarian tragedy, perhaps a lack, or an excess, which made him feel out of place in European cathedrals and on the bridges of Europe's rivers. And besides, the sky above Europe was not any better. He would return from there with relief, only to yearn for it again. He found this humorous, which was a certain consolation to him. For if he didn't see the humor, then all that would be left him would be a sense of being crippled. In the end it is better to have ears that stick out than one leg shorter than the other.

Was it Henryk who took all hope away from him? Pawel realized the senselessness of such accusations. The living Henryk would probably not have been much different from Pawel. Both had been robbed to the same degree. Henryk was in a better position because he didn't know about it. Dying, he could believe that one day it would be different. And indeed it was a bit different. After a certain point people were no longer being killed, at least not in Europe, and not even on its peripheries. It was an enormous step forward, and Pawel blessed the day when the war ended. Only madmen did not bless this day. Only fools did not see the difference, blinded by their principles. If Poland was not quite like the country they had wished for, even if it was not at all like it, for those who survived, the very fact of survival was difference enough so that they blessed it. After all Pawel was alive, and Henryk was dead. And Pawel understood the difference between those two states. Yet after ten years he felt weary, and after twenty a numbing boredom. How long can one celebrate the fact that a man was not killed? he would ask himself. It was an especially timely question, because all around him people were dying of old age, disease, as well as accidents of fate. And for those who died, it was all one how they crossed the threshold of eternity. There wasn't much of a difference between the old man shot on the streets of occupied Warsaw and his contemporary who died of cancer a dozen years later. It's quite possible that the one who was shot suffered less and was frightened for a shorter period of time. There also wasn't a discernible difference between the child burned in a wartime fire and the one run over by a drunk driver as it ran to school in peacetime. Their mothers cried the same tears. What had seemed miraculous in 1945, was merely commonplace a few years later, and later still became boring and banal. And it was no longer war that was dreadful, but peace. And for those who never experienced the war at all because they were born after it had ended, this banal peace, in other words the most ordinary life on earth, was becoming unbearable. Pawel was growing old, he remembered the past, and thanks to that was in a somewhat more fortunate position. He could, after all, always recall a more perfect hell. But this consolation wasn't durable or strong enough to allow him to live in hope. At bottom, he suffered from a sense of dignity. It was like a canker in his nose. Not being able to smell from where the wind was blowing, not being able to appear in public with his head held high.

Fortunately, the world was no longer as cruel as it had once been, during Pawel's youth, but it was becoming unbearably trivial. It was a world of shortages, of feigned order and public security. Of well-cared-for flower beds but stinking garbage dumps; true freedom but passage forbidden.

What was bothering Pawel? Could it be that Henryk had taken from him the right to freedom?

He was discussing this one evening with Gruszecki. Gruszecki had offered to give Pawel a lift in his car. They had met quite by accident at Sister Weronika's. Gruszecki was getting ready to leave when Pawel appeared, a rare visitor who had not been around for a long time. A vague and shaky bond tied Pawel to Sister Weronika brought about by an occasional correspondence. Both sometimes received a letter from Israel. "Please send my greetings to Sister Weronika." "My dear, when you see P., please give him my best." Pawel had just received a perfunctory postcard with the words, "Regards to dearest W." So he had come to give the old nun regards, a strange greeting whose faint shadow fell across continents, from a kibbutz on the West Bank all the way to the shores of the Vistula in Warsaw. He didn't stay long, having found Sister Weronika subdued and weak. She was nearing eighty. Kissing her hand, he had the impression that he was touching a dry leaf with his lips.

In the car Pawel said, "I remember her as a tall, sturdy woman. She's become so little. Don't you sometimes have the impression that everything is shrinking? As if life were constantly diminishing us?"

Gruszecki was looking straight ahead. The glow from the speedometer illuminated his thin face, his features both Anglo-Saxon and at the same time those of an old Polish nobleman. He held a pipe between his teeth in silence and shrugged his shoulders.

"She's almost eighty," he finally said, taking the pipe in his left hand, his right hand on the steering wheel. "That's how it goes, we're getting old."

"You still have quite a bit of time left," Pawel said. "With me it's different. I've got less and less. It's an unpleasant sensation. Something is running away and not returning. Endless losses."

"I wouldn't be so pessimistic. So far as age is concerned, there's no difference between us. There was once, yes. But that has no meaning today. It's all a matter of how you look at reality, it seems to me. You have somewhat romantic views, I daresay."

"Romantic?" Pawel repeated. "I've never thought so. I've always walked with my feet firmly on the ground."

"Well, well," said Gruszecki and suddenly swerved over to the side, scraping the tires against the curb, stopped the car, and turned off the motor. "I wouldn't say that, my friend. . . . I've heard a thing or two about your recent escapades. . . . What were they, if not romantic fantasies?"

The tone of his voice was almost accusing. He was sucking on his pipe again. Pawel burst out laughing. Gruszecki struck him as funny.

"You laugh? Go right ahead. But it's not just about you, about your affairs, even about your life. You can do whatever you please with that. But all of you together are endangering this country! Senselessly, because you don't have the slightest chance of winning."

"And what is it that does make sense, what does stand a chance, if I may ask? We're sitting up to our ears in muck, and when someone wants to get out of the muck, you say that it's senseless?"

Gruszecki nodded.

"Yes. Senseless. Because one can drown, one can sink to the bottom."

"So we're supposed to sit still and not move? Not a single gesture, right?"

"Not a single gesture! Every movement is dangerous. After all, since you insist on these not especially pretty comparisons, we may be sitting in muck up to our necks, but at least our heads are still above the surface. If we start to thrash about, that's the end of us! And that was thrashing about, nothing more than thrashing about! And it happened. Didn't you notice? We had been sitting in the muck up to our necks, but now we can breathe only through our noses. One more dangerous movement and that's it!"

He lit the pipe. The flame of the match illuminated his angry face.

"That's a matter of interpretation," Pawel said coldly. "After all it was always this way here. . . . For two hundred years, or even longer. The nation exists thanks to the fact that it constantly thrashed about. If it hadn't thrashed about, it would no longer be here at all. . . ."

"How do you know that? Why this certainty that our antics were the basis of our survival? That we must of necessity purchase our identity with such sacrifices? And what if it was just the opposite?"

"Engineer Gruszecki, I don't believe that history has a conditional tense," Pawel replied. "What happened, happened. What matters is what happened. . . . Poles are what they are, because what happened happened. Do you consider that romanticism? After all one must think historically, think with the nation's memory. Learn from the past. Whatever else may be the case, there existed a Wysocki here once. And Mochnacki. And Mickiewicz. Traugutt, Okrzeja, Pilsudski, Grot, Anielewicz, those people in the Uprising. They all existed. I cannot say what would have happened if they hadn't existed. And it doesn't interest me. That is where my realism lies. They existed. That fact cannot be crossed out or erased. And we are what we are because they existed!"

"What of it if they existed?" asked Gruszecki. "Does each and every generation have to be decimated? A sick fantasy. Look at the Czechs. How reasonable they are, how clear-sighted. Since the battle of White Mountain they haven't fired a single shot. They survived four hundred years of Germanization in peace and dignity. Without a single shot. And they exist, as you can see. Their presence is more palpable in the world than ours!"

"Different times, different methods, different regimes. Those four hundred Habsburg years caused less devastation than forty years of Soviet rule. What are you talking about? Old Kraków to this day fondly remembers the emperor. Austria, my God! What in the world are you talking about?"

"The Czechs didn't have all that much fun under the Habsburgs. And neither did we! Only the last decade . . . It's a question of options. This or that. How do you envision our existence without the protective umbrella of Russia? How do you envision it? Communism? It doesn't thrill me. But perhaps it's high time we understood that we are not the West. We are the Catholic East!"

Pawel burst out laughing again.

"I don't understand. That's one strange invention. The Catholic East? A swallow or an eagle at the bottom of the ocean. A creature not made to live."

"Why a swallow in the ocean? It could be a winged horse, for instance. Something very beautiful!"

"A monster! The first question one has to answer is, what is man? What is the point of his life on this earth? What does your Catholicism say to this, your belief in the dignity of the individual, his uniqueness and sovereignty in the world? How can you reconcile this with collective civilization?"

Gruszecki shrugged.

"Russia is also a work of God," he replied. "God never abandoned Russia, she never abandoned God. Don't measure Russia by the present moment."

"But it is what it is!" Pawel cried. "Don't you see that? And besides, this is not just about Russia. No one here aspired to save the whole world. To fight for a piece of authenticity, a pinch of one's own truth. That's all it was about!"

Suddenly he experienced a feeling of terrible hopelessness, an overwhelming sadness. It's too late, he thought. He's right, that Gruszecki. Something ended once and for all, long ago, before my very eyes, with my participation. It ended then. And it will never return. Where do you look for authenticity if Krucza and Marszalkowska streets no longer exist, and Mariensztat and Krochmalna? What authentic truth of one's own can revive this city, which was raised up from the ruins like a theater set; since the people are gone, there's not a single man on Kercelak Square, on Dluga and Koszykowa streets? Even the stones that survived are now somewhere else. Not a single drop is left of that water in the Vistula, not a single leaf from those chestnut trees in the Krasińskis' Garden, not a single look, a shout, a smile. He should know this, he of all people! Little Hirschfeld should know this. Something ended irrevocably, because the thread was cut that earlier had linked history to the present. Once, generations passed a flaming torch to one another. Where is the torch that I held in my hands, certain that it was the same that had been lit centuries ago? Where is the torch of the servant boy who lit up the way for King Waza and Prince Poniatowski as they passed through the streets of the city, the same one that burned in Kiliński's workshop, above Nabielak's head, in Traugutt's cell, on Castle Square, when Marshal Pilsudski rode to Kraków in his coffin, in the trenches of September, in the bunker on Gęsia Street, on the barricades near Mostowa Street? Where is this extinguished torch of truth and authenticity, which not long ago the shipyard workers of Gdańsk wanted to ignite again? Have we lost once and for all this time? Are these last forty years a new reality entirely, a transition to an irreversible state of the debasement of our soul? After all for the first time, the very, very first, Poland itself has dishonored Poland and trampled her into the mud!

"What are you thinking about?" Gruszecki asked softly.

"About my internment," Pawel replied. "A short, trivial affair. And yet in a spiritual sense it was worse than a camp. When I looked at the Mazovian and Galician faces of those boys in militiamen's fatigues, I would feel myself falling into an abyss."

"But they weren't brutal to you," muttered Gruszecki.

"They weren't brutal, but they simply were. With little eagles on their caps. Standing with their legs wide apart. And near the confessional as well. Because they went with us to Sunday mass, when the priest arrived."

"There, you see," muttered Gruszecki, "so after all . . ."

"I was joking. It's not about those boys, who probably had their dark dreams. It's about a new reality that is taking shape in Poland, something terrifying and hopeless, because after all—"

He broke off. It's pointless, he thought. He doesn't want to understand this. Poor old-time Pole, descendant of the Polish Commonwealth. He doesn't want to understand this, because if he does, the world will come crashing down upon his head. And have I really understood what it's all about? What is this conspiracy of mine against history? My God, it's not true after all that there was always a single torch, a common goal, solidarity! It's not true, it's the eternal Polish lie. He's probably right about my having a romantic soul. Differently than he imagines, but nevertheless romantic. I am ridiculous! That last trial was necessary. Indispensable. Blessed. At long last the myth of our uniqueness, of this Polish suffering that was always pure, righteous, and noble, has bit the dust. Didn't the torch illuminate the faces of traitors who were hanged? Didn't Crown Prince Constantine's informers flee from its glare? Who betrayed Traugutt? Who paid the Cossack regiments to attack the workers in 1905, in Lódź, Sosnowiec, Warsaw? Who beat people in Bereza and tortured them in Brześć? Who chased Henio Fichtelbaum through the streets of Warsaw? Who betrayed Irma, delivering her into German clutches? Who drove her out of Poland? Sacred Poland, suffering and brave. Holy Polishness, drunken, whoring, venal, its mouth stuffed with claptrap, anti-Semitic, anti-German, anti-Russian, antihuman. Under the picture of the Holy Virgin. Under the feet of the young ONR right wingers and old colonels. Under the roof of the Belvedere. Under the bridge. Holy Polishness under the pub and the cash-box. The dull mugs of navy blue policemen. The foxy snouts of *szmalcowniks*. The cruel faces of Stalinists. The boorish ones of March 1968. The terrified ones of August 1980. The boastful ones of December 1981. Holy blasphemous Polishness, which dared to call Poland the Christ of Nations and was rearing informers and denouncers, careerists and dimwits, torturers and bribetakers; who elevated xenophobia to the rank of patriotism, went begging among strangers, planted faithfully subservient kisses on the hands of tyrants. That last trial was necessary! Indispensable. Blessed. Maybe now Poland will at last understand that villainy and holiness dwell in one house, and here too, on the shores of the Vistula, like everywhere in God's world!

He looked sideways at Gruszecki's profile. I won't tell him this, because there is still a pinch of mercy left in my heart. He's carrying enough of his own misfortunes on his back, this Hirschfeld of mine—vice-chancellor of the Polish crown. God gave his battered soul a refuge. I am not going to disturb the tranquility, which was purchased with the suffering of generations. I like him. He's the last one who can dance the polonaise so beautifully! And in profile he reminds me a little of Henio. But perhaps I don't remember Henio's profile at all? I so wanted to remember it, I was memorizing it so fervently then, on the corner of Książęca Street, and yet I don't remember it! What sort of nose did Henio have? What shape was his chin? When he appears in my sleep, I always see him in full face. With a ski cap on his head. In that worn coat with the button coming off. But I don't remember his profile. Did he have a prominent nose? A Jewish one? Like this man here, who is sitting silent and worried, puffing on his pipe, and is probably thinking that I am one of the very few people in the world who knows his deepest secrets?

What has become of our freedom, if we cannot be ourselves? What has become of me, if I have gone astray?

XVII

The world lied. Every look was debauched, every gesture vile, every step abject. God still withheld the hardest trial, the yoke of language. He hadn't yet unleashed the tireless pack of words, covered in the foam of hypocrisy. Words bayed here and there, but they were still weak, still on the leash. It was not words that killed then, only later did a band of murderers grow out of them. The tyranny of words hadn't yet arrived when Bronek Blutman found himself face to face with Stuckler. Stuckler was standing in the bright rectangle of the window. Outside, a pale green branch was swaying in the breeze.

"She was lying," said Blutman. "I know her from before the war." Stuckler nodded his head.

"A Jew cannot cast doubt upon the word of a German," he said calmly. "It's not about a mistake, although they should not happen, but about stubbornness and self-assurance."

"Herr Sturmführer, my memory does not deceive me. Before coming here she didn't pretend that—"

Stuckler slapped him in the face. Bronek Blutman stepped back, bowed his head, and fell silent. The world lied. Its foundations were corroded by lies, deceit, and baseness. The ambiguity of lies, their duplicity and profusion, made one's head spin. The multitude of betrayals and humiliations. The diversity of the means, methods, and shapes of betrayal. I betrayed that Jewess, but she too betrayed me. Even Christ didn't foresee that. He was too artless for that. To Judas He said, "Friend!" To Peter He cried, "Begone, Satan!" Perhaps that was His sense of humor?

Stuckler slapped him again and Bronek Blutman again stepped back. The lying world. Everything upside down. Even Christ uttered sentences that were a kind of betrayal and lie. He said to the whore, "Go, and sin no more!" How could she not sin when she was a whore, and He after all hadn't ordered her to give up fornication and become a guardian of the anguished.

I remember her from before the war, that Jewess! No German, no Pole, has even the tiniest fraction of my instinct; I have inside me a Jewish compass the likes of which others cannot even imagine. A Jew will always recognize a Jew. This stupid, dimwitted criminal should know that. I can be trusted. Why? Because if I betrayed others, I can betray him too! I can betray everyone, because I was betrayed myself.

Stuckler slapped him a third time. His hand was a little sweaty, warm. This time Bronek Blutman didn't step back. The blow was lighter. Now he will kill me, he thought.

"Well?" Stuckler said. "It's a mistake after all, right?"

Why does he want to humiliate me even here, where I'm on infinitely surer footing than he is, than all of them taken together?! He looked into her ear, looked for markings that never existed. Maybe that Jewish ear, like a seashell fished out of the ocean, resounds for him with the rustle of the sands of Judea? Not the ear, Stuckler, but the eyes! I see it, Stuckler, no Jew has ever fooled me! In the ray of light that is reflected in a Jewish pupil I see old Moses, the holiday of Passover and Rosh Hashanah; I see clearly the Ark of the Covenant, the faces of all

the twelve tribes of Israel; and I see Garizim and Sychem and Betel and Hebron. I see everything in one Jewish eye, from Idumeia through Carmel, all the way to Tabor and Lake Genezaret, and even farther, because I see Dan, and I see farther still, all the way to Mount Hermon. Why does he want to humiliate me on my own territory? There was no mistake, it is he who fell into the snare of treachery. You shouldn't have built a world of treason, Stuckler, for now it has swallowed you up entirely, but I did not make a mistake; I am king on my own territory, no one will be stronger on it than I.

"Herr Sturmführer," said Bronek Blutman. "Everyone can make a mistake. This will not happen again."

It's pointless, my saying this. I'm going to be killed anyway. Everything's a lie, everything's disgraced and trampled into the ground. Why should I rise above par? So I say—a mistake. I say—a mistake, and once again I commit treason, I diminish my worth, for what use has Stuckler for a type who makes mistakes? Off to the Umschlagplatz with him. For mistakes Stuckler has his own fools, with their fat necks and bovine eyes, and he also has Poles, so what does he need a Jew who makes mistakes for? Jews are on this earth so they can be killed and so they won't make mistakes. I did not make a mistake and yet I will be killed. How can such a world exist?

"It's the last time I will tolerate a mistake," Stuckler declared. "Get out."

He didn't shout, he said everything in a calm tone of voice, even politely. He returned behind his desk. The rectangle of the window was empty. Only the green branch and a bit of sky. Bronek Blutman bowed with respect but without subservience. He stepped out of the office, closing the door behind him. He walked across the outer office, through the corridor, down the stairs. They'll kill m anyway. If not today, then tomorrow. He made a mistake, n killing me today. We both made a mistake, it's quite funny rea' I made a mistake because I didn't make it, he made it becaus expects me not to make a mistake, which will be a mistake, be if it will not be a mistake, then I will make a mistake. It' funny. Lies, betrayal, abasement, villainy, denunciation,

bestiality, whoring, mistakes, mistook, mistaken . . .

He stopped on the street. Green trees, blue sky. Green treason, blue lies. There is no world, thought Bronek Blutman. The world died. It ended. There will never be a world again. It died forever and ever. Amen. A mistake, he thought. If such a great, wise Jew like Jesus Christ made mistakes and erred, then who do you take yourself for, Broneczek! You're a little Jew, one meter, eighty-four centimeters tall, a big hunk of a Jew, one can say, and yet a little Jew nevertheless, Broneczek. A mistake? Fine, let him have his mistake. Starting today I'm steering clear of Mrs. Seidenman. I'm going to give a wide berth to all the Warsaw whores from the prewar dance halls with an arch whose bowstring will be my Jewish eye. I will shoot deadly arrows at the Orthodox, the peddlers, those about to kick the bucket. But I will avoid the Jewish whores, because their ears, like the shells from southern seas, sing the music of salvation. The world was founded on treason, lies, and abasement. You cannot hide the fact that Cain slew Abel. You can't disguise it! In the beginning there was treason, lies, and the abasement of Cain. So what else could he do but pick up a stone and beat Abel to death? What else could he do, since God left him no choice?

Bronek Blutman got into a rickshaw and asked to be taken to Narutowicz Square. The rickshaw driver wheezed and kept clearing his throat.

"What's wrong with you?" Bronek Blutman asked.

"I've got the flu."

"You should have stayed in bed."

"There are those who can, and those who can't," the rickshaw driver replied. They fell silent. Heavy wheezing continued to resound above Bronek Blutman's ear. When they got to Narutowicz Square, he gave the rickshaw driver a lavish tip.

"Here, put some cupping glasses on your chest," he said as he walked away.

"I'd rather drink a quart of vodka," the driver replied.

A mistake again, Bronek Blutman thought. You can't please anybody.

He went into a pub, sat down comfortably at a table, and ordered a proper dinner. Bronek's father, old Blutman, often used to say, "If you have a worry, don't worry, eat well first, and then you can worry." A mistake, Bronek Blutman thought. His father went to the Umschlagplatz during one of the first selections. For a long time before that he ate nothing and worried, as if there was any point in worrying. Old Blutman also made mistakes. And Jesus Christ. Everybody did, not excluding God. So what's the problem, Broneczek?

When he had eaten, he became convinced again that he would be killed. If not today, then tomorrow. In the beginning there was homicide, he thought. A mistake. In the beginning there was the word. But God kept this terrible pack of hounds at bay. The time had not yet come for the world to suffer the yoke of words.

In the evening Bronek Blutman visited his lover. He bathed, put on a cherry-colored terrycloth bathrobe. His lover was looking at him. She was sitting in a deep armchair wearing only her colorful underwear, silk stockings, and a garter belt with a blue hemstitch. She was sitting in the armchair, her large, naked breasts like hills, and her painted lips like a wound across the center of her face. She was looking at Bronek Blutman from beneath half-closed eyelids, because she thought that that's how one should look at Bronek Blutman. She was a silly woman, had grown up in poverty and in the cinema. Her father was an usher, and in the evening she would bring him his supper in a little pot and look at the films, standing behind the curtain by the door marked EXIT. She always saw films from a foreshortened perspective. Elongated faces and interminable gazes. It is just such a smoldering, interminable gaze that she now directed at Bronek Blutman. She wanted him to take her on the armchair, as he had never taken her before. A mistake, thought Bronek Blutman, I can't even think of such nonsense now. I'm going to sleep. A mistake, because she got what she wanted after all. Bronek Blutman wheezed like the sick rickshaw driver. Afterward he fell asleep. He dreamed that he was old. A mistake. He would be shot a year later in the ruins of the ghetto. He hadn't been mistaken in the least when he thought that they would kill him anyway.

XVIII

Professor Winiar, a mathematician who lived surrounded by the sympathy and respect of several generations of former pupils he had instructed for almost half a century in zero and infinity, stood at the streetcar stop holding an umbrella in his right hand and in his left a rolled-up copy of the *New Warsaw Courier,* which he hadn't yet had time to read that day. A stout woman in a navy-blue coat with velvet stripes walked up and stood beside him. The stop was near Krasiński Square, once a busy part of the city, where two worlds touched. Professor Winiar remembered the square well from past years, for he had lived on Świętojarska Street and always passed through here on his way downtown to the school in which he taught mathematics. In the olden days the square was an extremely pleasant place for the professor and even symbolic in a certain sense, for the mathematician was a liberal, a Christian, a supporter of independence, as well as a Semitophile. People like him were not very common, and in this part of Europe it was a mélange as noble as it was singular. But since a certain time the square on which Professor Winiar waited to no avail for the streetcar had changed in appearance, and it now struck him as dreary and repellent. Standing at the stop, he could see, thanks to his tall figure and supple neck, which supported a small but wise head, the red high wall separating the Aryan neighborhood from the ghetto. For some reason the professor always felt humiliated at this sight, rather than filled with pride at the thought that he belonged to the better race of humanity. But perhaps the feeling of dejection and humiliation that used to come over him whenever he looked at the ghetto wall stemmed from the belief that among those suffering on the other side were also some of his pupils, and among them the best mathematician he had come across in several years, a boy by the name of Fichtelbaum. The professor had seen Fichtelbaum for the last time three years ago, but he remembered very well the rosy-cheeked face with slightly capricious lips and dark eyes. The professor had an excellent memory for faces. He often confused his pupils' last names, didn't remember their first names almost as a rule, but he carried their facial features around in his head with an almost photographic precision. For example Kryński, a boy with a dreamer's gaze and moderate mathematical talents, would usually raise his hand, asking to speak in a very characteristic manner, holding his elbow to his chest and lifting two fingers, the middle finger and the index finger, in complete accord with Polish army regulations. This student, it seems, had some family ties with the army, something that the professor didn't approve of because after the Great War, on top of everything else, he had also become a pacifist.

And so the mathematician suffered. When the Jewish quarter was created, he left his apartment and moved close by, near the southern end of Krasiński Square, to a building on Długa Street. It was a mistake, resulting from the professor's mathematical logic. He wanted to remain in his own backyard and still be able to see his old house within the perimeters of the ghetto, because he counted on the war not to last long. He should have taken a different stance, perhaps less rational but visionary. Professor Winiar's neighbors, when the time came to abandon their home on Świętojarska Street, moved to the distant outskirts of the city. There was something of burning one's bridges in this, and Professor Winiar considered it small minded and perhaps even disgraceful. So he remained. And because of this he suffered. Day and night he was a witness to the triumph of evil. They were murdering his neighbors practically next door. He was comforted by the thought that God and Poland were scrupulously recording these crimes and on judgment day would pronounce sentence. God at a somewhat later date, in eternity, to be precise, but Poland when martial law had been lifted. And yet he suffered, because he knew that the most severe sentence would not bring his murdered neighbors back to life and would not dry Jewish tears.

The streetcar did not arrive. A cool wind started to blow. The woman standing near the professor buttoned up her coat collar. Shots rang out in the distance, from behind the ghetto walls. Professor Winiar had grown accustomed to these sounds. But now suddenly, to the astonishment of the teacher of numerous generations of high school pupils, another sound also reached his ears, an extremely peculiar one. The melody of a powerful barrel organ. One could hear the cymbals and the percussion and the drumroll, and also fiddles, violas, flutes, although the professor couldn't be sure of this because his musical knowledge was limited and his hearing dull. But there was no doubt, cheerful music resounded in the square, and the professor remembered the merry-go-round that had been built here recently. It stood practically against the ghetto wall, colorful and gay, like all merry-go-rounds the world over. There were white horses with red nostrils, Venetian gondolas, little carriages, sleds, and even a lordly coach. All of this twirled about in time to the music, the mechanism of the merry-go-round moaned, the horses galloped, the gondolas sailed, the sleds glided, the carriages bounded, and everything buzzed, whirred, rang, and twirled around in a circle, among bursts of laughter, squeals of frightened young ladies, shouts of young men, cheerful banter, giggles, and caresses. Professor Winiar looked at the merry-go-round, saw the rushing, brightly colored circle, the laughing faces, the young girls' wind-tousled hair, the white spots of naked calves and thighs, crops of hair, shirts, little skirts, boots, underwear, ties, flags, horses' manes, lanterns, benches, swans, butterflies. He saw this lovely, musical, mechanical, panicky whirl and heard the screech of the barrel organ, the crack of the machine gun, the screams of the Jews, the racket of the merry-go-round mechanism.

The woman in the buttoned-up coat said, "I prefer the streetcar."

They looked each other in the eyes. Had she pronounced these words earlier, perhaps Professor Winiar would have seized upon them as a plank of salvation, a towline—and pulled himself up on the shore of hope. But she spoke too late. Professor Winiar, the mathematician, dropped the newspaper, executed a pirouette, as if he were himself on the merry-go-round, and fell lifeless to the sidewalk.

It is not known what thoughts accompanied him in the moment of his final fall. The woman in the buttoned-up coat later informed his relatives that when he was already in a horizontal position, with his eyelids closed, still gripping the umbrella in his tightly clenched fist, he had whispered through ashen lips words that could have been, "Oh, Poland!" or "Oh, Poles!" but the matter was never cleared up. And yet during Professor Winiar's funeral, the speaker bidding him farewell, the high school physics teacher with whom the deceased had been close friends for years, announced to the assembled mourners that the mathematician Winiar "fell in the course of duty." It happened to be the truth. The coffin with the deceased's remains was carried from the cemetery gate to the tomb on the shoulders of his former pupils, among them Pawel Kryński, a student without great mathematical talent, and yet a boy whom the deceased had nevertheless liked. Missing at the funeral was the pupil Fichtelbaum and several other students of the Mosaic faith, whose fates weighed indirectly upon the fate of Professor Winiar. Those absent, however, as one could deduce, had gone ahead of the professor on the road to eternity.

A light, irritating rain fell during the funeral. The ladies took shelter beneath umbrellas. The men scraped their galoshes on the cemetery's gravelly paths. When the tomb was covered with wreaths of modest flowers, the mourners dispersed. Some of them, despite the rain, strolled for a while among the graves, read the names of the dead and the dates of their deaths carved in stone tablets and marble plates, commented animatedly on the fate of those they had known personally or remembered from Poland's past. The older people accustomed themselves during this walk to the thought of their own imminent departure, the young fortified their patriotism. Both pursuits were timely. Not many of these mourners were to survive the war and live to see the times when no one remembered Professor Winiar any longer and no one claimed any longer that he had fallen in the course of duty. Anyway, during the times that were to come after the war, a liberal Christian pacifist like Professor Winiar could not have counted on popularity. There was also no question but that he had fallen at a streetcar stop, not on a barricade, and when he fell he wasn't holding a rifle in his cooling fist but an umbrella, and on top of everything else an umbrella with patches because the mathematician was not a wealthy man.

On the day of Professor Winiar's funeral the merry-go-round on Krasiński Square was still turning, the little horses were galloping, the carriages bounding, the sleds gliding, the gondolas splashing, the flags whirring, the young girls squealing, the young men shouting, the barrel organ squeaking, the mechanism of the merry-go-round rumbling, the shots from the machine guns resounding louder and louder, cannonballs exploding, flames roaring, and only the Jewish moans could not be heard from behind the wall because the Jews died in silence. They answered with grenades and handguns, but their lips were silent for they were already dead, more so than ever before because they valiantly chose death before it even arrived, going out to meet it. In their proud eyes were reflected the fires of the ghetto, the terrified mugs of the SS men, the stupefied mugs of the gaping Polish crowd assembled around the merry-go-round, the sad face of the deceased Professor Winiar, and so also reflected in them were all the distant and near fates of the world, all the world's evil and the crumb of its goodness, and also the face of the Creator, cloudy and angry, sad and somewhat humiliated, because the Creator was turning His eyes toward other galaxies so as not to look at that which He had cooked up not only for His beloved people, but for all of the earth's peoples, disgraced, co-responsible, abject, impotent, ashamed, and among all the earth's people also for the man who, standing at the streetcar stop in precisely the same spot where a few days earlier Professor Winiar had fallen in the course of duty, said cheerfully, "The little Jews are frying till it sizzles!"

Yet no thunderbolt fell from the sky, enveloped in smoke, and struck this man, for this was written in the books of creation thousands of years ago. And it was also written that Professor Winiar should die a little bit earlier and not hear the words of this man, who laughed merrily and started to walk in the direction of the merry-go-round.

XIX

The saddle chafed him slightly. No doubt they hadn't fastened the girth properly again. He came across more and more bungling all the time. As if the climate of this country concealed some bacillus that infiltrated even the organisms of his subordinates. The gelding raised his head, a hoof rang out against a stone. He liked this harmony between himself and the looking glass. It was precisely at such moments that he felt most strongly the connection between his humanity and nature. The trees were turning delicately green; one could feel spring in the air; a gentle, warm breeze blew over the lake, ruffling the smooth surface of the water. Someday this will end, Stuckler thought. Arcadia does not last forever. The gelding was walking in the shade of spreading chestnut trees and lindens. The still bare branches exposed to view the pale-colored palace and fragments of antique columns, which seemed to grow up out of the water like the ruins of a flooded construction site. Everything here is a forgery, he thought, even the beauty they have created is fake. He hit his mount's rump lightly with his riding crop. The gelding passed into an elongated trot. The wind whistled, Stuckler could now hear the clatter of stones sliding away from beneath the hooves and a full, strong hoofbeat. He thought again that one day this will end. This terrible war will end one day, and there will be a return to banality. But if we lose the war, he thought, there will be no place for us in the world. It has always been that way. The horde will overrun Europe. The barbarian will triumph upon the ruins. He stopped the horse. The sun stood high in the heavens, shone through the crowns of the still leafless trees. The branches cast shadows across the lawn. The barbarians will proclaim that we were criminals, the refuse of humanity. We are conducting this war cruelly, but all wars are equally cruel. They will hold us responsible for the greatest infamy since the beginning of the world, as if all this were happening for the first time in human history. Whereas we are not doing anything that they would not have done. We are killing the enemies of our nation, so that we may win. We are killing on a large scale, because the world has gone forward and everything now happens on a large scale. It is comical and pitiful, but if we lose the war, the winners will proclaim that we committed mass murder, just as if murder on a more moderate scale were justified. That's what their morality, in the name of which they wage war, consists of. If we lose, they will draw up a balance sheet of victims and will reach the conclusion that we were criminals without conscience. I've ordered no more than one hundred Jews killed. Had I ordered only ten killed, would I have been more moral and worthy of salvation? It's nonsense, but that is exactly what they will say if they win this war. They will count the dead and it will not occur to them that I killed many in order to win. Were I to have killed few, spared my enemies, I would be betraying my own cause, because to show mercy in time of war is to act to the advantage of one's opponent, to diminish one's own chances. It has always been that way. Jews? Poles? Russians? Every Jew or Pole spared might be the cause of the death of a German, a man of my own race and blood. But if they win, they will charge me with having been merciless, they will forget that it has always been that way, they will forget too about their own cruelty and lack of mercy. I did not invent war, and neither did Adolf Hitler invent it. It is God Himself who made people warriors. It has always been that way.

The horse stopped. Stuckler felt the warmth of the sun's rays on his back. The water in the lake wrinkled slightly. It was empty all around, as if the horse had brought him to the very end of the world.

The fake columns against the fake water looked beautiful. Stuckler sighed deeply. He looked up at the sky. God? Does He really exist? In the twentieth century one doesn't easily believe in God. We have turned out to be so assiduous in uncovering the secrets of nature that there is less and less room left for God to hide in all of His mystery. If it is true that everything originates from Him, then He also enjoined humanity to war. And so we are good warriors.

But Stuckler did not possess a philosophical mind. He came from a family of millers, who one hundred years ago settled near Saalfeld, in Thuringia. At the start of the twenties he was himself a young miller. Later he chose another path. He was enamored of history. Ancient Rome, the wanderings of peoples, the German Reich. He loved times past. He found in them valor and a firmness of human character. His contemporaries, on the other hand, were mollusks. In the formations of the SS he discerned Roman lineaments. Stuckler's mind was not original. He called bolsheviks Huns. The hordes of Attila! This sounded a bit Wagnerian. He liked sublime, austere thoughts. He liked oak trees, tall horses, rocks, high peaks enveloped in clouds as if in the smoke from an invisible conflagration. He was the most ordinary SS man in the world, without intellectual ambitions and pangs of conscience. He belonged to the majority. Later, it was his Hamletizing friends who turned out to have been in the majority. But that was an adulteration. If Stuckler had lived to see those days, he would have declared them a joke. He personally knew only one fellow from the SS, a man named Otto Staubert, who was experiencing serious doubts and surrendering to moral anxieties. Staubert died on the Russian front in the fall of 1941. Stuckler was a level-headed man, he loved a strong Germany, despised Jews and

Slavs, waged war in such a way as to increase the chances of victory. But above all else he executed the orders of his superiors. It was they who assumed the responsibility. It had always been that way. Yet Stuckler was not the only one who embraced conformity. He lived, after all, in the twentieth century and was conscious of this. He was not the only one who harbored enmity toward Jews, dislike for Poles, contempt for Russians. One does not have to be a German fascist to think that way. When he was young, Stuckler had had the unpleasant sensation of being besieged by an unfriendly, alien world. He had experienced humiliation, he was snubbed as an uneducated man with coarse manners and a primitive way of life. He had lifted himself up thanks to his own stubbornness and favorable circumstances. He was self-taught, and cultivated in solitude his love of the history of ancient Rome and of the German Reich. He often renounced amusements in order to read history books or even to buy them for himself. People were incapable of properly appreciating these efforts. He always had the reputation of being a boor, and everywhere there were men better than he. The world was not kindly disposed toward Stuckler. It gave others more and at a lower price. Adolf Hitler claimed that those responsible for this were Jews, communists, and democracy. When Stuckler joined the Party and the SS, his unpleasant, annoying humiliations ceased. No one thought that he was a boor any longer, and they even started to appreciate his intellectual ambitions. Stuckler was not stupid, and so with time the thought dawned on him that he owed his new position to the influence of the NSDAP, and that his strongest support was the hierarchy of the Nazi movement. In this he proved more clear-sighted than many of his contemporaries. For he didn't consider himself wiser in a uniform than out of it. He remembered that he had read the Roman tales with a pounding heart when he was still a young miller's apprentice, and that his attachment for history stemmed from those times. His spiritual development did not begin with the moment he joined the movement. In fact just the opposite was true—it was then that he started to lack the time for educating himself and thinking about life. There were moments when he saw himself as merely an opportunist making a career for himself within the framework of the new reality. But this reality was no worse than the previous one; people simply changed roles, and those who once rode on the wagon found themselves under it, while others climbed up and took the reins. In his youth Stuckler had worked in the family mill and wealthy Jewish wholesalers exploited him. Later he lived elegantly and comfortably, and the Jews swept the streets. In a certain sense this was just; it agreed with the spirit of the times and also with human aspirations in general, for people desire change, metamorphoses, and new orders of things. The world is alive and transforms itself ceaselessly. It has always been that way.

The day came that the national socialist movement began violent persecutions of political opponents, and also of Jews in the Reich. Stuckler was by no means born a murderer without a conscience, for murderers without a conscience are never born anywhere. And no one ever started a criminal career by setting fire to the world or engaging in mass slaughter. Stuckler participated in smashing the windows in Jewish stores, which wasn't a very honorable occupation and looked rather foolish, in his eyes as well, but ultimately it didn't cause people great harm. Jews were rich and influential enough to put in new windows. And no doubt they could use such a lesson because it taught them humility and politeness. They were shown their proper place! Later, Stuckler beat up several Jews. One of them was sleeping with a German girl, who also got what she had coming to her because whereas it was true that she was the Jew's servant, she nevertheless had to understand that she had acted contrary to the law and had jeopardized the German race. The German race was better than others, about this there was no question in Stuckler's mind, just as there is no question for many Britons but that they are the finest nation in the world, just as for Jews who are faithful to the Testament there is no question but that they are God's chosen, and for Poles there is no question but that they are under the Virgin Mary's special protection; whereas Germans are Teutonic knights, Russians are peasant souls, the French are frog eaters, the Italians are mere mandolinists, the British are shopkeepers, and the Czechs are cowardly Pepiczeks. In this

Stuckler did not differ in any significant way from other people in the world. Perhaps he only donned a uniform rather early, sensed the power of community, and perceived the effectiveness of the whip. People are by nature rather weak, which is why they like force, and Stuckler was a run-of-the-mill man, which the majority are.

He killed a man after he had beaten, kicked, and wounded many others. Granted, this first act of homicide was not fully deliberate, rather even accidental. Stuckler hit too hard, medical assistance arrived too late. It was an unpleasant incident, and it is quite possible that Stuckler thought of it with reluctance, even tried to erase it from his memory. All the same, such incidents occurred more and more frequently later, and besides, war had broken out, and in wartime everyone kills one another because if they don't they will be killed themselves. One day Stuckler came to realize that he had killed many people, but once again he could repeat without fear of error that it had always been that way. And he was right, because it had indeed always been that way.

Stuckler whipped the horse. They set off again at full trot, in the shade of spreading trees, around the smooth lake, amid the rustling of nature. Stuckler felt tired and not especially happy, because in the past few months life had given him neither joy nor satisfaction, and the thought of eventual military defeat had an oppressive effect. Yet he didn't fear the future, for he was by nature a courageous man, and on top of that not a very intelligent and sensitive one; so knowing that he will die, like every man who is a mortal being, he did not imagine the moment of death and consequently it didn't terrify him. And he also did not fear God, for he considered his sins commonplace—everyone commits such sins in wartime—whereas the war was not Stuckler's doing. If it were up to him, he would gladly not participate in it. He did not find satisfaction in tracking down Jews and keeping a tight hand on this savage city. The war deprived Stuckler of the comfortable life to which he had grown accustomed during the several years when the movement exercised power in the Third Reich and Europe took account of Germans, showed them respect, and tried to meet their demands. Stuckler had a better life without the war and was less worried about the future. And yet it happened. He thought that he should fulfill to the very end his duties as a German, a citizen of the Reich, a party member, and a police officer. That was his obligation; it was a matter of honor.

Now the gelding's trot changed into an easy canter. Clods of earth and stones sprayed from under his hooves. Stuckler was no longer thinking about the girth, which in fact held well. He was thinking that if the Germans lose the war, Europe's decline will most likely never again be reversed. Its heritage will be destroyed. The barbarian era will set in. Stuckler could not picture himself in those landscapes. He also didn't picture himself with a broken sword, walking with a rope around his neck behind a Hun's shaggy horse, heading east. And yet something quite similar lay ahead of him. He didn't have sandals and a shield, to be sure, and didn't feel the rope around his neck, but he did walk east together with a large group of other German prisoners, and right beside him Red Army men passed by on small, nimble horses. He walked for many weeks, then rode on a railroad car across unending steppes. In the end he found himself behind the barbed wires of a camp on the Ob River. For several years he cleared Siberian forests, all the while growing weaker and more wild, until finally he died, and his corpse was thrown into a deep pit, which before long was covered by permafrost. Dying he did not regret his sins, because he no longer believed in God at all. Perhaps he didn't even remember that he had once been a German, a member of the NSDAP, and an officer of the Reich's security service. For several weeks before his death he thought only of food.

Then, too, he could have said that it had always been that way. If he didn't say it, it was probably for lack of physical and spiritual strength, which are necessary for deductive reasoning. Whereas he was dying from hunger and exhaustion, beyond all morality and ethical considerations, for which one undoubtedly needs a certain number of calories. At bottom, fate proved kinder to him than to all those who died similarly to him but somewhat earlier and through his agency. Stuckler's predecessors didn't have time to be either hungry enough or bestialized enough to forget about the centuries of culture they carried upon their shoulders. They were still capable of drawing conclusions, evaluating situations, and dispensing justice to the world according to the standards and principles with which they had been inculcated during better times. It is true that sometimes they accepted death as a release from suffering, but in general they died conscious of the fact that they were the victims of tyranny, crime, and the degradation of the world. Stuckler had been hungry too long to be able to understand anything at all at the end. The last months of his life were half a waking dream and half the dream of a sick and speechless animal. He probably didn't even remember his name, and so he couldn't very well remember his deeds. He died without contrition and consciousness, and so he did not know that this death was punishment for the evil that he had committed against others. In that sense the education by the shores of the Ob River misfired, at any rate in Stuckler's case. If they had put him on trial, listened to his arguments, confronted him with witnesses, and then punished him, as happened, after all, with certain of his comrades in arms, perhaps he would have had a chance to demonstrate contrition for his sins, which he would have comprehended, or at least appreciated intellectually. Expelled from the perimeters of the civilization that had called him into being, had shaped his mentality as well as his character; condemned to a long vegetation as neither man nor beast, he remained merely an unthinking ghost, beyond the sphere of moral critiques and choices. Even in this, humanity had no profit from him. But he himself could say, one more time, that it had always been that way.

The horse, obedient to the rider's hand, stopped. A white cloud covered the sun. The green lawn took on a purple hue. It was empty all around Stuckler. Only the present, he thought. He didn't like memory. Maybe he didn't even like life. He liked the distant past. It is there that he discovered himself as a symbol, a sign. Even as something more, because from history he derived the conviction that he was participating in a continuum that he had begun a long time ago, not in the physical sense, to be sure, as the son and grandson of millers from the Saalfeld area, a member of the movement, an officer, a rider on a pretty roan horse, on a purple lawn, beneath the crowns of leafless trees; no, he didn't physically begin so long ago, but he was one in a long line of those who carried out a certain spiritual mission, the duty of a certain fraction of mankind. It had always been that way. There were always conquerors and cruel men who trampled the earth to make it more docile, and there were also the others, the victims of pillage, conquest, tyranny, whose bones fertilized the earth. Such was no doubt people's destiny, and it was not they who chose their fate but some higher force marshaling history, according to whose decrees certain people ruled and others were ruled over. Stuckler knew with absolute certainty that it was his lot to rule. It was his duty to trample the earth, and not to fertilize it with his flesh. It had always been that way. Wasn't mighty Rome built on the backs of thousands of slaves? Who today knows their names? Who remembers their existence? And yet they supported the might of the empire, all the Roman edifices and conquests, all of Roman culture and civilization, which continues to be sacrosanct. The suffering of the slaves left no trace in history, while the Romans created the history of vast stretches of the world. There, where the sandal of a Roman legionnaire trod upon the earth, human history blossomed. How many slaves fertilized this earth with their ashes? Rome already applied the principle of collective responsibility and elevated the community of Roman citizens above all the rest of the earth's residents. Only they enjoyed freedom, were entitled to rights and privileges. It had always been that way. And thanks to that the world simply existed. If we lose the war, Stuckler thought, the thread of history will be severed. Some sort of monster without an umbilical cord will be born, humanity without warriors, and therefore weak, slothful, and condemned to slow extermination. Our enemies prattle on about democracy. In its name they want to defeat the Reich. What idiocy! After all even the Roman republic had its slaves. And the famous Athenian democracy rested upon slavery from the first moment of its existence to the last. It had always been that way. It was never different. It had always been that way.

Stuckler looked at his watch. It was past noon. He had to go back to work. The sun came out again. The horse moved at full trot. Stuckler felt buoyant. A warrior's life, he thought. A simple soldier's life. Even if we lose, they will envy us one day. Because there is an austere beauty in us, something of the angels. And the cut of our uniforms too is one of a kind, unsurpassed. They will envy us one day. It has always been that way.

XX

When she awoke in the morning, she was overwhelmed by a feeling of joyful wonder. Through the window she saw a patch of sky that was growing progressively lighter, the dark branches of trees, their delicate, green shoots. In the mirror of her dressing table she could see reflected the bed, the night table, the fold of the freshly covered quilt, the shape of a bare foot. It was her own foot, sticking out from beneath the quilt. A shapely, slender woman's foot. How wonderful it is that I'm waking up precisely here! Only now did she feel the joy of living and the attachment to her own body. She observed her foot in the mirror, moving her toes. And so I've survived after all, she thought joyfully; I am here, in my own house. But suddenly she grew frightened that she might die, that she might not live to see the end of the war, that she might share the fate of other Jews. She had taken that eventuality into account during the previous years, but she was nevertheless always convinced that somehow she would survive, would extract herself from this net. In the cell on Szucha Avenue she had been resigned to death, had thought about her past life, about all that which had been realized. She had been calm, perhaps even serene. She accepted with humility the sentence of fate, terrible and yet so obvious, one among those millions of sentences that were handed down every hour. That which was inevitable had come to pass. She was inclined to believe that that which is inevitable is a kind of duty; therefore, the thought of death did not incite her to moral protest. Only now, lying in bed, at the dawn of the following day, did she begin to realize that she had escaped something horrible, that the irrevocable end had been very close—and she became terrified. Never before had she felt such a strong desire to live. Fear seized her at the thought that today or tomorrow she might find herself again in the cell on Szucha, in Pawiak, or by the wall of executions. She pulled the quilt up over her head and lay motionless, her teeth chattering, out of breath, only now being killed, tortured with the most refined cruelty. She felt a trickle of sweat on her forehead, her back was wet, she was suffocating in a sticky, dark fear, as if she were only now about to find herself on Szucha, in the cell, in Stuckler's office; as if only now, in a few hours, was she to meet Bronek Blutman. No, she said to herself, I can't stand this! This has already happened; it will not be repeated.

Just then the doorbell sounded. And so they have come for me after all, she thought, yesterday they let me go, but now they have come. All at once all her fear evaporated. Yes, she thought, this is the end. Now they have come to kill me.

She got up out of bed, threw on her bathrobe. The doorbell rang again. Why don't they kick in the door, she thought, after all I'm not valuable enough that they should waste their time on me. . . .

She approached the door and looked through the peephole. On the other side stood Dr. Adam Korda, the classical philologist. He's gone mad, Irma thought coldly. What is he doing coming so early?

When she opened the door, he smiled shyly and said, "Please forgive me, dear lady, for coming at this hour, but I saw you returning from town yesterday and I couldn't sleep all night. . . . My God, you have been through something dreadful. I've come to offer you my assistance, if you—"

He broke off, cleared his throat. He stood on the threshold in gray knickerbockers and a dark jacket, his shirt collar out, his shoes carefully shined, with the expression of a dignified idiot on his face. In his hand he held a saucepan.

She wanted to shout, hit him in the face, or cry from relief and despair. And she started to cry because she managed to remember in time that this man had saved her, it was he who set into motion the assistance of various people, he who was the first link in the chain whose final link would be old Müller.

She started to cry, and Dr. Adam Korda, his voice breaking, said, "I just permitted myself to warm up some milk. Milk is very soothing. . . ."

They sat in the living room on chairs of pale ash upholstered in aquamarine damask, at an ash table, on which the classical philologist, quite idiotically, set down the saucepan with the milk. They sat for several minutes in silence, in the amber half-light of morning that was seeping into the room through the heavy curtains on the windows. They could hear the birds. Irma Seidenman wiped her eyes.

She said, "I don't know how to thank you. I can't express it. . . ."

"You should drink some milk," he replied. "I think I came a bit too early. But I really was so anxious."

He started to talk about this anxiety. He told her about his visit to Pawelek. She understood then fully that her rescue was the end result of the fears and efforts of many people. If one link had failed, she would have been lost. My God, she thought, here I was thinking that I was a lonely, unloved woman. I was wrong. I am not alone. No one is alone here.

Drinking milk under Dr. Korda's gaze, barefoot, her face wet with tears, trembling in the chill of the early morning, she understood for the first time in her life, with certainty and a feeling of joyous devotion, that here was her country, here were close and beloved people, to whom she owed not only gratitude for saving her life, but her entire future. Never before had she felt so deeply and painfully the sense of belonging in Poland, never had she thought with such bitter joy and devotion about her Polishness. Poland, she thought, my Poland. It is these people who are Poland. This decent, unintelligent man in knickerbockers is Poland, the most sacred thing that I possess in the whole world. Her heart welled up with gratitude to fate for having made her a Pole; for it was here—in this city, among these people—that she had to suffer and endure. Never in the past had she felt connections with her Jewishness, having been brought up in the milieu of an old intelligentsia, assimilated decades ago. Her father, admittedly, was an ophthalmologist serving the Jewish poor and went around tirelessly among the rickety, foul-smelling courtyards; clambered up the damp, dark stairs of Jewish outbuildings; tended to snot-covered, dirty Jewish children in the neighborhoods of poverty and abasement. But he was himself an enlightened, educated, and prosperous man, who knew so clearly where he himself belonged that he never gave the mother even one uncertain or worried thought. And her husband, Dr. Ignacy Seidenman, felt similarly, being an accomplished radiologist with scholarly ambitions, the product of exclusive schools, an alumnus of Montpellier and Paris, a man of the world, the truest European she had ever met. And it was these two men—her father and her husband—who shaped her, who molded her into a girl, a marriageable young lady, and finally a woman, free of all doubts and anxieties resulting from questions of religion or race, removed from Jewishness, with which she was linked only by a very distant memory of a bearded old man talking to her when she was still a small child in an incomprehensible language and caressing her face with a gnarled hand; the memory of her grandfather, who died when she was five years old, maybe six, a Jew from an era long past, who linked her impassively and painlessly with those mysterious origins, with the exotic aura of Jewishness that, it is true, was all around her on the street, made itself felt sometimes in a jarring note of anti-Semitism, but generally speaking took place on the peripheries of her life because she was a blue-eyed blonde, a pretty woman with an enchanting smile and a slender figure. So Jewishness had no connections with her, existed separately—without her and beyond her—

outside the sphere of her immediate experience, present, to be sure, and yet alien. Never in the past had she felt connections with Jewishness, that much she knew with absolute certainty! But perhaps for this very reason she also didn't feel any connections with Polishness, because Polishness was to her like the air she breathed—simply the self-evident. And only now, drinking milk under the watchful gaze of this comical man in knickerbockers and lace-up boots did she begin to realize that Polishness was the thing of greatest value in her life, that she was a Pole and belonged in Poland. And yet even in the cell on Szucha she hadn't thought that way. She had thought then about the damned cigarette case, the disastrous combination of circumstances that was going to cost her her life. There, on Szucha Avenue, she felt neither a Jew nor a Pole. Perhaps she was something more—a human being condemned to death and at the same time someone undefined and unfinished by fate, or rather undefined and unfinished in her own consciousness because she was suffering on account of a metal box. It was that object, she believed, that endangered her life, only it and nothing more! She was not going to die as a Jew or a Pole, for reasons of her criminal racial or national affiliation, but as a victim of a confluence of idiotic mistakes, crushed by an almost weightless object, by her own sentimentality about a memento of her late husband. And only now, in the presence of Dr. Korda, with the sounds of birds outside the window and swallowing warm milk, was she experiencing her liberation, defining herself, discovering her affiliation.

It would turn out in the future that the choice she made then, under the tender and watchful gaze of the lover of Cicero and Tacitus, was incorrect, or at least questionable. Not for her. For others. When she was leaving Warsaw, she did not remember Dr. Korda and the pan of milk. But if God had allowed her then to recall the memories of many years ago, she would have known with absolute certainty that she was leaving Warsaw against the will and wishes of Dr. Korda, that Dr. Korda's spirit, residing in eternity, had cried out bitterly and run to his Creator to complain. But it was not the dead who were deciding her fate.

Many years later, lost in foreign lands, rather comical, like most old and solitary women, she sometimes summoned up memories of Poland. She no longer looked at her slim feet in the mirror. They were misshapen and filled her with disgust, like the skin on her hands, covered in dark spots, like the folds of fat on the once slender nape of her neck, and above all the smell of her body, faint and at the same time penetrating, the alien smell of old age, with which she refused to reconcile herself. She thought about Poland sometimes then, because old people remember the distant past very well, return to it therein to find the strength to endure, to see themselves young again, beautiful, surrounded by love. And so she was searching for her past, and thus perforce for Poland and her connections with it. Yet this was sad and unpleasant. Lovely, tranquil, friendly Poland was linked in her mind with that which long ago had ceased to exist, with the furniture in Irma Seidenman's conjugal apartment before the war, with the staircase lined with cherry-colored coconut matting, adorned with the statue of a woman with a torch in her hand. Tranquil and friendly Poland was the view from the living-room windows onto the busy street, along which groaning streetcars rolled, horses with traces of sweat on their rumps pulled flatbed wagons, rectangular-shaped cars flashed by with small boys chasing behind them trying to catch in their hands the smoke flying from the exhaust pipes. It was also the face of Dr. Ignacy Seidenman by the light of a lamp, his hands on the desk, amid countless charts, photographs, and notes drawn up on loose pieces of paper. It was the taste of cakes from the Lardelli firm, of chocolates from Wedel or Fuchs, the window of the Old England store, furs from Apfelbaum, the smell of good Elizabeth Arden cosmetics from the perfumery on Krakowski Boulevard, and also the smell of books in Kozlowski's reading room nearby, cafés, droshkies, pretty women, pleasant men, well-behaved children.

Irma realized that this was an incomplete and one-sided image, because the Poland of old was also poor, dirty, backward, dark, noisy, rebellious. For many years after the war, she belonged to that group of people who with great effort, totally devoted to their mission, tried to right the shortcomings of the past, shaped this Poland stubbornly, built kindergartens, schools, universities, and in accordance with the dictates of old-time poets, carried learning to the people to raise the country out of backwardness. So she was conscious of the fact that the image of prewar Poland that she recalled in her memory was incomplete and did not correspond to historical reality. Yet nevertheless only that Poland was friendly to her, only that one looked benign and beautiful. That was my youth, she told herself toward the end of her life—shuffling along the streets of Paris, tapping her cane on the Parisian pavement—that was my youth, and the only Poland that I truly possessed.

The wartime period was erasing itself in her mind. From the moment the war broke out, a black abyss yawned in her memory, without light or colors. She was present without a doubt in that chasm. But she did not remember herself—her face, thoughts, and feelings—because darkness blurred the contours. And the subsequent Poland, in which she spent the greater part of her life, was simply alien. My fiddle is probably cracked, said the Jew Irma Seidenman-Gostomska, warming her old bones on a bench in the Luxembourg Gardens; my fiddle is playing out of tune. When she immersed herself in the past, she wanted to call forth a proper, deep tone from that fiddle of hers. But it seems to have truly cracked then, in the spring of 1968. It truly cracked, and it could not be glued back together again.

Birds soared outside the window. A streetcar passed in the distance. The classical philologist rose from the chair, smiled, and drew open the curtains. The early sun shimmered above the rooftops. Irma felt a chill on her bare feet. I look ridiculous, she thought, I must get dressed. But the philologist seemed in no hurry to leave.

"Mr. Pawelek was terrified," he said. "He assured me that he would immediately make every effort. Your husband was probably his father's friend, isn't that so? . . ."

"Yes," she replied. "They served once in the same regiment. If you'll excuse me, I'll just put something on my feet . . ."

He smiled foolishly. But he wasn't leaving. So she got up and went to get dressed. She heard him clearing his throat in the living room. She threw on a dress, pulled on some stockings. She looked into the mirror. No, I will not put on my makeup, she thought, it would not be appropriate at a moment like this. She decided also that she must immediately change apartments. Her papers too. Maybe I'll leave Warsaw? But where will I go? That makes no sense. Only in Warsaw do I have support—there are friendly people here. And why should I change my apartment and documents? After all my name is Maria Magdalena Gostomska, I am an officer's widow. I'll never get better papers. Am I a Jew? That's absurd! My name is Gostomska. I was never anyone else.

Arranging her hair in front of the mirror, hurriedly and carelessly, she suddenly felt irritated with Pawelek for thinking of her as Irma Seidenman, for remembering her as a Jew. I am Gostomska, Pawelek, my husband served in the same regiment with your father! She threw the comb down loudly on the shelf, then turned toward the mirror. I'm going to go crazy, she thought, I must get control over myself, or else I'll drive myself out of my mind. Pawelek, forgive me, I know that I'm alive thanks to you! She looked into the mirror again and smiled. She had known for a long time that he was in love with her. Before the war, when he was a nice, polite boy, she had met him once by accident on the street and taken him to Europejski for ice cream. He leaned his blushing, embarrassed little face over the bowl. Later, whenever he kissed Irma on the hand, he turned red and scraped his feet a bit too loudly. She saw how quickly he was changing from a boy into a young man. No doubt he ran around after pretty girls, kissed them in dark corners, dreamed of them. But he dreamed of her as well. Less than a year ago they were riding together in a rickshaw. He was sitting stiff and tense, in an uncomfortable position, leaning over all the way to the right, so as not to touch her thigh under any circumstances. When the rickshaw made a sudden turn, and Irma leaned over, pressing her body to his, he called out in a hoarse voice, "Oh, please, excuse me!" His hand touched her shoulder. He withdrew it. He was pale, his eyes looked sick, like those of a dying animal. He's still sweet on me, she thought at the time, not without a certain happy satisfaction. He was not yet twenty, she a dozen years older. He's so pretty, she thought then. But above all he was amusing in his awkwardness and suffering. She knew that this would pass. She liked Pawelek. He was a nice, well brought-up, intelligent boy, he was a link to her prewar past, he belonged to the landscapes of her deceased husband. When Pawelek visited her sometimes in the apartment in the Mokotów district, she liked to reminisce with him about past times. Dr. Ignacy Seidenman had also liked Pawelek. Whenever he met him, he would ask him about his progress in school and give him candy. Dr. Ignacy Seidenman had liked children in general, and suffered a little because he couldn't have a son of his own. Pawelek's company, his engaging, slightly shy way of being, had a soothing effect on Irma. But once, during one of his visits, she caught his gaze. It was the gaze of a man who desires a woman. He did not realize this, being still awkward and sincere in his youthful sentiments. But from that day on Irma was on her guard. Pawelek's discomfort communicated itself to her and she was no longer so free and easy with him. Perhaps she even avoided his visits somewhat. Nothing more happened.

She regretted this only in the café on Avenue Kléber thirty years later.

Pawel said to her then, "You were the love of my youth."

He was wearing a gray suit, a blue shirt, a badly knotted tie. He looked at her from behind thick glasses in dark frames. His thick, graying hair still fell onto his forehead. She laid an old, withered hand on his.

"Don't say that. You shouldn't make fun of an old woman. . . ."

But they both knew that he was speaking the truth. They also knew that all that was past and done for. He smiled and nodded his head.

"When do you go back?" she asked softly and again stroked his hand.

"The day after tomorrow, Irma. Please, think about a visit in the near future. I don't want to insist, but—"

"It's pointless," she interrupted. "You yourself know best that it's pointless."

"I know," he replied after a moment. "I understand. But I'm still unable to accept it."

"I've already accepted it."

"You have the right to," he said reluctantly. "I don't."

"Why not? What binds you to those people? From where does this solidarity of yours come from, this feeling of some kind of complicity? What do you have in common with them?"

He shrugged his shoulders.

"Seemingly nothing. You're right. I catch myself sometimes reacting foolishly to certain things. I don't have anything in common with them, that's true! Except for one detail. That I am there, and they are there too. . . ."

"But you are not responsible for what they did, and still do. . . . For God's sake, Pawel, one cannot assume such a responsibility."

"And am I assuming it?" he cried. "But it's not so simple. You know that I'm not responsible, and a hundred thousand people know it too. And the rest? All those here? I am from there. I am one of them. You must remember this. It is the mark with which I have been branded. And besides . . ."

He stopped, took off his glasses, and began wiping them carefully with a handkerchief.

"Besides what?" she asked. He continued to wipe his glasses in silence.

"Say it, Pawel. What 'besides' are you talking about?"

"And don't you, speaking quite frankly with God as a witness, don't you feel the same? It is after all not they who chased you out, but Poland. You do believe that."

"Not at all!" she replied, but she knew that she wasn't telling the whole truth. Because he had placed his fingers on the cracked fiddle, touched the broken string. If then, on Avenue Kléber, gazing watchfully into Pawel's eyes and listening intently to her cracked instrument, she had remembered the day of the great fear, the day after leaving Stuckler's cell; if she had remembered the flight of those birds outside the window, Dr. Korda's face, the amber-colored curtains in the living room, the taste of the milk she had drunk; if she had remembered then all that was happening when, already dressed and carelessly coiffed, she entered the room again, addressing the classical philologist with the words, "Please, don't go yet. It's so nice that you're taking care of me at a moment like this!" and he, of course, had sat down eagerly on the ash chair upholstered in aquamarine damask to recount for another quarter of an hour the visit of the rickshaw driver who brought him news of the arrest of Mrs. Gostomska under the absurd charge of Semitic descent; if she had remembered all this in the café on Avenue Kléber, she would certainly have understood this simple truth, yet a truth of which she was never made conscious because after all she didn't really remember the past, only crumbs, fragments of it, like spots of light filtered through the dense crown of a tree; she would have understood then the banal truth that Stuckler had not humiliated her in the least. Not for a moment had she felt humiliated then, abased, stripped of her dignity, disgraced, because Stuckler had wanted only to kill her, whereas those others, who years later came to her office and would not let her take her briefcase with the documents, they took from her something more than life because they took away her right to be herself, the right to self-determination.

A pigeon was cooing outside the window when she returned to the living room. Like on the terrace of the café on Avenue Kléber. But she never paid attention to birds. She liked dogs, cats, and above all horses. Birds flew in the air, she walked on the ground. She didn't pay attention to them. After a quarter of an hour Dr. Korda finally left, and she went back to bed. She undressed quickly, threw her dress and lingerie carelessly on the chair, and slipped under the quilt. She fell asleep violently, in anguish and fear that she might not wake up again. She dreamed of Stuckler, who was walking behind Dr. Ignacy Seidenman's coffin. Many people were taking part in the funeral. She didn't recognize their faces. She searched for herself in the procession, but she was nowhere to be seen. She searched more and more feverishly, terrified that she was not participating in the final journey of her own husband, whom she loved so much. Eventually she found Irma. Stuckler was holding her by the arm. She was saying to him, "My name is Gostomska, Maria Magdalena Gostomska, the widow of an officer of the Polish army!" Stuckler answered, "But I know that, this is your husband's funeral. . . . Do you think that I would come to a Jewish funeral?!" And yet it was Dr. Ignacy Seidenman's funeral. Later she was in the cell again, and Stuckler was shouting, "You misled me! This cigarette case explains everything. Show me your right earlobe!" But her ear was missing. In its place was a bleeding wound.

It was noon when she finally woke. She lay in bed for a long time, staring at the ceiling. That same dream still haunted her. Will I ever be free? she thought. Will I ever have peace?

XXI

———————

Judge Romnicki smiled and said, "How pleasantly cool it is here."

Sister Weronika replied that the side of the building giving onto the vegetable garden is sometimes quite hot, but the cloister walls are thick, they go back to very distant times, and that is why it is usually cool inside.

"I brought the child," the judge said and stroked Joasia lightly on her dark head. "As we agreed."

"I understand, Judge," the nun said and looked at the little girl. "She is a little too dark," she added after a moment.

"One cannot pick and choose these days, Sister."

"I'm not insisting on anything, but you do understand."

"Today man understands more than he should," the judge pronounced sententiously and again caressed Joasia's hair. "This is a charming little girl."

"One must always have hope, Judge."

"In accordance with what was settled upon, Mother Superior has already received certain funds," the judge said. "The war will not last forever. Besides, should the need arise, I am always at your disposal."

"It's not that," Sister Weronika replied. "We know our responsibilities, Judge."

Now she caressed the child's hair.

"So her name is Joasia," she said. "We'll teach her her prayers today still."

"That might come in handy," said the judge.

Sister Weronika looked at him attentively.

"This will be a Catholic child, Judge. You brought us not only her body, in danger of terrible suffering, but also her strayed soul."

"Do you believe, Sister, that she has had the time to stray? She's only four years old, after all. Who is straying here, Sister?"

"I think it's understood that we will bring her up Catholic. It is our duty toward this child. You are a Catholic yourself, Judge, and so I don't have to prove . . ."

"Well, yes," said Judge Romnicki and wanted to end the conversation, when suddenly he felt a twofold pain. That he would have to part with this sweet, silent child. And that there was something seriously wrong with him, a feeling of deep anxiety, bitterness, or even disappointment.

So he said, "You should do what you consider right, Sister. But nothing will come of it."

"What will nothing come of?"

"This Catholicism, Sister," the judge said, and was himself surprised at the anger, and perhaps even the vindictiveness, that resounded in his voice.

"What are you talking about, Judge?" Sister Weronika said harshly.

"Let me tell you something, Sister! Just try to think for a minute. Are there different gods? Or is there one and ineffable Almighty God, who led us out of Egypt, out of the house of slavery? The same one, Sister, our merciful God, the one who revealed Himself to Moses in the burning bush, called to Jacob, stopped Abraham's knife as it was poised above Isaac's neck. That is our God, the Creator of all people. . . ."

"Judge, please, remember the Saviour!" Sister Weronika exclaimed.

"Let me tell you something, Sister, let me tell you something! I am a Catholic, a Roman Catholic down the generations, a Polish nobleman. I believe in Jesus Christ, in the protection of the Holy Virgin Mary. I believe in everything that religion and my beloved Poland have given me. And be so kind as not to interrupt me, Sister, because no one interrupts me when I am speaking—even President Mościcki didn't interrupt although I am certain he did not enjoy listening to certain things I said. So, what are we talking about, Sister?! After all it's God who led this child through five thousand years, it was God who led her by the hand from the city of Ur to the land of Canaan, and then to Egypt, and then to Jerusalem, and then into Babylonian captivity, and then once again into the Holy Land, and then out over the entire vast world, to Rome and to Alexandria, to Toledo and to Mainz—all the way here, to the shores of the Vistula. It was, after all, God Himself who ordered this child to wander across the whole world from one extreme to the other so that in the end she would find herself here, among us, in this conflagration, in this end of all ends, where there is no choice anymore, from which there is no escape other than into this cave of our Catholicism, our Polishness, because that is the only chance of saving this child's life. So how is it to be with the will of God, Sister? For all those thousands of years He led her so that others might come to know Him, might understand Him, so that the Saviour could come, our Lord Jesus, in Whom we believe and Whom we adore on the Holy Cross because He died for us, for our salvation He died under Pontius Pilate, so for all those thousands of years the Lord led her, so that now, at the very end, she should transform herself, should deny herself, because that's the way Adolf Hitler wants it? Go ahead, Sister, baptize her, teach her prayers and the catechism, let her name be Joasia Bogucka, or Joasia Kowalczykówna, I'll of course arrange it, in two or at the most three days there will be a certificate of baptism ready, one proof against any suspicion. Against any suspicion, in the name of a deceased Catholic girl. So everything will be in the best possible order. Go ahead. Work on this child, Sister. In a Christian way, in a Catholic way, in a Polish way too! I believe that one must. It is necessary for her future, for her survival. But I will tell you, Sister, what I think of this. We here are one thing. And God is something else. And God will not permit it! I believe in this strongly, Sister, that He will not permit such an ending. And she will be a Jewish woman, one day a Jewish woman will awaken in her and she will shake the foreign dust from herself, to return to where she came from. And her womb will be fertile, and she will bring forth new Maccabees into the world. Because God will not forsake His own people! I am telling you this, Sister. And now take her, Sister, and let her believe in our Lord, Jesus Christ, because that is, as you know very well, Sister, the bread of life. But one day Judith will awaken in her, will draw a sword, and will cut off the head of Holofernes."

"Don't cry, Judge," said Sister Weronika.

And just as he said, a Jewish woman did awaken in Joasia, but not like the one he had foreseen. Perhaps the judge did not fully understand God's designs, or perhaps it was for a trivial reason. Joasia survived the war as Marysia Wiewióra, a Catholic girl, an orphan from near Sanok, whose parents, poor farmers, had left her behind in this world. After the war, she lived like the great majority of her contemporaries, studied diligently, and considered a stomatological career, because she had agile hands and her presence had a calming influence on people. But when she turned twenty she heard a voice calling her. And she followed it, humbly and obediently. She emigrated to Israel, where she was no longer called Marysia Wiewióra but Miriam Wewer.

And she did not become a dentist. Some time after arriving in her new country, where the chosen nation was building its own state so as never again to experience persecution and humiliation, she saw strange Jews, who perhaps issued from her dreams and presentiments, or maybe appeared for quite earthbound reasons, just like others, who resembled them, had appeared before. These Jews wore berets, camouflage fatigues, and tall boots. Almost as a rule they carried loaded submachine guns under their arms. They had sunburned faces and used the sparse vocabulary of armed men. Miriam saw how with one kick they would break down the doors of Palestinian houses, and then at gunpoint lead out into the blinding desert sun the bewildered fedayeen, their women and children. A kind of wild, shrill joy then awoke in her heart, as if something was finally being fulfilled, something that had been awaited for millennia, as if a dream that had been kept smothered in the generations of Israel was being realized, a dream that had burned through to the core of the tormented bodies of millions of European and Asian Jews, given life for entire centuries to these groups of eternal wanderers, gloomy, dark, frightened, cursed, and at the same time chosen.

When Miriam saw for the first time a powerful man with one kick smashing a Palestinian door, it seemed to her that God Himself was present at this and was nodding His head in consent. Miriam did not think then about the frightened and helpless fedayeen, but about all of savage humanity, which one Jewish kick was finally calling to order. Her eyes were full of tears and her heart full of pride, gratitude, and ardent faith. She absolved the world of all evil, for the moment for settling scores had arrived, and Jews were never again to be held in contempt, humiliated, and persecuted.

But the rapture did not last long. Miriam was a sensitive girl, and she also had a good deal of common sense. But perhaps neither her sensitivity nor her common sense would have sufficed had she not seen the subsequent scene, quite banal in fact, the most ordinary in the world and yet always educational. The Israeli soldiers, as soldiers are wont to do, stood facing the fedayeen, but the fedayeen were stooped, they held their arms behind their heads, their children screamed, although nothing was going on, their women shrieked, although no one took any interest in them, and all the while the soldiers stood there with their legs wide apart, their faces stony, looking rather stupid and boastful in this stoniness, and they held their fingers on the triggers of their guns. They stood that way, immobile, awaiting further orders from the officer, who with a swagger stick was drawing circles and lines in the desert sand, so concentrated on the historic decision he was about to make that he looked like a brainless buffoon, something in which he did not differ from all other officers in the world.

But for Miriam this was a deeply affecting scene, for she realized that she was participating in an absurdity, that no kick dealt a Palestinian fedayeen will erase centuries of history or constitute reparation. She was not educated enough to see at that moment that she was participating in an immemorial act of imitation, and that these soldiers did not invent even their imperious stance, because that is the way a man armed and conscious of his power has always stood before an unarmed and defeated one. That is the way the Roman legionnaire stood before the overthrown Maccabee and Odoacer on the ruins of the Colosseum, the Frankish knight before the Saxons bound with ropes, Maluta Skuratow before the kneeling boyars, Bismarck in Versailles, Stroop on the street of the burning ghetto, the Vietnamese guerrilla near Dien Bien Phu. And that is the way all conquerors were to stand before those they defeated, until the end of the world. So it wasn't worth much, and Miriam walked away so as to forget this senseless scene as quickly as possible. And yet she couldn't break the shackles that bound her, any more than others can. Later she somehow got accustomed to them and no longer felt either satisfaction or any particular discomfort.

Only some time later, when she found out that she was pregnant and her Israeli husband rejoiced noisily and boastfully at this fact, as if giving your own wife a child were an event without precedence in this best of all possible worlds, Miriam experienced a night of great fear. It was hot. The moon was shining above the hills, olive and tamarisk trees cast bluish shadows. Miriam stood at the window of her house. She looked at the sky, the moon, the hills. She felt, as never before, an overwhelming fear at the thought that she would give birth to a human being. She was afraid of that and wanted to curse her womb. She remembered the strange words from her childhood spent in the cloister, which Sister Weronika read from the Gospel in her soft, gentle voice. And Miriam repeated those words, but loudly and vehemently, aiming them at the sky: "Lord, why have You deserted me!" At that moment Miriam's husband, who was forty-seven years old and had impaired hearing, walked into the room and said gently, "I have not deserted you, I'm right in the next room. Can I bring you something to drink?" These words reconciled Miriam to her destiny. However, when she gave birth to a daughter, she felt an immense sense of relief.

But it's possible that she would have felt the same sense of relief at bringing into the world a son.

Translator's Notes

131 BEREZA—Bereza Kartuska; an isolation camp in eastern Poland for political prisoners, 1934–39

131 FRONT OF NATIONAL UNITY—a political organization created by the military regime of the colonels, 1937–39

131 GLASS HOUSES—a symbol of hope for a better future in the novel *Early Spring,* by Stefan Zermoski (1864–1925)

131 NIKOLAI—Czar Nicholas II

131 STOLYPIN—a reactionary minister of the interior and the czar's prime minister from 1906–11

131 BESELER—the imperial German General-Gouverneur of Warsaw, 1915–18

140 KOTSIS OR CHELMOŃSKI—Aleksander Kotsis (1836–77) and Jozef Chelmoński (1849–1914); realistic Polish painters

150 ROMUALD TRAUGUTT—(1826–64); leader of the Polish January Uprising of 1863, executed on the embankment of the Warsaw Citadel by the Russians

150 ROKITNA—a military attack in Bukowina in 1915 that caused great losses to the Polish cavalry legions

151 NOWY ŚWIAT STREET—one of the main streets of Warsaw

156 WYSOCKI—Piotr W. (1797–1874); Polish officer who sparked the November Uprising of 1830 against the czar and was banned to Siberia from 1831–57

156 MOCHNACKI—Maurycy M. (1803–34); Polish journalist and politician

156 OKRZEJA—Stefan O. (1886–1905); Polish revolutionary (PPS), executed on the embankment of the Warsaw Citadel by the Russians

156 GROT—code name for General Stefan Rowecki (1895–1944), who led the Home Army (in the underground) and was murdered by the Germans in Sachsenhausen concentration camp

156 ANIELEWICZ—Mordechai A. (1919–43); commander of the uprising of the Warsaw Ghetto in April–May 1943

156 THE UPRISING—Warsaw uprising against the German occupation, August 1–October 2, 1944

156 WHITE MOUNTAIN—victorious battle of the imperial Habsburg troops over the Bohemian army, near Prague in 1620

About the Author

Andrzej Szczypiorski was born in Warsaw in 1924. He took part in the uprising against the Germans in 1944 and was captured and sent to a concentration camp. After the war he became one of Poland's leading writers, with eighteen widely translated novels to his credit. Increasingly engaged in opposition to the Communist regime, he was arrested along with other Solidarity leaders upon the imposition of martial law in December 1981 and kept in confinement until the following spring. In June 1989 he was elected to the Polish Senate on the Solidarity ticket. He was awarded the Austrian State Prize for European Literature in 1988. *The Beautiful Mrs. Seidenman* has been translated into fifteen languages.

VINTAGE INTERNATIONAL

VINTAGE INTERNATIONAL

VINTAGE INTERNATIONAL

Available at your bookstore or call toll-free to order: 1-800-733-3000.
Credit cards only. Prices subject to change.